analog / virtual

Lavanya Lakshminarayan is a speculative fiction writer and game designer from Bangalore, India. She has received an honourable mention from the A.C. Bose Grant for South Asian Speculative Literature 2019, awarded by the Speculative Literature Foundation, USA. She is one of the winners of the Nature of Cities Prize for Urban Flash Fiction 2018, and was shortlisted for the Toto Award for Writing in English 2019. Her fiction has appeared in the anthologies *A Flash of Silver-Green* and *Third Eye*, and has also been featured in the *Indian Quarterly* and other publications.

As a game designer, Lavanya has built worlds and designed narratives for highly successful game titles, including Zynga Inc.'s *FarmVille*, *FarmVille 2* and *Mafia Wars*. Her work on these games has been experienced by millions of players around the world. When she isn't writing, she enjoys a strong cup of coffee, travelling the world and spending time with her dogs.

PRAISE FOR THE BOOK

'In the best tradition of dystopian fiction, *Analog/Virtual* explores issues around class, society, power structures and values. Lavanya Lakshminarayan has skilfully crafted a series of interwoven stories about a frighteningly plausible near future scenario, rooted in the extrapolation of today's worship of technology and productivity. Spanning multiple points of view, writing styles and character voices, this masterful work of science fiction weaves its individual stories into a complex and engaging whole.' – **S.B. Divya, author of Nebula Award finalist *Runtime***

'Lavanya Lakshminarayan's debut drops us head first into a future Bangalore where a corporation rules the world and humanity seeks security and fulfilment in a thought-policed virtuality. I loved the razor-sharp writing and vivid detailing of her unfolding of the human situations and dilemmas of the Analog–Virtual divide in society. This is fiction playing for the highest stakes – and winning.' – **Chandrahas Choudhury, author of *Clouds* and *Arzee the Dwarf***

'Productivity is power. The monster under your bed corrects your social opinions. And if you slip too far you might just end up living in the real world... By turns horror, cyberpunk and biting social satire, *Analog/Virtual* is a high-velocity anthem sung through the shape of things to come.' – **Yudhanjaya Wijeratne, Nebula Award finalist and author of *The Inhuman Race***

analog virtual

AND OTHER SIMULATIONS OF YOUR FUTURE

lavanya lakshminarayan

hachette
INDIA

First published in 2020 by Hachette India
(Registered name: Hachette Book Publishing India Pvt. Ltd)
An Hachette UK company
www.hachetteindia.com

1

ISBN 978-93-89253-08-5

Hachette Book Publishing India Pvt. Ltd
4th & 5th Floors, Corporate Centre,
Plot No. 94, Sector 44, Gurugram 122003, India

Typeset in Adobe Caslon Pro 10.5/14.5
by R Ajith Kumar, New Delhi

Printed and bound in India
by Replika Press Pvt. Ltd.

FSC www.fsc.org
MIX
Paper from responsible sources
FSC® C016779

Amma and Appa,
this book is for you,
for plunging into unknowable futures with me

CONTENTS

Herein we outline the principles of a smart new world.
We seek to fulfil our human potential. We do not tolerate failure.

– from the Preamble to the Meritocratic Manifesto

THE TEN-PERCENT THIEF

NOBODY NOTICES ANYTHING BECAUSE nothing has happened. Not yet anyway.

This is how all things begin.

The electric shield thrums ominously. It cuts Apex City in two, striking across the crater that was once Bangalore.

She lives on the wrong side of the Carnatic Meridian.

They call her Nāyaka, their Champion. They pledge allegiance to her.

They're her people. The Analogs.

When Bell Corp ignored the cholera epidemic, she stole meditech from their laboratories. When Bell Corp stopped funding their water treatment, she began lifting holo-watches. She snatches hundreds each week. One solar-powered battery purifies a thousand bottles of water.

If raid-bots break into her pod-house, they'll find the 140-square-foot space filled with paperbacks. Nothing of value, no link to her crimes.

She is discreet.

Dead drops. Paper money. Forty-one safe capsules buried underground.

I am invisible.

The Virtuals know her as the Ten-Percent Thief. They have a price on her head.

I'm going to make sure I'm worth it.

She strolls towards the Meridian Gate.

Pod-houses form towering aisles; their circular windows are eye sockets in fibreglass skulls. On their eastern walls, a well-known artist directs a crowd of Analogs towards the completion of a mural. It reflects their past and celebrates their present.

Children scurry to the Institute – a cluster of pod-houses that lean in dangerously towards each other. It's architecturally unsound, but the children don't notice.

A small playground made of scrap metal and junkyard finds is laid out before it. Trash can lids form the seats of swings, a slide is cobbled together from scavenged planks of wood. A solitary child sits on a merry-go-round made from the ancient remains of a satellite dish.

Hawkers set up canvas tents along the path. They're selling homemade sunscreen and scraps of illegally procured ClimaTech fabric.

A stab of guilt. She sourced that ClimaTech.

They'll be arrested and sent to the vegetable farm.

She nearly intervenes.

They'll be put down. Harvested.

She steels herself.

They've been instructed not to sell it this close to the Meridian. You can't save everyone.

She chokes on a rolling cloud of dust and presses on.

She passes a structure resembling a giant tin shed. It's made from the rusty shells of freight trains, painted in bright colours that will fade in the relentless sun. The salvaged doors of washing machines form its windows. Hundreds of Analogs line up before the entrance to the Museum of Analog History.

Nāyaka feels a twinge of pride – over seven hundred Analogs participated in its construction, and even more came forward to supply the artefacts that fill its cavernous halls.

At the edge of the Analog world, she places her palm over a holoscanner.

Her silicone gloves fit like second skin. Their tips bear a set of 3D-printed fingerprints. She's about to impersonate an Analog gardener.

They volunteer. They trust me.

An armed patrol-drone scans her. The Carnatic Meridian sparks blue. A gap appears, electricity crackling on either side.

She passes through the Meridian Gate.

The light dims abruptly. A wave of coolth rushes over her.

The SunShield Umbrella orbits Apex City. It protects the Virtual side from ultraviolet radiation, providing climatic conditions optimized for human performance.

Her people are exposed to heat waves and dust storms.

Twenty-six towers form rank into the heart of the city. Thousands of employees are ensconced in bio-mat and frosted-glass spirals, absorbed in HoloTech experiences. She spies a game of Hyper Reality golf – no doubt a sizeable business deal in progress.

A block of pod-houses shares a cellular phone.

The Arboretum curves on either side of her, all along the city's borders. Thousands of trees flower in desolation.

Most Analogs have no conception of a tree.

They rely on the memories of Virtuals who have been deported to their side of the city. They hang on to the descriptions of a handful of workers who make their way through the Meridian each day.

She makes for the teleportals. Virtuals edge away from her grubby, shabbily dressed person.

I will not claim their holo-watches. I have a bigger prize in mind.

The port-bot's cyber-arm vibrates in disgust when she produces paper money.

She steps into the carbon-fibre capsule.

The Ten-Percent Thief is molecularly reconstituted upon the estate of Sheila Prakash, a HoloTech mogul from the top one percent of society.

Don't throw up.

The side effects of teleportation include nausea, but she's also never seen so much open space before. A holo-sphere arcs over the property, projecting clear blue skies overhead and verdant meadows along the horizon. The illusion eliminates all trace of Apex City's jagged skyline.

We can barely see the sky in the spaces between our pod-houses.

She's scanned and approved by a patrol-droid. The entire transaction is witnessed by the telltale flash of light on a PanoptiCam lens.

Once she's equipped with a jetpack, a sap-scanner, pruning shears and InstaBlossom compounds, her instructions are relayed.

Bring All Trees to Flower by 3.49 p.m.

Trim buds from each tree.

Analyse using sap-scanner.

Apply appropriate InstaBlossom compound.

Repeat.

She powers up her jetpack. It propels her into the canopies.

She rubs her hands over the bark, feeling ridges and knots through her gloves. She presses leaves to her face, trailing sap and dew across her skin. She sniffs the buds that lie in her palm, prying into their scents and secrets.

Trees.

I've never touched one before.

They're the exclusive right of the top one percent.

The Arboretum can only be accessed by the top twenty percent.

The seventy percent in the middle are allowed Hyper Reality gardens, the occasional houseplant.

I'm only given the right to breathe. And barely.

She is a member of the bottom ten percent, exiled in shame.

The threat of the vegetable farm creeps in my shadow.

Each year, more non-performers are deported across the Meridian. The ranks of the hopeless swell.

They don't kill us; they watch us suffer.

It is immaterial that Bell Corp's system of governance came as a welcome relief to the ruins of an erstwhile civilization. It seemed optimal – even utopian – for a world divided along social and communal lines, faced with the threat of dwindling resources and hostile climate, to be redesigned.

Every system believes itself to be the perfect solution.

The PanoptiCam scans the grounds. She locates its blind spot – a thick 'W' formed by two intertwined trees.

She begins to whistle. She works her way to it, unhurriedly.

Her heart pounds an erratic rhythm.

The resistance needs a symbol. I will give them a dream.

Three buds fall into a tight space between her glove and her wrist.

An InstaBlossom sachet disappears under her wig.

She takes a deep breath.

It can't be this easy.

She returns to the gaze of the PanoptiCam, unchanged. She finishes her assignment. Whistling.

Her palms stay damp until she's back at the Meridian Gate.

The patrol-drone's scanners don't detect the contraband on Nāyaka, covered in dirt as she is.

It is this easy.

She feigns listlessness as she enters the Analog city. She makes for a confluence of alleyways at its heart.

She tears off her gloves. Digs.

She drops a bud into the shallow pit.

She packs it with InstaBlossom, then sacrifices a bottle of water.

A sapling plunges through the earth.

Her breath catches.

It shoots upwards with a shriek, reaching for the sky.

Her eyes sting.

It bursts into flower, a whisper of jacaranda falling to the ground.

There's a face at a grimy window. Gasps of wonder. Footsteps.

She melts into the shadows, invisible.

Tomorrow, there will be consequences.

Today, there is hope.

Bell Corp declares that civilization is free from discrimination.
A universal system of Merit determines an individual's worth to society.
We are a Meritocratic Technarchy.
We are the future of the human race.

– from the Preamble to the Bell Charter on Human Rights

MONSTERS UNDER THE BED

JOHN HAD A MONSTER. She lived under his bed. Her name was Op.He.Li.aA.

It was stencilled onto the side of her silicone and metal body. John might have named her Kree, after the strangely mechanical whirring emitted by her each time she filed down his opinions, like a dentist making repairs to his brain.

She'd become a part of his life after a troubling conversation with Mr Morris, his supervisor at Bell Corporation. The Opinion Homogenization Limitation and Alignment Unit had arrived in the mail, or so he supposed. He'd never actually figured out how she'd emerged from under his bed that first night.

There had been no user manual. She'd seemed perfectly functional and completely sentient.

It had taken John an entire week to understand what her purpose in his life was going to be.

Op.He.Li.aA had worked on him with the utmost care and patience. She had smoothed him over, teaching him the names of all the superheroes from the Vindicators franchise, educating him on the finer points of neo-Acousta, preparing him for tonight.

Tonight. Tonight was the big night.

Mr Morris, Vice President of Bell Corporation's Investments Division, sat across the virtual table from John. Motivational quotes cycled across the wall behind him, holo-rayed from a device the size of a paperweight.

'Productivity is Power.' 'Passion is Priceless.' 'Persona is Prime.'

They were at their routine monthly meeting, conducted via VirtuoPod.

John waited for Mr Morris to review his performance.

Mr Morris prompted John to discuss his views on culture.

John stuttered through his opinions.

On sports. He didn't follow the League of Champions.

On movies. He watched documentaries about the Outsiders.

On music. He listened to anatronica.

'John, I'm afraid we have a problem.'

'I'm sorry, sir. I don't understand.'

'You make Bell Corp millions of BellCoin each month.'

'I'm sorry, sir. I can do better. I've only been working twelve hours a day. I can put in fourteen hours a day, let's say...three days a week?'

Mr Morris sighed.

'All right, I can do fourteen every day.'

'John. John, John. Your Productivity isn't an issue. I've looked through your reports. Your Productivity Points are through the roof.'

'Oh.'

'There's no need to work longer hours.'

'Oh. Good.'

'However. Your opinions, John.' Mr Morris looked at him gravely. 'Your opinions just aren't right.'

John frowned at this, confused.

'They simply do not work, John. Listen to me.' Mr Morris lowered his voice to a whisper. 'There are rumours that you're up for a promotion, John. A big one. One that will bump you up from the seventy percenters to the twenty percenters.'

John took a deep breath. For several moments, he forgot to exhale. He couldn't believe it. This was his life's ambition.

'You're a strong contender to head Apex City's Policy and Governance Division. You're young, but your work ethic is precisely what we're looking for. We believe that you're the right man to get the job done.'

John fought the grin that was threatening to replace his expression of studied blankness.

No doubt he had it made as a seventy percenter. He had the best technology he could afford, he'd been on a virtual vacation, and he'd successfully racked up enough Productivity Points to distance himself from his Analog beginnings.

With its dusty streets and pod-housing, its roadside stalls and paper-money transactions, its promiscuity when it came to marriage, the Analog world was a lawless landscape to which he would never return.

And then there was the vegetable farm…

As a twenty percenter, he'd be so far up on the Bell Curve that he'd be untouchable. He'd ignore the pains of the Analog world and never look back. He'd possess exclusive HoloTech and Sentient Intelligence machines.

He'd go on vacations. On-site vacations.

A real night in Premier City…

'But.' Mr Morris's voice sliced through his dreams like a laser sabre. 'There is absolutely no way it can happen unless you repair your opinions. Do you understand?'

'N-no. Not yet. I mean, how do I repair my individually formed views of the world?'

Mr Morris sighed, flicking his ruby cufflinks and fiddling with the sleeves on his silk-lined jacket.

'I've made an appointment with Mrs Naidu.'

'The counsellor?'

'Yes, the company counsellor. Don't worry, it's off the record. I'm doing this as a favour. I believe in you, John.'

John exhaled. He arranged his face to wear a mask of gratitude.

At least it was off the record.

John was relieved that he had invested in a holographic keyboard. His palms pooled moisture where they met the fabric of his trousers, blotting against the skin on his thighs.

He took several deep breaths and surveyed the counsellor's office. He had a 360-degree view of it from within his VirtuoPod. The walls were painted white. The occasional happy kitten frolicked within its mounted frame. Motivational quotes cycled across the walls to his left and right.

'Persona is Prime.' 'Conform, don't Question.' 'Progress is Perfection.'

For several seconds, he wished he'd attended this session via his unidirectional flat-screen monitor. Instead, a perfect cylinder of glass cocooned him in its curvature, the Bell Corp insignia discreetly etched onto its surface. It simulated his surroundings to a fault.

John had invested in his set-up at home. He could transport himself to any Bell-approved location in the world and it would surround him, immersing him in high-fidelity reality.

He'd experienced sweeping Hyper Reality views from atop the Bell Towers in Crown City, awestruck as its nano-fibre constructions reoriented themselves with clockwork precision. They crested and descended, swivelling to make the most of their solar-harvesting capabilities, absorbing snatches of power from the sunlight that peeked through whips of rain lashing down from the sky.

He'd experienced a Hyper Real reconstruction of Apex City from decades ago, when it had still been named Bangalore. The immensity of the azure sky had left him speechless, arcing dome-like overhead and reflected in thousands of mirrored-glass buildings rising into the sky. When Bell Corp had taken over the city, they'd redesigned its architecture to eliminate all its heat islands. Now Bell Corp's twenty-six towers mushroomed over the streets, a bio-mat canopy that all but obscured the clouds. John would never forget his brief glimpse of the infinity that lay beyond the city's skyscape.

If he made it to the top twenty percent of society, he'd gain admission to far more elaborate experiences; rumour had it that the apex of the Curve could access olfactory simulations.

Mrs Naidu cleared her throat. John returned to the present.

She was probably seated in a set-up similar to his own.

She looked at him indifferently. 'John Alvares, I want to get to know you.'

'Okay.' His throat felt dry.

'I'm going to project a series of images onto your screen. Name them.'

'Okay.' His throat seized up. He wasn't expecting a test.

'Ready?'

A sequence of cards appeared on the screen. The first was open-faced and had a timer beneath it. He surmised he had ten seconds to guess who each figure on the cards was.

He stumbled through his guesses.

'The Vindicators, that superhero group. Um. Barthöven, I dunno, all neo-Acousta composers look the same. Um, Steel Man. Er, wait, I know this one... *I really do* – no, let's skip it. Um, *Battle Arena* champion who's a famous VR fighter? I dunno, I really don't follow the League of Champions. Star Masters, the sci-fi franchise, not sure what the bad guy's name is. Ahh. *Clash of Empires*, the docudrama. I think this one is a start-up queen from the 2000s...the founder of FreshGoodz? I give up.'

He fell quiet. He didn't recognize the next ten characters.

Mrs Naidu let him fail. Repeatedly.

She could have stopped the sequence at any time, but she seemed to revel in his inadequacy.

When the sequence ran out, she didn't say a word.

She typed away soundlessly on her holographic keyboard.

'Is that all?' John broke the silence.

Mrs Naidu looked up at him.

'Hardly.' She paused. 'Tell me, John, is there a specific reason you refuse to engage with the contemporary and the classical alike?'

'What, no...'

'Do you believe yourself superior to your peers? Or perhaps superior to the creators of all these cultural phenomena?'

'No.'

'Or maybe you think this makes you special? Your *non-conformity*?'

'No, er,' John stammered. 'I mean, I guess I'm just not interested in this stuff. My interests are different.'

He couldn't tell her the truth. This meeting might be off the record, but truth was more valuable than BellCoin, and his would be his undoing.

'How did you come to possess this very specific disinterest?' Mrs Naidu probed. 'Is it because you have very specific interests?'

'What? I *like* the things I'm into.'

'The world around you doesn't *like* the same things, so how did you come to be so special?'

'I…I don't know.'

'Are you a rebel?' she spat.

John flinched, and pushed his chair back. She was looming over him, a terrifying presence, even though they were only conversing through the technology of their VirtuoPods.

'A closet punk? An Outsider activist? An Analog *sympathist*?'

'What, no…' John was horrified. Were therapists supposed to display such obvious biases?

'What's your position on Outsider immigration?'

'I…er –'

'What's your *opinion* on the Analog world?'

The words scrambled their way out of John, rushing out in a single breath as he rose to his defence.

'It's a terrible place. People don't have access to technology. To portals. They have printed newspapers. They're forced to talk to each other in person every single day, experience the weather without being able to control it… Many of them are used by the twenty percenters in their Pleasure Domes, and many of them are forced to serve us – the seventy percenters, I mean – whenever we demand it of them. And the most Unproductive Analogs, they're, well…the vegetable farm…'

'Hmm.' Mrs Naidu seemed to nod in approval.

'I've never belonged to it, and I never want to,' John finished conclusively and, he hoped, convincingly.

'You're a seventy percenter, John. Life is good, yes? Well, it can get better when you belong to the top twenty percent. You do want to make it, I suppose? You want legal avenues to get married, be popular, own property, travel the world?'

She waited for him to supply a nod.

'Then you need to know this. Your opinions, your interests, they're not just infra-Bell, they're positively *anti-Bell*. I could write up a report that states the same. Of course, it will only ensure that you never make it to the twenty-percent club. The rest of your downward spiral will be your fault.'

She paused.

'I've seen it all before. You'll be so demotivated that your Productivity will start to slip. Before you know it, you'll be downgraded to Analog status. Maybe you'll make a living on the other side, *somehow*...but it's far more likely that you'll wind up in the vegetable farm.'

John shuddered.

'So why don't you tell me the truth? What went wrong with you? Were your parents rebels?'

'My parents died when I was young.'

Reflex.

Muscle memory took over.

'I was raised by their housekeeper. An Analog woman.'

Lies.

A spasm shot through the nerves in his neck as he felt his humanity crack.

'That explains your non-conformist streak.' Her tone was sympathetic with notes of contempt.

John watched her eyes scan something on her screen.

She clucked twice.

'Peace Riot, really! That's as cultured as a bottom feeder. Subscriptions to *Outside Matters* and a history of streaming HoloTube shows about *their lot*. A signed petition for trade negotiations to resume between the Delhi Aqua-Soc and the Krishna–Godavari Agro-Soc... Why does it matter to you if Krishna–Godavari's drought remains unresolved? So what if Delhi refuses to supply them with water?'

'I believe in being informed –'

'I've got the entire report here, you know? Nearly every search term you've ever typed into your devices has been flagged on the Nebula by Bell Corp's Seditious Activities Unit. All the conversations you've ever had with your co-workers have been recorded. You've raised several eyebrows, and not in the right way.'

She paused, encountered stony silence, and pressed on with her interrogation.

'Are you a *nationalist*?'

'What, no –' John almost rose to the bait, but caught himself.

'Then you know this, John Alvares. I repeat it for your benefit. The Outside is none of your concern. Your allegiance...your *focus* should rest on all matters within the Bell Corp domain, *particularly* within Apex City. Do you understand?'

He seethed in silence.

'Good, good, you're learning.'

The woman's gaze was appraising.

'That's good. Mouldable, pliable, you're open to changing.'

'Changing what?' John snapped, caught himself again, and repeated the words more civilly. 'Changing what?'

'Every single thing about yourself.'

John felt hollow. It had been this way since he had first crossed the border from the Analog to the Virtual world.

The lies, they ballooned.

Soon, they would slip from his grasp and float away.

What would be left behind?

Tonight's interview wasn't one in the strictest sense. John had been invited to Mr Morris's penthouse, located on the two hundred and forty-fifth floor of a condo in the Central Business District, right at the heart of Apex City.

The building was state-of-the-art, built from bio-mats designed to self-regulate temperature and heat emissions. Its upper floors divaricated into a delta of planar platforms, enabling solar harvesting across the entirety of their curved surface area. Looking up from the street, one saw what appeared to be a cluster of lily pads hovering in the sky. Each lily pad – for that's what they were called by passers-by and tourists – powered its own en-suite apartment. The building boasted the newest developments by Bell Corp's Sustainable Architecture Division, and had been aptly named the Lotus Blossom.

John had always likened it to the Venus flytrap sitting in a bright yellow planter on his dresser. He was about to step within its reach.

He exhaled slowly. If he landed this promotion, he'd be able to move out of the seventy-percenter housing units in the Hexadrome. He might even be able to afford one of the flytrap's – no, the *Lotus Blossom's* – apartments a decade from now.

All he had to do was impress.

Mr Morris had called the event a cocktail party.

'It's tradition,' he had said.

It's theatre, John had thought.

A way for twenty percenters to make him the evening's entertainment. A worthy proposition for which they'd leave their upscale residences to be physically present in the same room in order to examine him in person. A performance so they could decide if he was ready to be elevated to their circles on the Curve.

John's Social Persona would be under intense scrutiny. Mr Morris's guests would hover around him like vultures, pecking at his eyes and skin until they found the nicks in his smooth facade.

Step right up!

John smiled at himself in the reflecto-screen. He was fresh out of the shower. His clothes hung on the rack – a semi-casual collared Brunieri T-shirt, a carefully fitted fawn jacket from Bijou, and tailored blue trousers. The buttons on his jacket were dark topaz, hand-carved to reflect the Bell Corp insignia. Each one perfectly articulated the shape of a rising curve, swelling into its crest and descending into a flatline – a symbol of his commitment to Bell Corp's philosophy. His spectacles lay on the dresser; vintage with thick frames, for a bit of drama. The entire ensemble was worth his annual bonus in BellCoin, but it was nothing he couldn't recover if he landed this promotion.

He was almost ready. There was just one last thing he needed to do.

He sat on his bed. Op.He.Li.aA glided across the floor towards him.

She had been waiting for him. She was good at waiting.

#lifegoals, he thought.

This was their own strange code, a series of hashtags they used to let each other know what they were thinking and feeling.

She had the uncanny ability to understand every phrase and idea that popped into his head, continually relayed to her via the Bell Biochip implanted behind his ear. He wanted her to know that he was looking forward to this moment, that this would be the culmination of all his work over the years.

He wanted her to know that he couldn't have done it without her.

Op.He.Li.aA radiated an air of tranquillity, her amorphous, globular being thrumming with the energy of earnestness. It spread through the room like a very still breeze.

She was going to help him. She had no eyes and no limbs, but she was here to help John, and John was there to receive her.

#letsdothis, he thought.

Op.He.Li.aA stood still on the floor beside his bed.

John felt her filling his vision, enrapturing him. His eyes lost their usually sharp focus. He smiled, emptying them of all concern.

He'd learnt so much about her that he recognized she was smiling back at him. She had no eyes and no mouth, but he could tell.

He reached out to touch her, patting her on the head like she was a well-behaved child.

#allinthistogether

He pulled his OmniPort from his pocket, and her being began to expand so that she loomed over him. She wasn't intimidating. She was soothing, encouraging him to be his natural self.

John accessed a portal on his OmniPort.

Op.He.Li.aA extended a slender appendage from within her mass. She placed it on his shoulder. It wasn't cold, but it wasn't warm either.

John looked up at where her eyes might have been, and felt her staring at him. They shared a quiet moment, and then he returned his attention to the device in his hand, swiping at the holographic icons hovering over its surface.

Op.He.Li.aA sent a wave of warmth through the point where she touched his skin.

#goodvibes

He absorbed himself in the contents being beamed by his OmniPort.

The wave became a steady pulse…

John started, disrupting the flow of warmth.

White Noise had a new single out.

He loved White Noise! He'd owned every album of theirs in his Analog days.

She felt his heartbeat rise.

John tapped on the HoloTube link. The holovid popped up, hovering a few inches above the screen.

Op.He.Li.aA sent a jolt of electricity through him.

He gasped in pain.

#nocookie

The appendage she'd placed on his shoulder had gotten sharper, more pointed. It had acquired the shape of a very small chisel. She pushed the point of the chisel into John's ear.

John didn't wince. The sensation was more ticklish than painful, and he'd got used to it. This was how Op.He.Li.aA was designed to rewire his natural opinions.

She pushed the chisel deep into his ear, and began to tease something out of his head. A wave of sound emerged, impaled upon the tool. The beat of an electrotemp, accompanied by a simulosynth loop and the rhythm of a holofret filled the room, each of the musical instruments no more than a Hyper Reality simulator.

A large hole began to open up in the sentient silicone machine, into which it placed this mysterious sound artefact.

John heard a snatch of lyric.

'To get ahead I sold…'

Op.He.Li.aA swallowed and grinned, and the rest of the words were lost to vacuum.

She had a mouth now.

John didn't notice. He was immersed in a neo-Acousta performance, a form of music as unfamiliar to him as the Virtual world had once been.

La Ménagerie.

Only three songs, but forty minutes long. Someone had told him that neo-Acousta was meant to celebrate the purity of sound. It was only ever performed using physical acoustic instruments. An immaculate expression.

Op.He.Li.aA pressed another appendage to his chest.

Empathy and tenderness rippled through his skin, opening up his pores. The sound was rich and robust. He was receptive, welcoming of its invasive tones.

He experienced a musical epiphany.

Why had he listened to White Noise in the first place? This was aural ambrosia, even if it was so curious that he couldn't name more than three of the instruments being played.

Op.He.Li.aA supplied the list.

A grand piano. Two acou-violins. A glass flute. A double bass. A wood-guitar…

John mouthed the words and they rolled off his tongue like caramel. They stuck to his palate and his teeth, refusing to dislodge themselves with grace.

#satire

#polychromatic #microtonal

#allusion

Op.He.Li.aA projected keywords into his mind that he would later be able to use in conversation.

John digested them without recognizing the meaning of most.

She listed homages to past neo-Acousta composers, a list of unpronounceable names that John stored away in his memory. She drew attention to the innate cleverness of the construction. She pointed out that this arrangement featured a wood-guitarist, a rare occurrence in a world dominated by the holofret.

She emphasized the satirical nature of the work.

The glass flute played a lofty air accompanied by piano trills, elevating the piece titled 'Les Cochons'. The weight of the double bass accented 'La Voliére des Rêves', playing counterpoint to the rest of the arrangement.

His mind reverberated with the crash and chime of unfamiliar instruments beating upon an alien vocabulary.

'La Voliére des Rêves,' he spoke the French out loud. It flowed like toffee.

Op.He.Li.aA looked at him with undisguised pride.

#progressisperfection

John felt a rush of pleasure pulse through him.

Once the last movement, 'Les Singes', had played itself out – it was downtempo, extensive dramatic passages building up to triumphant crescendos – he breathed in the silence.

Then he brought up *Outside Matters*, his news-reading portal of habit.

> Tidal waves batter the coast of Kochi Contingency-Soc. Apex City denies aid until the Malabar Trade Treaty is upheld –

He'd barely made it through the sentence when Op.He.Li.aA sent electricity shooting through him.

She was growing a third appendage now. It was long and flat with a serrated surface. She held this delicately over John's left eye, rubbing it over the soft tissue of his cornea.

He felt the information he had just absorbed flaking away, specks of dust that would lie on the floor of his mind, unnoticed. A low series of scrapes filled the air as her silicone and electronic being filed the edges of his vision, curbing the radius of his thought.

She then lifted the tool and, holding it over his right eye, repeated the process.

John felt no discomfort at his temporary blindness. The first time he'd experienced it, he'd panicked. Now he knew Op.He.Li.aA was leading him to a safe place. When his vision returned, he'd see the world in an entirely different light.

With a chorus of beeps and whirs, she stuck out her long, slithery tongue. She placed a handful of small shavings on the gluey surface and began to retract it with care. Sight was a delicate thing, and it needed to be carefully moderated for human consumption.

John's vision returned to him in a rush, blurry at first and then in high definition. The impulse to learn about the latest world issues had left him.

The portal he was looking at was of no use. He accessed the *Pop Vulture*, which supplied him with cleverly written editorials.

11 Ways We Thought the Vindicators Movies Would Be Cooler

John's eyes widened. He'd been exposed to dozens of superhero arcs through these lists. He began to absorb its criticisms of the franchise so that he could parrot the observations away to the twenty percenters who, no doubt, had read the same article tonight.

27 Things about *Clash of Empires* That Will Blow Your Mind

The series was a fictionalized account of the start-up wars that had ravaged Apex City, back when it was still a disorganized town called Bangalore. The programme was set in the days just after the Population Catastrophe had resulted in the collapse of nation states. Every city had been forced to fend for itself in a world starved of resources and ravaged by climate change, taking to bartering resources to maintain peace and stability. Bell Corporation had emerged in erstwhile Singapore, and had systematically invested in technologically forward hubs across the world, including what was then Bangalore. It instituted a system of meritocracy, mapping civilization onto the Bell Curve. Grim, gritty and filled with lo-tech political drama, the series had captivated Virtual denizens with its account of their roots. Obscure trivia about the show would further prove to the twenty percenters that he was *socially relevant*.

Top 40 Hype Tunes for Every Party

He'd never heard most of this music until Op.He.Li.aA had introduced him to it. It was nothing like the politically charged and often introspective music of anatronica. Hype was digitally created as well, but it radiated positivity. It was the aural equivalent of sunshine, with its songs about fast cars and ballads about travel. He'd surprised everyone at the most recent office party with his expertise on the genre.

It would help to go over the list again so he could impress both neo-Acousta lovers and Hype aficionados with his versatile interests.

If only he didn't have to be ashamed of his love for anatronica…

Op.He.Li.aA watched his thought process play out in silence. Her appendages hovered mere millimetres from his shoulder. She was entirely prepared for him to fail to come to a socially approved conclusion. She had electroshocked him into the right opinions several times over the course of the last month.

John's mind looped itself around the anti-acoustic sounds of White Noise and the Fracas. He thought of the pacifo-punk band Peace Riot and the alt-tronica moodiness of the Placebo Effect. Brilliant musicians restricted to using virtually created sounds to express themselves.

Why did Virtuals prize the possession of a grand piano when they shuddered at the sight of a newspaper?

His great-great-grandmother had owned a grand piano, according to family legend. It had been seized during the Bell Takeover, to be handed back to the family should they demonstrate sufficient merit on the Curve. John had never laid eyes on it.

Op.He.Li.aA placed her appendages on his shoulders, preparing to administer a sharp poke of electricity.

And then John was immersed in a preview of Edie Taylor's insipid new Hype single, 'Summer Sunshine'.

John caught himself and smiled. Did he think insipid?

He laughed.

No, he meant *inspiring*. She was a role model, after all.

His eyes lost the lustre of thought, and he watched the video with his mouth agape.

Op.He.Li.aA grinned, displaying an array of teeth filed to points within the rubbery gash that served as her mouth. He'd made progress.

When John was midway through the holovid, a notification popped up.

His heart skipped a beat and his eyes flicked to where Op.He.Li.aA stood.

A line of furrows rippled over silicone. Op.He.Li.aA scowled.

John didn't like it when she got angry. Notifications from his other life made her mad.

#triggerwarning, she said.

He read the text message. It was from his father.

> Hey John,
>
> I heard you got an interview today, kiddo. Good luck. I wish you'd call sometime.
>
> Lots of love,
>
> Dad

John fought the urge to reply right away.

He felt his fabricated existence begin to crumble.

He had been raised an Analog, and both his parents were very much alive. They looked upon him with love and pride, while he categorically denied their existence. But he'd come from a black hole where technology meant a cellular phone, where all social interactions were face-to-face. They'd raised him there without ever trying to do better!

He'd had to create his opportunities for himself. He'd studied long hours to win an extremely rare scholarship to a university in the Virtual world. He'd worked more hours than anyone he knew. He'd clawed his way up the ranks of the seventy percenters. Each time he looked down, he saw the long shadow of his past. He had begun to hack away at his roots, tearing at his tethers in the hope that it would set him free.

The pinnacle of his achievements was in sight, if only he could soar to reach it.

He couldn't lose focus. Not now.

If anyone from tonight's cocktail party caught the stench of his lineage…

He would come crashing down. Get passed over. Be a seventy percenter for life.

#TRIGGERWARNING

Op.He.Li.aA's appendages had begun to burn uncomfortably warm.

He continued to feed his thoughts, ignoring her.

Twenty percenters carried their lineage like a badge. Most of them were second-generation, at the very least.

He'd ignored his parents and sister for years, visiting unannounced and on the sly, covering up his absences. His co-workers were competitive, bloodthirsty. It would take but one rumour –

A ripple of shock rocked through John's body, sending him into convulsions for what felt like an age. When the shaking stopped and his limbs fell away from him, weak, his thoughts scattered.

Op.He.Li.aA swept John up in an embrace. A part of her gelatinous corpus had climbed onto the bed.

#worthit #dontworrybehappy #toughlove

John nodded in agreement. A wave of ecstasy passed through his tired muscles, and he surrendered to it.

He reconfigured his thoughts. He constructed his past with care, emptying his mind of memory.

His parents were dead. They'd disappeared while on a twenty-percenter expedition. They'd been visiting an exotic Analog village on the fringes of Apex City. Rumour had it that they'd been murdered by the Analogs, their technology scavenged and sold to the highest bidder. Their bodies had been burnt so it would be the perfect crime.

He'd ensured that it would remain the perfect crime when he'd read about a similar attack that had left countless dead. He'd falsified his genealogy and claimed to be a survivor, paying extensive sums of BellCoin to keep the document trail a secret.

John dismissed the text message from his father and swiped through his portals. He accessed Woofer, the social media platform with a signature holovid-enhancing technology. It allowed Virtuals to post immersive videos of their surroundings – 360-degree explorations of worlds both real and fantastical – that could be explored using nothing more than an OmniPort and intel-lenses. Olfactory simulations were supposed to be their most exclusive offering.

John accessed the first Woofer handle that appeared: *@lifeinthedustbowl*. It was a popular stream from the Outside.

Op.He.Li.aA shot a warning bolt of unpleasantness through him. John nearly dropped his OmniPort, not having recovered from his previous shock yet.

Drought and famine were problems of the Outside. Political awareness, particularly regarding unpleasant events, was not prized by the twenty percenters. They perceived it as dangerous, a sign of activism.

John typed a suggestion from Op.He.Li.aA into the search field: *#vacayyaycay*

He scrolled through a list of woofs from twenty percenters across the world. They were in real-life vacation spots – the kind he'd someday visit himself.

He picked a holovid to immerse himself in. It was a rare glimpse of a secret beach untouched by climate change. White sand spread around him for miles, water of the most pristine aqua lapping at its shores. The holovid wrapped itself around him like a waking dream, the reality of his apartment fading in the cloud of pixel dust.

The only vacation he'd ever been on had been a Virtual one, the kind offered to seventy percenters via their VirtuoPods. He'd experienced an immersive Hyper Reality tour of the Musée d'Orsay in the historically preserved town of Paris.

John couldn't wait to be a twenty percenter, to earn the right to travel the world by physically teleporting to locations outside Apex City. For the moment, though, this would do.

Op.He.Li.aA shrank to a third her size and hauled herself up onto the bed, sitting on his bare chest.

John gazed at the endless ocean of possibility that beckoned him onward, and the two shared a companionable silence.

He liked the woof.

He continued to browse his feed, looking at 360-degree fitness routines and attending the high-fidelity birthday celebrations of the rich and famous. He liked many of the experiences appropriately.

Each time he responded to them, he felt the dopamine centres in his head fill to bursting.

Op.He.Li.aA had sprouted a raceme of stubby appendages. She resembled a gelatinous anemone. She placed them all on his chest, sending billions of little pulses of pleasure into him.

John laughed so much that he couldn't remember anything else that had happened to him that day.

She grinned at him.

He knew in that instant that he was ready.

He would blow the twenty percenters' minds with the seamless way in which he fit into their society.

He would make them laugh, he would make them think, he would offer them the prompts and cues that were endlessly reproduced at every single party, and he would elicit all the right responses.

It was a behavioural experiment.

They would like him. They would love him.

He had moved outside of his real self. He had discarded it like an exoskeleton, crawled out of it and turned into a green bird with a red beak, its wings clipped.

Who was he, anyway, if not for his plumage?

They would love him because he was filled with all the things they liked to hear. They would love him because he was empty.

Ask and turn up empty.
Seek and you find lies.
Take. Settle for nothing.
Take the world back.

– Password to the Electric Underground

SYMPHONY FOR THE DISENFRANCHISED TEENAGER

AN UNOBTRUSIVE PACKAGE LAY on the doorstep wrapped in brown paper and grime.

It was addressed to no one. It might have been meant for his parents, but they weren't around and Arun was a nobody too, so he reasoned that it was fair game.

He shut the door and carried it carefully into the gloom of his 140-square-foot pod-house. Streaks of light broke their way through a filthy porthole. He stood before the glass and unwrapped the object, ignoring the filth that rubbed away onto his fingers.

A cassette lay in the palm of his hand.

He gingerly held it between his thumb and forefinger, turning it over to see if it was marked. Anatronica artists regularly distributed their work in the neighbourhood this way. Each artist was known by their unique symbol. A peace sign on fire was the emblem of the Fracas. A black flower meant it was a Peace Riot album.

This cassette was unmarked.

Arun should have been on his way to his latest apprenticeship. He was only a week into it, and was under pressure to demonstrate his value to the thieves of the Sutae tribe. He acknowledged that he was a terrible pickpocket, and he was only slightly more skilled at keeping their accounts. Try as he might, he seemed destined to fail. He debated going to work, but decided this cassette was far more interesting.

He reached for his Walkman where it lay on a cardboard box. He hoped its batteries were working.

He popped out the Placebo Effect album he'd been listening to a few days ago, the band's distinctive purple pill shimmering off the plastic. Most anatronica albums were produced on the Virtual side of the city, their lyrics carefully monitored by Bell Corp.

This cassette felt *original.*

He carefully placed it into its slot and snapped the listening device shut. He pushed his earphones in and hit play.

A gentle hiss filled his ears.

He heard a button being pushed down. The noise receded.

'Like what you hear?'

The voice was jagged, echoing as if its message had been recorded several times over.

'The password's in the chorus. We invite you to join us.'

A peal of bells playing a musical scale followed, only for the sound to shatter. The pattern repeated, escalating in tempo. There was the thwack of a heavy object repeatedly striking something fleshy, followed by cries of pain. This was swallowed by a rush of electronic dissonance, as if every machine ever created had gone haywire all at once. An accelerating beat emerged from this wall of sound like a panic attack. Spewing forth from a haze of static were vocals thick with rage.

Arun felt the music pound against the insides of his skull. The song was over before he realized that he hadn't caught a single lyric.

He hit rewind. Listened to the message again. Listened to the wave of sound drown him in its fury. Tried to listen to the words, but found himself lost in a sudden rush of anger.

He repeated this process again. And again.

On his eleventh listen, the lyrics began to emerge.

Arun fumbled for a scrap of paper and a pen.

He began to scribble out the chorus. He missed a few words.

He hit rewind.

His ballpoint was running out of ink.

He stabbed at the paper, desperately trying to etch the words onto its surface as the pen began to trail pools of ink across the page.

He hit rewind.

The last few words fell into place.

He had found the password. Now he'd have to find the right door.

Arun emerged from his pod-house that evening running on a frenzy of energy. He'd listened to the song until his batteries had run out of power. He'd swapped a week's ration of nutro-shakes with his neighbour for a brand-new pair.

He'd neglected to show up at his apprenticeship today. His parents had returned from labouring in Bell Corp's vertical farms to discover him brooding over another cassette, and had politely asked him to take to the streets if he wanted to express his angst.

Arun was used to this. He'd never amounted to much at the Institute. He'd been bored, but in cramped classrooms filled with dozens of children they'd believed him slow. He'd dropped out early and had taken to doing odd jobs to save up. A wad of paper money lay hidden in the cover of a Systems Warp cassette, stuffed into a hole in the ground outside his pod-house.

Most Analogs saved up to buy smuggled fresh fruit. Arun was going to buy a tent of his own, far from his mother's disappointed gaze. A pod-house was unattainable, but a tent would do. At eighteen, it was about time he struck out on his own.

He hit play again as he walked past Market Square and down the dimly lit streets. The jacaranda tree was a dense shadow in the firelight. Ever since its appearance, a cavern of need had yawned within his chest. He longed to discover a way to fill it.

He was sure the cassette had been meant for him. He was convinced it had chosen him. For the first time in his life, he felt awake and filled with the stirrings of an unnameable desire.

He headed straight to the Burnt Crusader. It was the first anatronica club on his list of suspects.

The club was a makeshift tent made from tattered fabric. It lay at the heart of the Vitae tribe's tent city and was frequented by scavengers trying to sell their salvaged finds. Its unwieldy wooden speakers boomed the latest offering from White Noise. He was admitted freely, but not before he was offered a set of weathered bone buttons, an ancient car battery with juice in it – the scavenger had demonstrated that it was fully functional by sparking a light bulb – and a thick overcoat whose seller promised it would keep him cool.

'It's always sweltering, here.' Arun had laughed.

'Just put it on and stay indoors. Stay very still. It's better than ClimaTech, it'll keep the cool in.'

'Sorry, not looking to buy today.' He'd shrugged.

'I have the password,' he told the woman at the bar as she poured him a drink of home-brewed StarShimmer.

She laughed and walked away.

It was an unsuccessful evening.

The next night, he tried the Rusty Forager, right at the edge of the Junkyard. The structure was riveted together from scraps of metal. Bulbs hung on naked wires and its speakers – cobbled together from electronics and tin cans – spat out the sounds of the Fracas. When he claimed to have the password, the other Analogs at the bar gave him a wide berth.

He hurriedly made his way across the length of the city of dust, back to the pod-houses. He stepped through the door of the Cracked Spine, on the ground floor of a wrecked pod-house. It had been restored sufficiently to let it function as a dingy club. He looked around for signs of clandestine activity and found none.

He turned to leave. His shoulders sagged, the weight of disappointment settling heavy upon him.

As he walked out the door, someone placed a hand on his shoulder.

'I believe you're looking for the Electric Underground. Try the sewers.'

Arun started. He turned to catch a glimpse of the speaker, to ask for directions, to ask how they knew that he had the mysterious password, but the stranger was gone.

The underground drainage system formed a network of passages beneath Apex City, spanning the area of the Analog side and running beneath the Carnatic Meridian all the way to the Virtual city. It had long since dried out from disuse in the Analog world, once Bell Corp had cut off their access to running water, but a veneer of mould coated its walls and it reeked of the damp.

Arun knew that the club – the Electric Underground – was unlikely to be nested too deep within the labyrinth. If they'd sent the invite, they expected people to show up, and that meant they'd be near civilization.

He was near the workshops of the Tatae craftsmiths, somewhat south of the pod-houses and the Cracked Spine, somewhat north of the tent city and the Rusty Forager.

His candle flickered in an unexpected draft. Arun's hands involuntarily touched his pockets to make sure his matches were still on him.

He'd been following a series of heavy pulses that seemed to reverberate through the concrete floor of the tunnel. They were either from a booming bass or from the Tatae craftsmiths' experiments with flammable material. The floor beneath him seemed to rock again. He quickened his pace, trying to reckon where the vibrations were strongest. Whether through actual skill or sheer dumb luck, he found himself at a door after an hour of wandering in the dank.

A heavy metal door, locked and barred.

Arun wiped the sweat from his brow. He lifted his hand to knock when a slit in the door slid open.

'Password,' a voice rasped.

Arun had carried the scrap of paper in his pocket, just in case, but he'd listened to the song so many times that he knew all the lyrics – not just the chorus – like the back of his hand.

He recited the phrases nervously.

The door opened, and out spilled the powerful, raw anger of an anatronica song he'd never heard before.

'Welcome to the resistance,' the woman said. 'Stop gaping at us and hurry in.'

Arun stepped into the club. The noise drowned his anxiety and filled him with manic energy. He began to process that the woman had called this 'the resistance'.

He went to the bar and ordered a drink of StarShimmer.

A woman with short, spiky hair was seated beside him.

'I just got here too.' She smiled. 'The resistance – it's so exciting!'

Arun downed his shot of StarShimmer and his head spun with anticipation.

'I'm Rohini.' She offered a hand. 'My friends call me Ro.'

'Arun,' he said, accepting it. 'What happens here?'

'I don't know. I suppose we wait around for them to make speeches or something? The invite wasn't very clear.'

'Did you listen to the tape too?' Arun asked.

She rolled her eyes. 'How else could I have gotten in?'

'Oh, right.'

'Wasn't it incredible?' she gushed. 'So raw.'

'So much anger!' He nodded, then added, 'It…it really riled me up.'

'Don't you feel like you just want to *do something*?' she asked.

'Like what?' he said slowly.

'I don't know. Set things on fire. Blow stuff up.'

He looked at her cautiously. Her eyes glittered in the yellow light.

'You should be careful what you say to strangers,' he said.

'What do you mean?'

'Everyone knows the Virtuals have an informant or two in our midst. You don't want to end up being…' He swallowed and said the word, 'Harvested.'

She seemed taken aback for a moment, but then laughed.

'We're in a top secret club. We were invited here to join something that's imaginatively called "the resistance". I believe we're going to topple the Virtual world order.'

She eyed him over the top of her glass. 'Our problems are going to amount to more than just routine harvesting if we get caught, don't you think?'

Arun ordered two more shots of StarShimmer.

The thought hadn't occurred to him up until this moment.

At first, it had been about solving its puzzle. But the song…

The song had cracked him open. It had left him with an ache in his chest, a burning in his skull. The very air he exhaled felt molten.

'Are you scared?' Rohini eyed him curiously.

He was. Terrified, in fact, but he was also –

'Ready,' he clarified. 'Scared too. But more than anything, ready.'

Productivity is Power.

– from the Meritocratic Manifesto,
'Concerning Virtual Citizen Reports', Article I (a)

ANALOG/VIRTUAL

PIP.

The Bell Biochip implanted behind my ear beeps. It has clocked the exact moment of my waking.

I blink. The world around me is blurry.

It must be close to noon. I can tell from the way the sunlight falls on the wall.

I've learnt to tell time by gazing at patterns of light, this past month. It's one of the perks of being unemployed.

My Bell Biochip beeps again, reminding me to get a move on. If I don't clock sufficient neural and physical activity today, I'll slide further down the Curve. That's a slippery slope all the way down to the vegetable farm.

I laugh and it comes out as a hoarse chuckle. I wonder what the Bell Bio Portal will recommend today. I've been on its Productivity Improvement Programme ever since I was laid off.

I procrastinate, ignoring the persistent thrum of my OmniPort. If something important had occurred, it would be holo-rayed across my walls.

I need a coffee before I take a look at what the hamster wheel has in store for me.

I roll out of bed and shuffle to my refrigerator.

It turns out that a day is made up of more minutes than I ever thought possible.

It used to be easier, of course. As a Bell Corp employee, I once had a calendar filled with meetings. All my free time was carefully calibrated with recommended productive, social and learning activities to ensure that my mind and body were optimized for performance. I was trained to rise to the top twenty percent of high-functioning individuals in society. I'd been so close to achieving my goal…and then they'd taken my dreams away from me.

My mother died.

My motivation slipped. My Productivity tanked.

Here I am. Unemployed.

There's no room for error in Apex City.

Yes, I'm bitter.

I reach for the milk.

'Bottom feeder!' I swear.

I'm out of milk.

I haven't ordered groceries off the FreshGoodz portal this week.

I sink to the floor, crossing my legs beneath me. The refrigerator bathes me in its unhealthy glow. There are scant findings within.

No more cheese.

The only food left is a solitary head of broccoli. I wonder how old it is.

It's funny that I haven't noticed this up until now. I don't exactly have a job that provides me with a constant supply of food through the day. Or with free candy and alcohol.

Come to think of it, the Bell Bio Portal should have prompted me to buy groceries last night.

I pull my OmniPort from my pocket and gaze at its camera. Its iris-scanner acknowledges my identity, and the transparent glass interface lights up, reflecting my face.

Dark circles and unkempt hair.

I take a photograph and the device unlocks, simultaneously uploading my picture onto the Nebula, where it'll live on the Bell Corp database. I've checked in as alive and productive for the day. Productive with a capital 'P'.

I wait for a holo-ray of portals to appear in the empty air above the OmniPort.

Several seconds pass by.

I look down and nearly drop my device. Where I'm used to seeing a slew of three-dimensional portals hovering over the surface, I see right through it. There's only my hand resting on the underside of the device. At the centre of the glass interface is a flat envelope with an enormous red tag on it.

One unread notification.

'Ten percent!' I swear. Sweat beads upon my forehead.

It's a message from Bell Corp. It's unacceptable to leave a notification unattended at the best of times, but for someone who's unemployed and on a PIP, it could have disastrous consequences.

I take a deep breath and tap on it.

Dear Anita,

It has come to our notice that you have currently crossed 31 days of Unemployment. Until further notice, your Unemployment status has been transitioned from Acute to Chronic.

My throat seizes up. How could I have lost track of this?

In light of this unfortunate circumstance, we have taken the liberty to recalibrate all portals associated with monitoring your Productivity.

Your PIP will now recommend tasks that will gently guide you towards life in the Analog world. We have taken this measure to help you adjust to Analog living, should you fail to achieve your targets.

We hope that you will bounce back and be worthy of being a Virtual Citizen once more.

Have a great day!

Gentle reminder: Failure to achieve your PIP targets will lead to deportation. You will be labelled Unproductive, your Virtual Citizen Report will be terminated, and you will be relocated to the Analog world.

My heart hammers an irregular staccato within my chest. I read through the notice again, and twice more.

A single slip could send me straight to the vegetable farm –

I rise and slam the refrigerator door shut.

I will not be an Analog.

I wonder if I should call my father. He's in his seventies and still at the top twenty percent of the Curve, in spite of his wife's untimely demise.

I reach for my OmniPort, then stop myself. I can't face his disappointment. He's worked twice as hard as all his peers to earn his place at the top and stay there. He's made his mark, in spite of being an immigrant from the Outside. He's had to realign his thought processes to internalize Bell Corp's ideals of meritocracy, a concept alien to someone from a cooperative Agro-Soc like Kodagu. This will break his heart.

He doesn't know that I've been fired. I'd rather keep him in the dark, halfway across the world in his retirement village in Crest City.

In fact, I don't think he knows that I was passed over for that promotion, that it was handed to Mark Morris's protégé, that ruthless cut-throat who surged ahead when my performance started to slip...

I cringe at the two-dimensionality of the graphics now playing on my OmniPort. A series of animations shows a woman racing towards radiant light. It plays on loop – its colours bright and unforgiving – compelling me to tap on it, if only to dismiss it.

I comply.

Welcome back, Anita!

Hi, there!

I realize I have to *tap* on the auto-generated response to proceed. I stare at it for several moments before I hit the button. Another line of pre-programmed text appears in place of the last, my suggested response highlighted in blue. I grit my teeth and tap.

Are you ready
for your new life?

You bet!

This is horrific. They've replaced every piece of HoloTech on my phone with technology that hasn't been used in decades. They're downgrading me from the Virtual world already.

The graphics aren't holographic, or even 3D. There's no audio.

I can't believe I have to read all this input.

You might feel like you're
on your way to Unproductivity
right now...

I'm scared.

This might be true, but it's presumptuous of the program to expect me to admit it. I wouldn't, except that I have no choice.

Never fear!
The Bell Bio Portal is here!
We're going to help you
get your life back on track!

Yay!

I grimace and tap.

All you have to do is
master a new quest
every single day!

How?

Let's start with
today's little challenge.

An envelope appears on screen. It animates itself open and presents me with a task:

Buy groceries and make yourself dinner!

I'm reeling from the flatness of this experience, but I know that I need to get a move on if I want to avoid the vegetable farm.

'FreshGoodz!' I say out loud.

The portal should open up in front of me.

I should be able to view a holo-ray history of my previous purchases.

The OmniPort doesn't respond.

'Ten percent!'

I touch the glass. The icons wriggle. I sigh.

Do I have to move them around with my fingers now?

I swipe. The mess of icons is replaced by another.

I manually swipe through the images on the glass. They're two-dimensional. There's a lag. Precious seconds tick by and I'm on the verge of imploding with impatience when I finally locate the orange FreshGoodz icon.

I tap on it.

No holo-ray.

I wince.

'Slacker,' I bite out.

I swipe through my shopping history. The great thing about FreshGoodz is that it syncs with my Bell Biochip and recommends exactly what I need to eat to ensure maximum Productivity. Its MealPlanner subscription gives me a personalized healthy diet, all for 5000 BellCoin a year.

I begin to tap on items to add to my shopping cart, my fingers unused to the physicality of the action, when a pop-up blocks the screen.

Naughty, naughty!

I'm sorry!

Wait, what? I tap to proceed.

You're in Chronic Unemployment, Anita.
No shortcuts.
How else will you adjust to Analog living?

Help me!

In order to score points towards your PIP,
you'll have to complete these challenges
in the Analog world.

I'm on it!

I did not agree to be on it. I do not want to be on it.

I need to shop for groceries in a store today.

I glower at the clutter of text on my OmniPort.

I say it out loud, just to make sure I've understood it right.

'I'm going outside to shop for groceries in the store. In a real store. I'll pick my own fruits and vegetables. There will be a real-life shopping cart. I'll carry them home.'

It sounds completely wrong.

The vegetable farm.

It isn't, as one would assume, a market for organic vegetables. It's a Bell Corp facility on the Analog side of the city, separated from us by the Meridian. It's a windowless building with bio-mat walls that electrocute you if you get too close without having the security clearance to pass through them. It's where the most degenerate Analogs are sent to be permanently removed from society.

Even if an Analog manages to avoid being taken to the farm, everyone knows what it's like to be one.

I could be one of them.

There's a reason for the saying 'Unemployment is the first step towards Unproductivity'. It was printed at the top of all our textbooks in university, right beneath the Bell Corp insignia – a short line tending into a gradual curve.

Pennants flutter against the bio-glass structure in front of me, dancing in an artificially induced breeze. Each of them bears the Curve, rising gently before it arcs into a smooth descent, flattening out at the other end.

All across the glass, holo-rayed posters cycle through official Bell Corp messages.

'Suspect your neighbour of Anti-Social tendencies? Report to Bell Corp.'

'Unhappy with your Productivity targets? You CAN do more. Report to Bell Corp for a recalibration.'

The face grinning at me from the posters belongs to none other than John Alvares, who seems to be taking his new role a tad too seriously. If I'd landed the promotion, I might have implemented my regulations with a bit more tact.

I peer past the noise of the images and into the Hexadrome's supermarket.

It's completely deserted. So are the parking bays outside.

I stand in the courtyard.

Hexadrome 3 spreads itself wide around me. The six-sided residential complex occupies an area of four square kilometres. I'm in the South Wing, where Block 1 converges with Block 6. The six blocks arc gently towards the centre as they rise, like the petals of a colossal glass flower that will someday snap shut, swallowing us into obscurity.

The lower floors house restaurants and shopfronts. On the upper floors, the hexagonal glass doors that mark each living space are equidistant from each other, a ribbon of honeycomb unfurling into the distance. Flowering creepers rush downward from the upper floors, growing from within the very fibres of the construction.

I haven't been on street level since I was fired. Most employed Virtuals have no need to leave their homes, except to meet the face-to-face requirements of working in the Towers, or to take part in events prescribed to enhance social and emotional development.

Needless to say, all of these have been wiped from my calendar.

I have a feeling that I'm going to be seeing a lot more of the outside world in the days to come. I probably won't be allowed to have my dry-cleaning picked up and delivered by Door-2-Door Fabrics, or have my make-up and shampoo delivered by SkinDeep Services. I'll need to drive myself around physical reality –

Scratch that. I'll need to walk. The PIP has disabled my personal-transportation capsule.

Walking is a great way to earn Physical Productivity Points towards your PIP target!

That was what my OmniPort flashed when I tried to unlock my capsule's door. Right after:

Naughty, naughty!

I'm sorry!

I won't be whizzing about the Hexadrome any time soon.

I was once empowered to disengage from the mundane physicality that comprises reality. I'd revelled in the services offered by the multitude of convenience portals that criss-cross their way across Apex City, creating a grid of connections to everyday life that didn't require me to engage with it. My world was engineered so that I'd be capable of being 100 per cent Productive in Bell Corp's Towers, safe within my mirrored-glass cocoon.

If I'd landed my promotion, I'd have had the chance to sample the very best technology had to offer all over the world. Cutting-edge Social Influencer algorithms in Crest, nanobot microsurgeries in Pinnacle, bio-hybrid personal transportation vehicles in Premier…

All those dreams taste like ash.

Harvest John Alvares and his immaculate record.

Here I am.

I will rise.

I take a deep breath and step towards the front of the supermarket. The bio-glass takes less than a second to scan my Biochip, ID me on the Nebula, and molecularly pull itself apart to form an opening large enough for me to step through. The silken whoosh of air conditioning envelops me.

The aisles are empty except for the ferriers. Each of their glossy black frames forms an approximation of a human physique, their shoulders dwarfing the rest of their proportions as if emphasizing their utility – lifting and carrying heavy loads. In a half-hearted attempt to humanize them, their squat heads possess a pair of glowing LEDs that burn blue when they're active. In their present state of inertia, their eyes are wide and staring, reflecting the emptiness of the automaton within each shell.

They still achieve the overall effect of intimidation. They stand like sentinels, guarding deep corridors flanked by shelving, converging to a point in the distant horizon. There are shelves stacked with so many products that it makes my head spin. Baskets of fruit and fresh produce are piled in a large space off to my left.

I look around uncertainly for directions.

Is there really no map?

My head pounds, but I force the panic down.

Confession time. I'm expecting a holo-rayed walkthrough of the store's layout. I'm used to my chip transmitting my neurological signs of uncertainty to my OmniPort. I'm used to its algorithms taking over, offering me guided maps and appropriate activities based on my location, my mood and my day's Productivity. I want a set of holo-ray labels charting each aisle in the store, with recommendations on what to buy, with a list of vegetables that will complement each other in the perfect salad and a list of which ones will comply with my Burn Stomach Fat Diet.

I let out a small noise of frustration. My OmniPort is so silent that I can hear the rustle of paper in the quiet of the store.

I glance towards the sound.

At the billing counter sits a shabby old man reading the day's newspaper.

I gasp.

An Analog.

With a newspaper. *A physical copy.*

I consider making actual conversation to ask for directions, but I don't want to engage with an Analog until I'm forced to.

Instead, I take a tentative step forward. My legs wobble like they've turned to jelly. I'm sure I'll be swallowed whole by the store, chewed to pieces by its shelving.

Nothing happens.

I take another step. And another one, my legs still twitching.

That's when I hear a series of beeps scream a warning.

My head snaps up and I look around. At the counter, an antique flat-screen monitor displays an order of groceries from FreshGoodz. The ferriers whir, their outsized bodies swooping through the aisles, reaching up into the shelves to grab various boxes and packages with their metal claws.

One rushes straight towards me, its eyes blazing like the heart of a star. I raise my hands over my face in self-defence.

Several seconds pass.

I peer through my fingers, anticipating impact –

It veers off to the produce section to grab a box of apples.

My knees shake. My shoulders retreat into my person.

The ferriers glide serenely towards the counter. In under a minute, their goods are packed and dispatched to their destination.

The Analog behind the counter hasn't flinched. It flicks the newspaper to turn the page and carries on reading.

The ferriers return to stillness.

Adrenaline pumps its way through the small of my back.

I force deep breaths into my lungs and take hesitant steps towards the produce stands.

Tomatoes. I can use those to make pasta sauce.

A wave of nostalgia crashes into me.

I once went to a farmer's market with Mum. There was a time when physically shopping for artisanal vegetables was a sign of prestige, not failure.

Mum taught me how to buy tomatoes. *'Make sure they're firm, but not hard.'*

I reach out slowly to touch a tomato. I recoil the minute my skin grazes it. It's smooth and cold, covered in a fine layer of dust.

I shake the revulsion from me. It's just a vegetable. I've even cooked with it over the last month, once I ran out of shows to watch on HoloTube.

I grit my teeth and pick it up, giving it a gentle squeeze. It'll do.

Mum's voice echoes in my head. *'Make sure they're the right colour.'*

I see red, orange-red, deep red and several other shades of red in the produce basket. I try to remember the last delivery I received from FreshGoodz. Those tomatoes were red. Non-committal red.

I look for the most average red colouring amid the tomatoes, and select half a dozen.

I let out a sigh of relief.

I step towards the next basket, and then the next one.

I drop two lemons – lemony yellow, smell like citrus – into my cart. A dozen onions join them. I'm not sure if those top layers should be flaking off like that, but the uncertainty is titillating. I pick up a bagful of potatoes.

Do potatoes have an ideal firmness, make a specific sound when you tap them, or have a perfect shade of brown? I take a leap of faith and drop them in my cart.

I pause, suddenly terrified by my adept decision-making. I shouldn't get used to this. This is exactly what Bell Corp wants me to do. Embrace the Analog, so they can pull the plug on me.

I empty my mind of any sense of achievement and roll the cart towards the next set of baskets.

Beans.

I can't remember which type I usually pick on FreshGoodz. I'm pretty sure I buy string beans, but I can't tell if these beans are runner beans or broad beans or French beans.

Which one has the least calories? Which is the most nutritious? What's the most versatile in the kitchen?

I hurriedly reach for my OmniPort, hoping I can sneak a glance at some information, but the portal refuses to launch.

The Bell Bio Portal pops up instead, beaming the full censure of my PIP.

Naughty, naughty!

I'm sorry!

I hurriedly put my OmniPort away.

I close my eyes and point at random. I throw a selection of beans into my cart and hurry away from the vegetables.

I begin to giggle. I can't remember the last time I didn't run an algorithm to make a decision – calorie count, popularity based on user ratings, price points… My impulsive behaviour feels reckless, dizzying.

STOP.

My brain shouts so loud that the vastness of the store seems to echo with the full force of my panic.

This is what Bell Corp is preparing you for. They're trying to make you accustomed to life in the bottom ten percent. Is this the life you want?

'Ten percent,' I mutter, squeezing my eyes shut. 'Ten percent. It's going to be okay.'

I find myself before six aisles diverging in the yellow light of the store.

I choose the one farthest to my left. I'm confronted with a line of oversized freezers filled with dairy.

Milk.

Or the lack of it. That's where my day started.

I wheel my cart down the aisle. Do I want low-fat, 1%-fat, skim, soy, whole or some other form of milk altogether?

'Bottom feeder!'

I pick up two cartons of skim milk when the store is filled with beeping once again.

A ferrier barrels down the aisle straight towards me. I yank the freezer door open and throw myself to my right, pressing against the shelves. Wind rushes through my hair as the ferrier swooshes down its path. I push myself as far into the shelving as I can, ignoring the cold wet condensation from the milk trickling down my back and sides.

The store goes still in an instant but I can hear my thudding heart and my ragged breathing magnified within the crush of the refrigerator. I press my face into the cold glass. My cheeks are wet. I can't tell if it's from my tears or the freezer door.

Steadying my breathing, I force myself out of my cramped confines. I lean against my grocery cart for support until my brain emerges from its fog.

I open my eyes and look straight ahead of me. The cheese section glows with the unwholesomeness of processed dairy.

I look into the display and find dozens of unmarked tins, each one displaying a bar code.

I find my OmniPort.

'ScanMan,' I say out loud, before I remember that I have to tap on the glass to elicit a response.

I swipe. My fingers hover over the ScanMan icon, when I'm interrupted by the PIP. Again.

Naughty, naughty!

I'm sorry!

'What the harvest –'

I'm beginning to hate this PIP.

I refuse to accept it. I will not be an Analog. Ever.

I need to get out of here, make my dinner and rack up enough Productivity Points for another shot at employment. I'll even take an evaluation that puts me in the middle seventy percent for the rest of my life. They may not have olfactory simulations, but at least they have basic HoloTech.

I push my cart as fast as I can towards the exit. Instead, I find myself in the midst of a jumble of bottles, jars, bags, boxes and packages.

Jars of olives – each indiscernible from its neighbour – are crammed onto a shelf. I reach for one at random.

I will not attempt to make a conscious decision, not when I have only my assumptions and no data. It's the way of the Analog, and I will resist it until I'm dragged through the electric shield, kicking and screaming, onto the other side – a situation that will never come to pass, because in a month, this PIP will be over, and I will return – triumphant – to a life where my algorithms, portals and simulations will collect, share and analyse data to decide for me.

I repeat my indiscriminate process of selection to a bottle of capers and some pre-made pasta. Whole-wheat, multigrain, millet – I don't really care.

I'm not sure how much time has passed, but it feels like I've spent the entire day in this store. I finally arrive at the billing counter, desperate to escape the ongoing nightmare.

The old man pushes a button, and a ferrier zooms to my side. I flinch.

'It's okay,' the Analog says. 'It's only here to help.'

I ignore the man, hoping it won't address me again. I'm not sure whether my Social Persona will suffer if I engage with an Analog.

The ferrier weighs my vegetables and packs them in what seems like an instant.

The old man eyes me up and down.

A chill runs down my spine. I've heard about the things that happen to Virtual women who are caught unawares by an Analog.

'Are you new to the neighbourhood? Haven't found employment yet?'

I don't reply.

Its face twitches. It fights a scowl. I glower at it until it drops its gaze to the floor.

'I'm so sorry for disrupting your day, madam.'

I'm flooded by a savage sense of satisfaction at having terminated the conversation.

I swipe my hand over the holoscanner. When my BellCoin transaction is approved after an agonizing three-second wait, I let out an audible sigh.

They haven't relegated me to using paper money – yet.

I reach for my shopping bags. I loop one around my right forearm, the second around my left, and straighten up. My back is pulled downward by the weight and I roll my shoulders back to relieve the pressure.

I take a tentative step forward, and then another one.

My footsteps are unsteady.

'Ten percent.'

My hands are shaking. I've never been addressed by an Analog before.

I stagger through the bio-glass as it rearranges itself for me once more. My apartment block is all the way across the courtyard. A system of roadways, parks and recreational centres stretches before me, arranged around a central pillar mounted by a statue of four lions seated back to back. Nobody knows why it's there, or how long it's been there, except that it's an ancient monument from the nationalist days.

It's warm outside. The afternoon sun has crept up on me. A trickle of sweat runs down the back of my neck, pooling where my T-shirt clings to my back, despite the SunShield umbrella keeping the worst of the heat at bay.

I've never noticed the temperature before – of course, I used to work out of a climate-controlled office space where it was perpetually daylight. I can now conclude that I much prefer the simulation to the reality.

I shudder at the thought of the Analog world without air conditioning. If I'm downgraded, I'll have to pay for electric motors to run a fan. With paper money that I'll have to make from services I'd rather not imagine…

I shake my head to dispel the darkness.

My OmniPort beeps. I twist uncomfortably to reach for it.

An animation plays on its screen. A group of horrid little cartoon men in costumes celebrate. Its jerky, lo-fi quality is only improved upon by the fact that it's low-budget enough not to have been able to afford a sound patch – the horrid men are playing trumpets.

Congratulations! You've bought your own groceries
and earned 375 Productivity Points!
You're doing well on your PIP!

Hurray! Thank you!

I grin at the approval. I'd like to see the Analog world take me now.

I hitch the bags up my forearms, their bands cutting into my skin, colluding with gravity to make this walk as uncomfortable as possible.

Personal-transportation capsules undulate past me, riding the micro-thermals a few inches above the road. A self-driving cab rolls past me every three minutes, with scheduled precision. I'm tempted to hail one of them, but the threat of losing Productivity Points makes me walk on.

Pedestrian traffic in the Hexadrome is scant at this time of day.

A couple of people glide past me on their hoverskates, their dogs racing beside them. They stare at me curiously as I shuffle past. I see judgement in their eyes.

A nanny-bot pushes a perambulator. A man runs past me wearing neon activewear that flashes Bell Corp's insignia. He must be racking up Physical Productivity Points.

I wish I had his lightness and speed today.

The bags in my arms drag me down.

I look up and see Bell Towers V and W blotting out snatches of sky beyond the Hexadrome. Thousands of employees stride through glass corridors, all focused on making it to the top of the Curve and staying there.

Sweat trickles down my forehead.

My arms begin to ache. My legs feel like lead.

A bike-bot messenger nearly bumps into me as it races away, one with the wind.

I pass a happy family lining up for ice cream at the Corner House. They're definitely tourists on a Bell-approved real-world vacation. I can tell from their appearance, their relaxed demeanour, and the fact that all of them are relishing the Corner House's world-famous hot chocolate fudge sundaes.

A light breeze stirs, shifting the air around me. I shiver, but enjoy the coolth. I'm about to step off the street to take a walkway up to Level 49 when I notice a florist's shop across the way. There's a beautiful array of lilies on display.

My mother loved lilies.

A memory sparks.

I'm in tears.

I've just returned from a horrid field trip to the Analog side of the city.

My mother is the only parent from my fourth-grade class waiting at the Maglev station.

She gives me a hug, and a posy of bright white lilies…

In that moment, I am safe from the horrors of the Analog world.

I cross the street hurriedly, dragging the weight of my bags with me.

I make an impulsive decision to buy flowers. *For Mum.*

I shove through the gap as the bio-glass reconstitutes itself open and drop my bags. They've left their marks on my skin, a reminder of the inescapable pull of reality. My arms and shoulders burn.

The air conditioning in the store carries the scent of freshly cut blossoms. I haven't smelt fresh flowers since the last Bell Corp bonus I won – a trip to a real-life farm.

I resist the urge to bury my face in the nearest display, to breathe in deep and lose myself in its scent.

At the counter sits a young Analog woman.

'I recommend the carnations – nice bright hues this year!'

It flashes me a forced smile. I ignore it. It drops its grin.

I walk past the giant pots and vases, first turning flowers towards me and then away from me. I enjoy the firmness of their stems and the lightness of their petals. The physical nature of examining them – touching, smelling, observing them – relaxes me.

My OmniPort beeps.

Going for Gold!

You're really making an effort in the Analog world today!

Flowers win you 500 Bonus Productivity Points!

I'm on it!

I grin. Of course they do. And when I make it up to the top twenty percent, I'll be buying them every week.

I settle on some white lilies and a peculiar yellow wildflower.

As my selections are wrapped in paper, I glance at my shopping bags. I cringe at the thought of hefting them again, but I'm almost home. I know I'll make it.

I hoist the bags up, my muscles protesting against being abused again.

'It looks a bit heavy, ma'am. Perhaps I can help?'

I don't acknowledge that it has spoken.

I grab the flowers in my right hand and step through the glass, back onto the street.

It's warm. My shoulders sag.

One step at a time, I remind myself as I make my way back onto a walkway. The tug of the scents and sounds on street level release their hold on me as I'm enveloped by air conditioning once more.

The walkway whirs steadily upward. I pass the Indoor Nursery that runs across all six blocks of the Hexadrome, occupying the entirety of its third floor. I pass Brunieri, Moskovitch and several other clothing stores. Award-winning restaurants whirl past, intriguing installations and art galleries fall away.

I ascend level after level of housing units. My heart soars when I finally catch sight of my floor.

I step onto Level 49. I look down at the street through the glass walls and marvel at the insignificance of the distance I have travelled today.

I make for my front door.

I set my bags down.

I pass my hand over the holoscanner. It glows green as the bio-glass entrance pulls apart.

My OmniPort beeps.

Congratulations, Anita!
Keep at it,
and you'll be Productive again
in no time!

Woohoo!

Soon you'll have access to all your HoloTech,
but as a reward,
we're going to unlock FreshGoodz
right away!

Awesome!

I grin. I'm making progress.

Soon I'll never have to step out into the real world again.

The citizens of Apex City forgo their rights when they neglect to uphold their commitment to Bell Corp's manifesto.
We will owe them nothing.

– from the Bell Charter on Human Rights, Article I, Section 1(a)

...INTO THAT GOOD NIGHT

THE ROOM IS DARK. I know you're listening – someone's always listening. I'm saying this out loud so you can hear me.

The room is dark. It's Sasha here, by the way. Just clarifying.

It's dark, and I'd really like a light. I've never experienced darkness. I know this is part of my punishment, but it's *really* dark.

Listen, I'm not panicking. I'm perfectly calm, see. You can tell from the tone of my voice.

I'm going to stay perfectly *calm* because that's what you want. I know this. If I stay calm and behave myself, you'll reward me. That's how the system works.

I know I'm being deported, but there's still the system right? I'm a part of it, even though you're sending me...*there*.

I'm going to behave myself. Did you get that?

I have faith in you. The system always rewards good behaviour.

It's still dark. I know I've been in here for forty-eight hours. I read the fine print when I was taken. I get my nutro-shakes once a day. I've received two nutro-shakes. That's two days.

I know you expect me to lose track of time in here. Well, I'm not going to. You'll see how smart I am. That this is all a big mistake.

This is Sasha, by the way. I'd like some light.

I haven't burst into tears or screamed or hammered on the doors, like some of the others in here. I know that's bad behaviour. And the system always rewards good behaviour.

It's day three, and I still don't have any light, but I'm being patient.

Also, you know, keeping track of time. I know you expect me to lose my mind, but I'm telling you, I'm better than all the others who have gone before me.

You'll realize that you've made a mistake. You'll probably let me back in. I make an excellent seventy percenter, just look at my track record. I only slipped in the last quarter, but that's because I had –

Look, I know I let you down. I was *unwell.* I was sent to the counsellor. I fixed myself, right?

I didn't hit my targets but I fixed myself. And now I can hit my targets. Just let me back in and give me another chance to prove myself.

This is Sasha, by the way. I know you're listening.

I keep waking up and reaching for an OmniPort that isn't there. It feels like an itch in my brain.

I've accepted that I don't deserve my HoloTech, though. I surrendered my holo-watch and my OmniPort without protest. You should have seen the man beside me. He screamed when they made him give up his intel-glasses. He was so loud and angry that they had to put him under. Then they carried him to another room on a stretcher – I suppose to deactivate his chip, maybe to get the rest of his tech off him.

I didn't scream. I barely cried during the electro-surge that fried my chip. The scar tissue still itches, but I haven't made a big deal of it.

You can ask the ward-bot that comes in with my nutro-shakes. I speak only when I'm spoken to during my daily medical exam. I make no unreasonable requests, even though my brain feels like it's on fire without my OmniPort. My fingers twitch all the time, but I can still focus. I get all its questions right.

Name: Sasha Sundaram. Age: Twenty-eight. Address: C-19, Hexadrome 3. Profession: CommSat Performance Analyst. Date of Birth…

Thank you. Thank you, Bell Corp. I knew my patience wouldn't go unappreciated.

The ward-bot just gave me a candle and a box of matches. I don't know how to use them, but I'm going to learn.

If this is a test, I'll pass.

Was that an accident? Did you send me wax-tipped matches by accident?

It's Sasha here. I've been in the dark for a week now. I tried to light every single match but none of them work. I removed each one I struck from the box and laid them in a neat pile on the floor, but they shifted somehow – or maybe I lost track of them in the dark. It was hard gathering them off the floor without a light, and there was a lot of crawling involved. I found them all, though – they're back in the box and you can count every single one.

So could you send me another box of matches, please?

'Summer Sunshine' by Edie Taylor has been stuck in my head, but I don't know all the words. Could you please send them with the ward-bot tomorrow? It's playing on loop.

I've been trying to sing along to songs I know, but I realize that I never bothered to learn the lyrics because they were always on the

Nebula, and I was always uplinked to it. It's amazing how silent the inside of my head is without live-streamed ambient sound from my InEars.

I'm not asking for my OmniPort back, though. Or for my InEars. I don't deserve them. I'd just like the lyrics to one song. And another box of matches. Please?

This is Sasha. Just in case you're listening.

I get that the Analogs don't have free electricity or running water. I get that you're trying to acclimatize me to a life in the dark. But this feels like punishment, not sensitization. It's taken me two weeks to come to this conclusion.

I thought Bell Corp was humane. This does not feel humane.

I'm sorry, I didn't mean to yell at you. I only meant what I said as constructive feedback.

I'm so sorry.

How many days has it been?

Bell Corp does such a great job designing these simulations. I wonder how I'm doing on this test.

Name: Sasha. Age: Twenty-eight. Address: Where are we right now?

You're letting me leave! You're blindfolding me because it's a big surprise, aren't you?

When I open my eyes, I'll be back…somewhere outside the dark. It must be my birthday. Is it my birthday?

Where are you taking me? I hope there's cake.

The future of the world depends upon perfect alignment.
We must begin with the children.

– from the Bell Charter on Human Rights,
'On the Matter of Free and Compulsory Primary School Education',
Article III, Section 6(c)

WELCOME TO THE MACHINE

'WELCOME ABOARD! THIS IS Maglev Adventures's Mission Analog!'

Children sniff, wiping runny noses on clean white handkerchiefs.

In the world outside the windows of the train, the towers of the Bell Corp technarchy mushroom against the clear blue sky. Narrow at their foundations to facilitate adequate air circulation at street level, the upper storeys widen gradually until they umbrella overhead, casting a net of shadows upon the pedestrians below.

The station is nestled beneath the canopy cast by Bell Towers C and D. A series of interconnected bio-glass domes is supported by skeletal bio-mat beams, trailing bougainvillea and firecracker flowers from the substrate that constitutes their material. Perma-Day skylights shine an everlasting noon.

Twelve exits, all shaped in the form of a smooth curve tapering at either end, ensure that Bell Corp makes its presence felt.

'We are about to embark upon a thrilling and terrifying journey into the heart of the Analog world. At Bell Square – formerly known as Minsk Square – we will pass through the Carnatic Meridian into Analog territory. This ride will speed up as we pass the Analog Rehabilitation Centre, so hold on to your hats! We will then take a leisurely tour of Market Square, where you can observe the Analogs in their natural habitat.'

Teresa Fernandes takes a sip of her Vita-Hydration Solution. She'll need all the energy she can get today.

Little girls and boys press their faces to the glass. Lower lips tremble, tear-streaked cheeks wobble. They hope for parental intervention.

None will be forthcoming.

This ride is a mandate for all children over the age of ten. Analog Sensitization is an integral part of their education.

It will fall to Teresa to keep them in high spirits for the next few hours, a task she has managed to perform adequately for several years. Of late, though, her own spirits have been flagging.

Her time is running out.

'We have ahead of us a day packed with adventure. Please follow the safety instructions and enjoy the ride.'

'Please remain seated and keep your hands, arms, feet and legs within the boundaries of your assigned seats. You will see dotted lines indicating the extent of this area. This is to help us maintain order and decorum on the train. We don't want to disturb the Analogs.'

Teresa has conducted hundreds – perhaps thousands – of these tours. She's yet to see an Analog react to their presence. They barely register the Maglev's progress through their side of the city, even when it's filled with twenty percenters making rude signs and calling them names. And yet, she follows the script – she doesn't have much of a say in the matter.

'Sound frequencies might interfere with the infrasound waves that we transmit to keep the Analogs tranquil. Please do not play any music. Do not sing or chant school anthems. You may talk in hushed voices. If you must laugh, do so quietly. You may take photographs, but refrain from flash photography – it might upset the Analogs.'

Another dubious statement.

It's broad daylight. There's no use for flash photography. The Analogs have many concerns, but being photographed by a train full of children on a field trip probably isn't one of them.

Each tour she conducts gives Teresa further reason to doubt what she's paid to say.

Then again, what does she know for sure? She's been a seventy percenter her entire career, a tour operator shielded within the glass walls of a Maglev train all her life. She marks time on the Bell Curve with what could pass for success – she has neither progressed nor fallen behind.

She's never been on the other side of the glass. She's never seen and felt what *they* do.

Her life has been carved from routine. It's the same script, every single day.

Now everything is about to change.

'This train will slow down when we enter Market Square. You are encouraged to record your experiences for further study.'

'All set? Welcome again to the ride of a lifetime!' Teresa ends on a note of excitement.

The children look at her sullenly.

The train ascends.

A child shrieks. It is infectious.

Another child hiccups. A third begins to wail.

Teresa sighs.

There was a brief period of heightened Analog unrest during which the Analog Sensitization Programme was conducted using a Hyper Reality simulator. Behaviourists conducted several long-term studies on the schoolchildren who had undergone this method. They concluded that the terror induced by experiencing the physical environs of the Analogs yielded more positive results, and so the Maglev Monorail had been recommissioned – with bulletproof glass.

'The visitors on board the train are reminded that they must keep silent. Please refrain from hysteria as it might upset the Analogs. This ride will not depart until the children are calm and placid. If the accompanying Magistra could intervene –'

Magistra AB43 emits a shrill whistle from her speakers. The children snap to attention. The edu-bot chides them.

Things were different when Teresa was in school. They still had human facilitators, for a start.

Magistra AB43 is calm but stern. Teresa has discovered that she – for the bot's pre-assigned gender is female, just like all edu-bots and nanny-bots – is programmed to be *feminine*. Bell Corp has designed her Sentient Intelligence algorithm to favour emotional sensitivity and heightened skill at handling children.

Teresa questions the validity of these assumptions regarding womanhood, but as with most other matters, she does so in silence.

The edu-bot speaks in soothing tones. She firmly reminds the class that it is their duty to go on this field trip. If they refuse to cooperate, they'll never be promoted to a higher grade.

– You don't want to fail a year, do you?

– No, Magistra.

No, indeed.

Failure is unacceptable for a Virtual student.

Teresa used to belong to the upper percentiles in most of her classes, but so did everybody else. As evidenced by her life experiences, being smart only guaranteed employment. Being successful demanded genius. Academic prowess wasn't special; it was expected.

Magistra AB43 reminds the children that the education they receive today will help their holistic development.

– You don't want to be bad citizens, do you?

That shuts them up.

Teresa smiles unconsciously at the bot, who pats her hand with a metal claw. Teresa winces at the touch. It brings her back to the present.

When did I start treating droids like they were human?

She can't remember. Nobody can.

They've managed to assimilate into Virtual society like a creeping presence. When they're revealed to be lurking in the shadows, it's already too late.

Teresa is scheduled to be replaced by a guide-droid next week.

It is known that the droid will be able to mimic human vocalization, complete with inflections and tones to convey dread, excitement and enthusiasm.

It is believed that the droid will be less likely to develop independent opinions on the Analogs, a purported side effect of spending too much time in their presence. Many a human tour guide has had therapy to help cope with Analog Desensitization and Sympathy Disorder. Treatment for ADSD is expensive, and Bell Corp no longer wants to support it.

It is plausible that the droid will do a much better job than a human possibly can.

After today, Teresa will have only one more trip to the Analog city as an official Bell Corp tour guide.

'This ride has departed. Pay careful attention, class. This is what awaits your hopes and dreams should you fail to be a good citizen.'

Teresa watches terror sink into the faces of the little boys and girls.

They gaze at her, round-eyed and anxious.

The ride hums gently, bobbing up and down along its magnetic track.

The children watch all that is familiar slide by in silence. The irregular skyline of Apex City is a rampart that shields them from the terrors beyond. The six-sided residential Hexadrome 1 peels away from them to the left. The lily pads of the Lotus Blossom flower from their bio-mat frame into the skies on the right, solar panels glinting in the sun. The well-preserved brick-and-tile buildings of the Historic School District slip away like jet-trails streaking their peripheral vision. A child presses his hand to the glass as they zoom over the verdant Arboretum. The tree line yields to arid scrub and then dust.

'We are about to pass through the Carnatic Meridian and into Analog territory.'

The children study the view through the bulletproof glass of the train.

The Carnatic Meridian thrums. Jagged blue sparks flare across its smooth, curving surface. Light passes through it and into shadow; the world beyond is the gullet of a beast that is about to swallow them whole.

The electric shield begins to swirl, spiralling in on itself before pulling apart to reveal a gap large enough for the train to pass through.

'You may gasp in quiet wonder at the beauty of the Carnatic Meridian. Developed and patented by Bell Corp's Secure Civilizations venture, this shield has prevented the Analogs from corrupting us with their Unproductive and Anti-Social thoughts and behaviours. It is all that stands between our Virtual model of civilization and anarchy. For more on its history and development, you can watch the official HoloTube documentary *A Shield against the Night*.'

The children gasp, for the shield always makes a magnificent first impression – but also because they have finally been permitted to expunge the dread they've been forced to swallow.

Hiccups and nervous giggles follow.

Teresa feels the tension build up between her shoulders. She's passed through the Meridian hundreds of times. She still hasn't found what she's looking for.

That could change today.

It's the normalcy of this thought that saddens her, the familiar feeling of anticipation that she knows will fizzle into nothingness as the ride wears on.

Teresa will persist. Teresa will strain her eyes for a glimpse of her sister.

'This rail levitates at a height of five feet over the Analog streets. Stay vigilant. Analogs might approach the train as it slows. Do not shout or wave out to them. They are not friendly. Do not make eye contact. Do not smile. And, finally, do not – I repeat, do not – display your food to the Analogs.'

The children's smiles fade. Some hurriedly swallow their candy, stuff their sandwiches and snacks into their backpacks. One bursts out crying and has to be shushed by the entire class. All of them place their intel-glasses over their eyes so that they can record their experiences. It will be years before they're permitted their lens implants.

Teresa fervently hopes that one specific Analog approaches the train.

'On either side of you are the pod-housing facilities. Bell Corp believes in the humane treatment of all life, and it is through their goodwill that the Analogs are permitted to live here. These houses are built of carbon fibre, and every Analog is allotted a room measuring 140 square feet for itself and its personal belongings. You can find more on their structure and development in *The Engineering Marvels of the Bell Technarchy*.'

The children narrow their eyes, imagining cramped confines.

Teresa routinely contemplates the hardship of living in a single room the size of her bathroom. Her sister had dreamt of living in a sprawling bungalow serviced by a staff of server-bots. It was inconceivable that she would one day be deported, and yet…

She is here. Somewhere in this maze of nondescript Bell-provisioned housing.

Teresa chokes her thoughts down. She continues to recite from a script she knows like the back of her hand.

'The Analogs express deep ingratitude, make note. Their lot continue to have children. Their population continues to grow.'

She wonders – as she often does – if she's an aunt to some child destined to a life of poverty and discrimination.

'An epidemic of Unproductivity and Anti-Social tendencies is beginning to thrive. We are not immune to it. Look around at your classmates. Some of you might be struggling with your schoolwork, others with your conversation skills. Commit now to improving them, to being the best version of yourself. You are the future of this world. You hold the hopes and dreams of Bell Corp in your hands.'

All eyes slide over a wide-eyed little girl, as if in silent acknowledgement that she'll be the first of them deported in ten years' time.

Teresa feels a pang of pity for the child.

She wonders how her sister's life went wrong. She'd been bright, talented and ambitious. She definitely hadn't been a mousy-haired girl with a vacant gaze.

Teresa peers out the window at the streets rolling by.

'Observe how narrow these streets are. Bell Corp has stopped building pod-houses on the limited real estate available, owing to the rising demands of overpopulation. The Analogs have taken to living in tents deeper within their city. They refuse to obey Bell Corp's guidelines on family planning, and must pay the consequences. Their sort is discouraged from propagation, yet they persist. You can look up the guidelines on Reproductive Rights in the Bell Charter they blatantly defy.'

Expressions of disbelief appear on the sea of small faces. The Analog world can't be overpopulated, for the class is yet to have spotted a single Analog.

Teresa is impatient as well. She has to see as many of them as possible before her time on the train is done. She is unlikely to receive authorized permission to enter the Analog city – her history as a tour guide will lead to ADSD suspicions and a possible quarantine. And as much as she'd like to find her sister, she doesn't want to be deported to do so.

'We are about to enter an Analog living facility. You will observe the average Analog in its own home. We will slow down so you can record this experience. Remember your safety instructions and do not communicate with the Analog on display.'

Eyes snap ahead to the front of the train. Looming before it is what appears to be a pod-house that has cracked down its spine. Its structure is hollowed out in the centre, and its walls lean away from each other in a gravity-defying curve.

The train slows.

Teresa holds her breath in anticipation. She deflates when she sees that today's Analog specimen is a man.

'Observe the Analog in its domestic confines. Make note of its sparse surroundings. A mat on the floor is used to sleep and laze upon. A single bulb provides illumination when the Analog can afford to run an electricity generator. There is no climate control, or even air conditioning, on this side of the Carnatic Meridian.'

Teresa thinks of her sister sweating in the sultry heat of an unknown pod-house. She had always hated humidity because of its effect on her curly hair.

They'd told her of her imminent deportation through a message on her OmniPort. All her HoloTech had been wiped, replaced by a faceless, emotionless notification. It had informed her that life as she knew it was over.

Teresa comments on the features of the pod-house. They have been carefully orchestrated for this display by the directors of the programme.

'This Analog appears to like to read. You can see physical copies of newspapers and pamphlets spread all over the floor. There is no technology in this dwelling – you will notice the absence of Hyper Reality devices, sentient machines and HoloTech of any kind. Analogs are not permitted to own these.

'Magistra, please take this opportunity to ask the class why it thinks these privileges have been denied to the Analogs.'

Magistra AB43 complies.

– They are bad citizens.

The class is united. Magistra AB43's facial features turn upward in a pixelated LED smile.

'Take a close look at the Analog. Observe that this male member of the species has dust and mud streaked across its face. It has probably neglected to bathe in days, a common affliction here. Bell Corp generously provides Public Bath Facilities to their lot. Each Analog is allotted an entire bucket of water a day, yet most Analogs fail to take advantage of this luxury.'

The children withdraw towards the centre of the train, repelled from the glass windows on either side.

Her sister had been the beautiful one. Teresa cannot imagine her covered in grime and filth, unable to access running water.

'Observe that this Analog is content with lying on the floor of the house all day. It was probably deported for being Unproductive. Laziness is an incurable disease.'

From what Teresa knows of the Analogs, the man has probably spent all night toiling in the Junkyard and is too exhausted to move a muscle. Knowledge of this sort is dangerous – it means that she has been reading illegal pamphlets, handwritten and physically distributed to keep their contents off Bell Corp's records. She keeps this thought to herself, along with another, far more dangerous revelation.

Perhaps I am an Analog sympathist, after all.

She checks her thoughts and steels her gaze, her face a neutral mask. The on-rail lenses of the PanoptiCam have recorded her emotions since her very first tour, live-streaming their feed onto the Nebula where complex algorithms continue to scrutinize her every expression and inflection. The Policy and Governance Division has reinforced its zero-tolerance policy towards sympathists. None dare express their pro-Analog sentiments on Woofer or InstaSnap – not that they were encouraged to, in the past – but the Seditious Activities Unit has been more vigilant than ever before.

She cannot drop her guard. Not now. Not with one ride left.

'Think of your parents. Each day, they strive to do their best for Bell Corp and our society. Bell Corp's model of meritocratic technarchy succeeds because of them. You must aspire to be exactly like them.'

The children gaze at the Analog in silence. Each one believes that their parents are not just good citizens, but the best citizens.

Teresa's sister had been a good citizen. She'd been the talented one. Her career had skyrocketed straight out of university. She'd built the first interplanetary communications satellite, using alternative technology to radio waves. She'd been absorbed by Bell Corp's Star Charters programme, developing commercial manned flights to Enceladus.

They'd come for her in the dead of night after the first commercial spaceship exploded in its orbit. There had been consequences for the entire family when they'd discovered that she was missing.

There is no room for error in Apex City.

'To your right, you'll catch a brief glimpse of Bell Corporation's Analog Rehabilitation Centre.'

'Here we give the most Productivity-challenged Analogs the chance to fulfil their lives with purpose. Through humane, perfectly sanitized limb- and organ-harvesting techniques, an Analog can finally serve our society in the way it normally fails to. In many cases, it is one last act of redemption for the system's most Unproductive, their greatest service to the wider Bell community.'

A squeak. A gasp. Eyes grow wide as saucers.

This is the vegetable farm. This is the home of the VeggieMaker, that urban legend their parents have threatened to give them away to when they throw tantrums, stay up past their bedtime and refuse to eat their vegetables.

Teresa flinches each time she passes the facility.

When her sister had gone missing, the whole family had come under scrutiny. Teresa had been suspended and repeatedly interrogated by the Seditious Activities Unit. Her parents had been harassed.

A full week later, her sister was discovered attempting to pass through the Southern Wall using false papers that identified her as a conservationist from the Nagarhole Eco-Soc. She'd filed down her fingerprints and dyed her hair, but a full-body holoscan had put an end to her charade as an Outsider, identifying her as a fugitive from her dental records.

Teresa had never had the chance to say goodbye.

'We're now passing by the Analog Kitchens. Bell Corp provides the Analogs with nutrition-rich food, but the Analogs are ungrateful.'

Teresa can imagine why. The food that's given to the Analogs looks distinctly unappetizing. It comes out of vacuum-sealed pouches and sachets and preserves for up to three years.

'Look down through the glass bottom of the train. There are piles of protein-porridge and nutro-shakes littering the ground. Analogs are frequently dismissed from employment for food theft. There's a common saying: "Hide the fruit, not the HoloTech."'

The children giggle.

Teresa cannot imagine her sister living on formulaic food supplies. Perhaps she's been imprisoned for stealing an apple…

She catches herself falling behind on the timing of her script, and quickly remedies this.

'Magistra, you may recap the basic principles of the Bell Curve.'

– Topmost twenty all deserve
  tech in plenty
  to rule the Curve.
Seventy mean have the right
  to be seen and heard –
  climb the Curve they might.
Bottom ten
  deport, forget.
Mice, not men
  must live in regret.

The children chant their nursery rhyme, and Magistra AB43 beams in approval.

Teresa recoils at the sound of it. She hopes that her sister won't need to live with the weight of her failures for the rest of her days. She looks at the line of Analogs heading into the bathhouses and scrutinizes each face for one she might recognize.

'To your right are the Public Baths.'

She stands as if to address the class, but it is to provide herself with a better view through the port-side window.

Teresa scans the faces in the crowd. Her nerves catch fire when she spots an unmistakable build, a crop of curly hair…

Her heart races. *It must be her.*

She's deep in conversation with another woman. She tilts her head in that familiar way.

It must be her.

The woman turns towards the train…

Teresa's shoulders slump. Her insides are hollow.

She soldiers on.

'We will soon arrive in Market Square. Please remember that it is of utmost importance that you remain as silent as possible.

'The Analogs will appear both fascinating and incomprehensible, but I urge you to observe them with an open mind and attempt to understand their ways.'

The children appear eager to please.

Teresa stifles a gasp when she realizes that she has spoken her mind instead of delivering yet another warning from the script. She forces her face to stay neutral, but she can feel a surge of anxiety pressing against the walls of her skull. She has been caught on the PanoptiCam's live stream making what could be construed as a pro-Analog statement. She needs to be careful.

She wonders if she will follow her script and ignore the Analogs if she should spot her sister – or jeopardize the lives of all these children for selfish gain. She's never seen an Analog turn violent, but that doesn't mean it can't happen. There will be consequences, and they will undo her.

The train zooms over dusty warrens. She soldiers on.

'We are arriving in Market Square. This rail will gradually descend so you can observe the Analogs on street level.'

The train decelerates, descending to the level of the street.

Teresa forces herself to act natural. Perhaps nobody's listening to the live stream of her tour – after all, it's a routine one, conducted every single day.

No more slip-ups.

Her eyes remain fixed on the small crowd of people in the square. She turns her head from left to right, looking for the curve of a smile, a well-known gesture of the hand, for a stride that bounces as if trying to balance itself on the clouds.

There is only dust.

'Look into the tents and stalls that have been set up all around you. Most of them sell indigenous Analog crafts.'

Teresa stares at the familiar faces of the craftsmiths as they pass by. She's seen the same array of careworn eyes and sunburnt skin every day.

'Many Analogs make a living from craftsmanship. Their goods include improvised batteries, cheap handheld fans and mirrors, notebooks made from scavenged paper, and pens with ink made from organic dyes. Sometimes they even make hand-carved toys. For a list of Analog handicrafts, refer to *A Virtual in the Analog World*, a biographical account of Leslie Schnyder, an anthropologist who lived among the Analogs for over a decade, studying their ways.'

Teresa wonders if her prospective niece or nephew plays with wooden dolls or tops or animals. She cannot imagine it. She and her sister grew up playing Hyper Reality games.

'Keep in mind that Analogs do not have any access to technology. Some are permitted cellular phones if they can afford them. Cellular phones are an archaic technology, a predecessor of sorts to our OmniPorts. They were a communications device in the days before the Bell Takeover.'

She fidgets. She's losing focus.

I'm running out of time.

'We permit the Analogs to craft and trade in these articles so that they find a peaceable way to pass their time.'

The children do not understand this statement. The slow passage of time is inconceivable to them. They are all trained to attain maximum Productivity.

'We encourage them to engage in art projects, such as this pair of magnificent trees built from scrap metal, on either side of this pod-house.'

Teresa's hands move to her mouth involuntarily, but she forces them back down.

Her script calls attention to the trees, but says nothing of their magnificence.

The children appear confused by her statement. The alleged trees in question do not conform to any standard of beauty that they have been trained to appreciate.

I cannot slip up again. Not now.

She races to catch up with her script. She needs to stick to it.

'None of the stalls sell restricted goods, at least not openly. The consequences are dire for any Analog that breaks the law on contraband.'

The classroom cannot understand restricted access to things. They have been raised with unlimited resources.

Teresa wonders, as she often has, if her sister has taken to smuggling. She could succeed – she's certainly smart enough. Perhaps that's why she hasn't seen her all these years.

She imagines her sister as a thief lord – perhaps she is even the Ten-Percent Thief – hovering in the shadows and melting into the dusty streets after providing food, water and shelter to the starving throngs that comprise her loyal following.

'The fascinating thing about visiting the Analog city is the outdated technology that is available here. Look to your right,' Teresa prompts, then bites her lip in despair.

My facade is cracking.

The script reads, 'The Analogs make use of outdated technology because it is all they deserve. [The tour guide must now ask the children to explain why.]'

She quickly poses the question.

– They are bad citizens.

Magistra AB43 beams her pixelated smile yet again.

Teresa ploughs on.

'This shack sells restored Walkman Personal Stereos. They're used to play music, and they haven't been seen in the Virtual world since the days of the OmniPort. In fact, they're older than cellular phones.'

The children gasp in wonder. That's a time too old for them to reckon.

'These devices are battery-operated, and play an archaic form of technology called the cassette tape. Analogs use these cassette tapes to listen to a form of music called anatronica. Bell Corp officially permits this activity, as it provides the Analogs with enough entertainment to keep them happy. Here is the anatronica currently being played within the Walkman shack.'

Heavy synth beats play over the train's speakers. They are accompanied by a loud and dissonant chorus of instruments that the children have never encountered before.

They throw their hands over their ears to block out the noise.

Teresa secretly enjoys the strange and alien nature of the sound. Perhaps her sister is an anatronica artist – she was always adept at playing the piano. She wraps herself in the daydream that she is listening to her sister, but quickly terminates the fantasy before she starts bobbing her head to the music.

There is no more room for error.

The music fades.

'Anatronica is completely digitally synthesized. Several of you will be overwhelmed by its sound. That is to your credit. It's loud and primitive with no aesthetic sensibility or finesse.'

She makes this last statement resound with vehemence, hoping it will atone for her lapses on this ride.

'Analogs trade in paper money. You can see them handing over bundles of paper money in exchange for goods. These notes have no value in the Virtual city. Bell Corp has eliminated all paper-money transactions, thereby simplifying our lives.'

Teresa pictures her imagined niece or nephew earning a living and feels a crack appear in the walls of her heart.

'The Analogs only speak Trad, an old language from when Apex City was still called Bangalore, divided on the basis of cultural identity. This language has been outlawed as part of Bell Corp's efforts to unify our world towards the common goal of Productivity.'

Teresa chokes down a laugh. She cannot imagine her sister

speaking the language. When they were children, they would sometimes jabber at each other in gibberish while playing at Virtuals and Analogs. The object of ridicule was always the Analog – the incoherent, bumbling idiot blabbering in Trad who had to be captured and harvested.

Teresa now doubts that this is the reality of Analog communication. The handwritten pamphlets she has read are perfectly articulate, and several ex-Virtuals are now on the other side of the Meridian, her sister included. Surely they are capable of more than Trad.

'You might wonder where many of the Analogs are, this morning.' Teresa's script echoes her own thoughts, for a change.

'They are in the mines, greenhouses and vertical farms around the city. They harvest and tend to the resources that keep Apex City running. As your history textbooks will tell you, most modern cities on the Outside survive on the basis of trading resources they are rich in for resources they do not have access to. It is our technology that permits these cities to trade with each other in the first place, which is why we occupy a position of tremendous power in the post-nation world. We are almost entirely self-sufficient, and will come into being completely self-sufficient in the next decade.'

Teresa pauses, then states slowly and with great emphasis, 'It is a privilege to be born and raised in Apex City. Do not squander the opportunity you have been given. Be the best Virtual Citizen in the world.'

The train ascends slowly.

'You've all done very well to ignore the dozens of Analogs that, no doubt, approached this train or attempted to make eye contact with you.' Teresa forces herself to repeat the words on her script.

As for the Analogs who approached the train, there were none.

The train begins to gain momentum as it exits Market Square, making for the periphery of the Analog city.

'You're privileged to have been able to witness the Analogs in their natural habitat without untoward incident. They can often resort to violent behaviour when confronted by Virtuals, even Virtual children.'

Teresa has never seen this happen, and balks at the obvious bias. She cannot afford any further deviation from the prescribed text – she has probably already merited a review. She cannot risk saying any more. Not with only one ride left.

A weight settles in the pit of her stomach. She has failed to find her sister. Again.

The train is now at the outskirts of the city.

'Behold the lush, verdant vertical farms that lie in the distance. It is a privilege for the Analogs to tend to them. We will shortly be replacing all of them with agro-droids, once the technology is perfected. Analogs cannot be relied upon.'

Just like tour guides. She swallows the thought.

The vertical farmlands rise above the barren landscape in the form of large, asymmetrical greenhouses, each capable of rearranging itself to ensure that the crops and plants grown within receive an optimal dose of sunlight by the hour.

'If you use the magnification lens on your intel-glasses, you will see Analogs gathering lilies on Farmland 7. Look to the eighteenth floor. The lily is a flower that Apex City is famed for all over the world. We export our lilies to every major event in Pinnacle, Crown, Crest and Premier.'

The children applaud politely. Some of them have probably attended these events.

Teresa uses her intel-lens implants to zoom in on the blurred shapes in the distance. She imagines that she sees her sister bending over the crop of millet. She pictures her tending to a patch of white lilies.

The attention of the class is beginning to waver. Only the most diligent students continue to pay attention. Most of them are relieved, unzipping their backpacks to access their precious stores of candy and chocolate.

A murmur spreads through the hitherto silent train, as comments are exchanged for giggles.

Magistra AB43 does not intervene. The children have been put through a harrowing experience and have done her proud.

The electric shield thrums on the horizon. The train slides through, but the children barely notice. They have begun to chatter freely now, with the promise of safety so close at hand.

'We are nearly at the end of our adventure. Remember all that you have seen within the Analog city. Make a solemn promise to yourselves to always be good citizens, and to uphold Bell Corp's values so long as you live and breathe. Magistra, you may encourage the class to recite –'

The children recite the Pledge of Conformity.

The train draws into the station, passing beneath the protective arc of the Bell Curve-shaped exit. A few anxious parental faces look up at its carriage as it descends.

The children stream out, flush with joy at their safe return.

Teresa remains seated.

One more ride.

She will persist. She will continue to look for a face in the crowd.

She will find her sister.

She could not have been captured.

She could not have been harvested.

She could not have been in that delivery from the vegetable farm.

Her laugh was too big to fit into that tiny titanium box.

She could not have been turned to ash all those years ago.

The greatest gift of art lies not in its beauty or its horror,
but in the manner of its creation.
It has the power to bring people together. It urges us to recognize in each the other.
It makes us more than Analogs. It makes us human.

**– Bashir Rehan, Keeper of the Lore,
on the Inauguration of the Garnet Tree (anecdotal)**

FULL METAL FOREST BREATHING

SO MUCH DEPENDS UPON her hands.

A feat of evolution, their potential is shared by much of the human race but seldom explored to this degree. Her fingers aren't long and slender, but she has mastered the nuances of each muscle within them. She can do this in the dark, blindfolded, if she must.

She sometimes thinks she'd prefer to.

When she looks down at them working, she sees them covered in phantom crimson spatter.

She has taught herself not to look, over the years.

In a tiny box held in her palm lies an intricate array of semiconductors. They have been neatly welded into place, their positions optimized within the unforgiving limits of the space available. They're Junkyard finds and bear telltale signs of rust. This is an additional reminder of the wreckage from another day.

Marie Fernandes is widely regarded as the most capable engineer on either side of Apex City. She no longer correlates her abilities with her sense of self – something she has learnt to do the hard way.

She flicks a switch and the box in her hands lights up, along with the string of solar-powered lights it's attached to. She places it on the table before her, watching it flicker in the dim light of the bunker.

She picks up a cellular phone, another salvaged find from the Junkyard. Her fingers fly across its hard-button keys with an ease she'd have thought impossible in her other life.

No, she thinks. *My former life.*

A bulky piece of hardware the size of a notebook is the only other object on the plane surface before her. Its screen is cracked, but its processors work just fine. Line after line of numbers begin to crawl across its screen. A cluster of graphs occupies the right side, updating as the machine runs through its computations.

'What are you testing?' Tariq's voice interrupts her careful scrutiny of the data.

'Signal strength from the trans-comm. Determines whether an OmniPort is likely to uplink to it. Harvest speed – how fast can we port data. Accuracy – how true is the data relative to its source.'

'And?'

'It's performing within our conservative estimates. It should fit in with the rest of the network.'

'Excellent. We're at twenty-three devices, each harvesting credentials from twelve to fifteen OmniPorts every day.' Tariq nods. 'Our developers were blocked for a bit on some changes to the Sentient+ syntax, but we're on top of it now.'

'Our window is at three to five minutes to scrape each device when it passes within range,' Marie says. 'When Codename: Dissentient goes live, we'll need to keep this in mind. It'll be slower when we start pushing our data onto the Nebula.'

'We're aware,' Tariq says. 'Any chance we can improve the trans-comm's transmission rate?'

'Not with these processors, I'm afraid.' Marie shakes her head. 'Besides, most of their power is used in connecting to the old radio-wave satellites in the first place.'

Each of her trans-comm devices is made from less than desirable components. Sasha has done her best to stick to Marie's specifications while scavenging, but microprocessors covered in dust and exposed to the elements for years on end tend to lose much of their efficacy, even if they can be brought back to life.

She tuts at the harvest speed. It's far from optimal, but it will have to do.

Marie puts the cellular phone down. Her hands begin to shake. She does her best to hide this by holding onto the edge of her table.

She glances up at Tariq.

'Ever heard of a wire?' he says.

'A cable?'

'No. A wire, like a recording device.'

She stares at him, confused.

'Ancient technology. Most primitively, a tiny microphone carried on someone's person to eavesdrop on conversations.'

'Oh!' She laughs. 'Espionage stuff! Like those old thrillers –'

'Yes. Exactly. We've just built the most complicated wire of all time, and we've managed to do it against near-insurmountable odds! The components in this box are eavesdropping on electronic conversations... All the data that's registered, recorded and transmitted by OmniPorts – we've got access to it. We can listen in on the world!'

'Yes, Tariq,' she says slowly. 'I'm well aware. I designed the system.'

'What I'm trying to say is, Marie... We have an all-access pass to hundreds of Virtual credentials, every single day.' Tariq grins. 'I – the resistance – wanted access to the Nebula. *You* built it for me, for us. *You are brilliant, Marie.*'

Marie laughs out loud. Her palms flutter against the tabletop, and she presses them down to staunch their hammering.

'Run along.' She smirks. 'Report back to Nāyaka and the Suzerain Rasae. Tell the leaders that everything's going according to plan.'

Marie takes a circuitous route from the underground caverns of the Tatae craftsmiths, buried in an erstwhile sewage system, to where the Amethyst Tree stands.

She passes the clothesline that marks the beginning of Rasae territory. The members of the warrior tribe are led in an intense routine of the Sand Arts by the fluid figure of their Suzerain. They engage in drills every dawn, well before the first Maglev arrives with its load of tourists.

She walks past the Sapphire Tree and the Topaz Tree where they stand guard over the northern edge of the tent city. Their canopies spin gently in the swirling dust. Decorative lights twinkle silently in the light of dawn, hiding her secret in plain sight.

The Jewel Forest fans out over the breadth of the Analog side of Apex City. It holds the living, breathing jacaranda tree at the heart of its spiral. Close to two dozen glass-and-metal structures, made from scrap that's been meticulously gathered in the Junkyard and recycled, raise their shimmering branches towards the sky. They're celebrated by most of the Analogs as a symbol of their indomitable spirit, a piece of this world that they have built together – one tree at a time – beginning with the Garnet Tree. The Virtuals might deny them their rights and seek to negate their existence, but the Analogs will always come together as a community.

Unknown to most of the Analog world, each of their precious trees carries one of Marie's handcrafted trans-communicators. Each device harvests data from every passing Virtual, scanning their OmniPorts and all their HoloTech. It scrapes them for every single Virtual's credentials – passcodes, bank account information, access to every single contact they possess across their address books, passwords to social media accounts and workplace databases.

The Forest serves as a parallel network to the Nebula. It pools its finds into a central database made from outdated computers and servers salvaged in the Junkyard. The machines have been restored and installed in a dingy room at the top of the highest pod-house structure.

In time, the resistance will gain access to the Nebula. They will soon be ready to use it to destabilize Bell Corp's very foundations.

It's not personal. New world orders never are.

The network of the Jewel Forest is primed to enable this. It amplifies the signals of archaic cellular towers that lie abandoned on their side of the city. It uses defunct radio-wave technology to communicate with satellites from the old world. Virtual devices are compelled to uplink to it whenever they come within range. Their hubris prevents the Virtuals from thinking any of this possible.

It is Marie's proudest creation. Her hands have lent the Analogs the backbone upon which they will mount their revolution.

The Amethyst Tree is still incomplete. Of its seven planned branches, only three are currently attached. Its trunk is welded together from metal pipes of all dimensions, riveted to the ground to hold it in place. Its canopy is flexible – it sways and rotates on a set of gears and springs to help it withstand the dust storms that ravage this side of the city.

It is the final piece in the biggest community art project the Analogs have ever undertaken. The Jewel Forest – *her forest*, as Marie likes to think of it – has become their pride and joy.

Once the branches are raised, each Analog citizen will be able to lend their work to filling out its canopy. The other trees feature fluttering scarves, decorated CDs, leaves made from broken glass…

And, most importantly, Marie's module. A nondescript piece of scant decorative value that has given this forest a life all its own.

'Four more branches to go,' she says brusquely when she spots Tariq.

She jams her hands deeper in her pockets. He doesn't need to see them shaking.

'I need to talk to you,' Tariq says urgently. 'Alone.'

'Well. Go on.'

'We're being watched.'

Marie frowns. 'We've always known there were informants, Tariq. The entire Electric Underground exists to throw them off guard. *Electric Underground* – with a name like that, we're feeding them exactly what they're looking for. All those incendiary speeches, recruiting a bunch of repressed teenagers using music… They'll be looking for a resistance fuelled by guns, hormones and explosives.

They don't think we'll come for them on their territory – on the Nebula itself.'

'I think they might know about this. The Forest – our technical capability.' Tariq furrows his brow.

Marie knows that it's his job to be paranoid – that's why he's so valuable to the leaders of the resistance – but this seems like a serious concern.

'Well, you know what to do then,' Marie says.

'Find the spy and try to turn them.' Tariq sighs.

'Otherwise, use them. Feed them false information. Send them looking down the wrong rabbit hole,' Marie says. 'If they're convinced we're using technology, then weaponize it in their imaginations.'

Tariq nods. 'I thought I'd tell you first. Keep the trans-comms safe.'

'Nāyaka and the Suzerain Rasae need to know immediately,' she replies.

'I'm going to tell them. Right now.'

Tariq begins to melt into the shadows of the breaking dawn.

'And, Marie… Keep yourself safe too.'

She is used to loss but not to absence. Absence implies the possibility of return, and it is this hope that wears one down. Loss promises finality.

When the Star Charters flight she'd designed exploded while orbiting Enceladus, all lives had been lost. When she received that dreaded notification on her OmniPort, intimating her of her immediate deportation, her value to Bell Corp had been lost. When she'd attempted to sneak across the Southern Wall and into the Nagarhole Eco-Soc, her family had been lost. She would never see her sister again. When she'd been captured, her own life had been forfeit.

Imprisoned in the vegetable farm with her and primed for harvesting was a complete stranger. He'd been extracted by a shadowy figure named Nāyaka, and had insisted on taking Marie with them.

She'd hated him at first. Thanks to him, she'd been forced to reckon with the shadows of her failures. With the tremors in her hands.

She'd tolerated him then. He'd been persistent in checking in on her welfare.

She was grateful to him after a while. He'd roped her into a top-secret project. It had languished until she'd taken over its design. The Jewel Forest is what gives her a sense of fulfilment; every day its radio waves and electrical signals beam their way into the skies, she continues to breathe at ease with their ultrasonic hum.

There's more to the Jewel Forest than the fact that she's designed it. She's enjoyed building it together, *with him*.

The Amethyst Tree is nearly ready to be inaugurated.

It seems unfair that Tariq won't be around to see their creation completed. He's in pursuit of the mysterious Virtual informant. She misses him now. She doesn't know when she'll see him again. *Or if.*

It's a long day for the Tatae craftsmiths as they hoist and fasten each branch onto its welded base. They're working overtime to finish the Amethyst Tree as soon as possible. The inauguration is scheduled for three days from now. There are still three branches to go. They've had to stop each time a Maglev makes its tour of the city. That's too many interruptions to be truly efficient.

Marie calls time.

'We start tomorrow at dawn,' she says, clambering down a ladder from the crook of a branch she's been bolting in place.

She enjoys the repetitive nature of working with tools. It clears her mind. It stills her hands. Now the fog has returned with the twitch in her palms. Tariq's absence – held at bay for the better part of the day – rushes to fill the empty spaces within her.

She pulls off her weather-worn gloves and begins her walk back to Tatae territory alone.

'M-Marie!' calls a hesitant voice.

She turns.

It's one of the craftsmiths, following her down the path. She has short, spiky hair.

'Ro.' She extends a hand. 'Rohini, I mean. All my friends call me Ro.'

Marie doesn't take her hand. She doesn't know what to do with it. 'Nice to meet you, Rohini.'

She continues walking.

'I'm a hu-uge fan of your work,' Rohini says, hurrying to keep up with her.

'Oh.'

'I love how the Jewel Forest is designed,' she gushes. 'The flexibility that allows each tree to withstand the dust storms. The way the branches permit for ornamentation. The way –'

'You're new here, aren't you?' Marie cuts her off.

'Yes. I've only been here for about a year.' Rohini pauses. 'Why?'

'No reason.'

Marie assumes that this means their conversation is at an end. The Analogs have learnt to give her her space. When she'd first arrived, she'd rebuffed their every approach to include her in their conversations, and they had long since left her to her own devices.

The only reason they continue to tolerate her, and occasionally respond to her, is because her genius demands so.

'I – I was thinking,' Rohini continues, cutting through her thoughts.

Marie stifles a sigh.

'I would love to apprentice with you. I'm okay learning about the mechanics of bolting the trees in place, but I'd love to explore the thought behind how you design them. And why.'

Rohini has rushed through her words until now, but she lays this desire out clearly.

'Sorry,' Marie says curtly. 'I work alone.'

'I can't draft, but I can write Sentient+.'

Marie stops short in her tracks.

'I'm sure – I'm sure over time...' the woman says, 'you'll be able to automate some of the design, and I could –'

'I have no use for Sentient+, Rohini,' Marie says coldly. 'None of us do. We're Analogs. We don't use code. We don't have computers. Or have you forgotten which side of the Meridian you're on?'

A lie, but a necessary one. Nobody but the inner circle of the resistance knows that they have access to computer hardware.

'I – I know about the resistance,' the woman says. 'I've been to the meetings at the Electric Underground.'

'I don't know what you're talking about,' Marie says flatly.

'I know the Jewel Forest is more than just an art project.' A hint of desperation creeps into her voice.

'You're right,' Marie says. 'It's a piece of our identity as a community. You can contribute to it on Inauguration Day too. Bring a piece of artwork. Bonus points to the tribe with the most originality.'

She tries to walk past the woman but Rohini stands her ground, eyeing her coldly.

'I only hope your delusions of grandeur don't get us all killed this time. Another Star Charters incident, except the casualties won't be the rich and famous.'

Marie reacts before her brain can process what her body is doing. She pulls her fist back and cracks it into the side of the woman's head.

The woman cries out and reaches for her jaw, but does not retaliate. A thin trickle of blood runs down her chin from a cut on her lower lip.

'Oh my goodness! I'm so sorry,' Marie rushes to apologize. 'You touched a raw nerve, I didn't mean to hit you –'

The woman turns and stalks away without a word, still gingerly tending to her face.

Marie looks down and sees that a spot of blood stains her knuckles. It isn't lost on her that her hands are still.

Persona is paramount.

– from the Meritocratic Manifesto,
'Concerning Virtual Citizen Reports', Article II (a)

THE PERSONA POLICE

'TANVI!' CATHY FLASHED HER most charming smile. 'My favourite client! We've been expecting you.' She regarded Tanvi's tangle of too-long bangs in silent disapproval. 'Congratulations! I saw your post on InstaSnap. You must be so excited.'

'Um –'

Cathy ushered her into one of the private StylePods reserved for her twenty-percenter clientele. Reflecto-screens surrounded them on all sides, beaming their high-definition likenesses magnified to showcase every flaw.

She offered Tanvi a seat, then tapped on her holo-watch.

The reflecto-screens faded to black to enable an optimal holographic experience.

An image from Tanvi's InstaSnap profile appeared in a swirl of pixels, beaming down at her. The holosnap was captioned 'Mama to be!'

'Well –'

'You look great! I love that top. Bijou, isn't it? I've got an eye for these things. It's flattering – practically hides your bump,' Cathy gushed.

'Tha –'

'According to our Timeline, you had a styling due three weeks ago.'

'Oh –'

'Better late than never though, isn't it? You must've been busy with the pregnancy and everything. Arjun must be so happy. I'm sure you'll make great parents...'

'Mmm –'

'But, Tanvi, your hair!' She let her words ring through the silence of the StylePod.

She lifted a lank section and tutted. It was crinkly. Definitely dry. She rubbed it between her fingers and little wisps detached themselves, falling dead to the floor.

'It's no good,' Cathy muttered. 'Haven't you been using SkinDeep's Sp@Home Hair Mask? And their ScalpMoisture Therapy? I know, I know – you've been busy, but think about your Social Persona!'

She tapped on her holo-watch again. A collage of holosnaps and holovids featuring Tanvi's person appeared on the blackscreen, encircling them in the glitter of her perfect white smile.

'Your comments and shares have dropped: 3,13,418 shares three months ago – that's the holosnap on your far left, near the top – to just 2,85,607 yesterday. That's the one right in front of you.'

Cathy let the import of this data sink in.

'You're losing virality. It's all because of your hair.'

The mass of holo-rayed images disappeared. The two images in question were blown up larger than life.

'When was your last styling?'

'I –'

Cathy rushed to answer her own question. 'Over three months ago! Tanvi, here at Primp & Preen, we're one call away from caring for all your style needs. You're a twenty percenter at the top of the Curve! You can't afford to let yourself go!'

'But –'

'I know, I know. You're pregnant. It's a new experience. It'll be easier once the foetus is transferred to its PregaPod.'

Cathy tapped her holo-watch once more. A fresh set of three-dimensional Tanvis in various states of stillness and motion presented themselves, all recorded at Primp & Preen.

'This is your style trend over the last two years. Long hair is still in, but with your current texture – it must be from your new diet, what with the pregnancy and all – we recommend something mid-length.'

With another tap, the images were replaced with a view of Tanvi's face up close. A series of measurements appeared – the width of her cheekbones from her nostrils, the height of her forehead, the length of her nose.

'You've gained about two millimetres of fat on either side of your face, so we recommend longer bangs. You'll look super cute.'

Cathy blew her a conciliatory air-kiss. She felt the need to reassure Tanvi after coming down so hard on her.

'These are our proposed styles.'

Cathy let Tanvi swipe through various styling options overlaid on her magnified likeness.

'You want your Social Persona to celebrate your new-found motherhood.'

She supplied her insights each time Tanvi paused to look at a style she liked, rotating it to view its effect on her likeness from every angle.

'We *could* do this, but blonde-and-brown highlights are too tame. You'd *own* the purple-to-red ombré, but is it mature enough for a new mama? Hmm…somehow, I don't think so. You don't either? Good. I like this option for you. Balayage. Blonde. We'll add nice blue highlights… You like, hmm?'

'Well –'

'Once the baby is released from its PregaPod, we'll take it down to a bob. It's an edgy new look for an edgy new mama.'

Tanvi continued to swipe through the options on offer.

'You know what Sheila Prakash did when her daughter's foetus was in its Pod?' Cathy lowered her voice. 'I heard this from Dr Binny, who's also my client – not my favourite client, though, that's you!'

She waited until Tanvi acknowledged her flattery with a smile.

'Sheila modified almost all of the child's DNA. Her bright green eyes – ugh, such a cliché – under those jet-black bangs? Sheila prototyped a biotech application to screen and pick her baby's features. She went through *hundreds* of possible outcomes and then created the most clichéd pretty baby possible. And then she named her *Anastasia*!' Cathy giggled.

'Oh –'

'Like ordering a baby from a catalogue.' Cathy smirked.

'But –'

'You should do the same thing. Here's my advice, though. Keep their appearance either natural or edgy. *Commit.* Don't be indecisive.' Her voice dropped to a whisper. 'Do you know the barbarians on the other side *don't* have PregaPods? No wonder they all turn out hideous.'

'Well –'

'They give birth the *old-fashioned way*. Don't care about their Productivity, but we knew that already, didn't we?'

She began to giggle, fumbling over her words.

'They're too busy making art. Did you see that Woofer post that someone shot from a Maglev? They're building…t-t-trees!' She began to laugh. 'From trash!'

She quieted her laughter when she noticed that Tanvi hadn't joined in.

'I guess you haven't seen it yet, what with the pregnancy and all.'

She kept her tone bright.

'I'm just saying. *That lot* can afford to let nine months go by. Like that.' Cathy snapped her fingers. 'No commitment to self-improvement. But look at you! You're a celebrated Bell Corp treasure, my darling. You're at the apex of our society, and you're *only* thirty-one. InstaSnap is lucky to have you.'

'Thank –'

'You transfer that foetus soon, drop the pounds, come in for your stylings on time, and you'll be back on top of your game in no time!'

Cathy sensed Tanvi's attention begin to waver. She quickly brought the conversation back to business. 'Have you chosen a style?'

Tanvi pointed to the blonde balayage with blue highlights.

'Ooh!' Cathy squealed. 'That's my favourite!'

She tapped her holo-watch and the walls transitioned back to reflecto-screen. A snipper-snapper and a dye-n-dryer popped out of a panel in the wall.

'Do you know that natural colours are making a comeback in Premier City?' Cathy shook her head in disapproval. 'I mean, there's a reason that Crown is the fashion capital of the world. We'll keep the blue highlights nice and rich.'

'I –'

'In Crown, getting temp face tattoos that contrast with your highlights is really in vogue right now.'

'Well –'

'But we won't do that to you yet, doll. You transition into motherhood and then we'll talk.'

'Okay –'

'So when are you going to have your PregaPod transfer, hon?'

She pointed the snipper-snapper at a long lock of hair and monitored the machine as it snipped the section in a feathered pattern.

'I can pick the length of your bangs depending on when you're going to lose the puffiness around your cheeks.'

A rule-tool hovered before Tanvi's face, offering options for the length of her bangs.

'Hon?' Cathy prompted patiently. 'The PregaPod transfer date?'

'Oh,' Tanvi said. 'Right. Look, I'm not sure I'm going to have a PregaPod transfer.'

InstaB!tchezz <3

Nit@Insta	<u wont believe this,,,>
Suman_182	<Wut>
Saba_Rocks	<Tell>
Nit@Insta	<tanvi nair is preggers>
R0chelle	<v kno>
Saba_Rocks	<Yeah, old news>
Nit@Insta	<u kno she isn't doing a pregapod transfer?>

Saba_Rocks <Get out!>

R0chelle <who told you>

Nit@Insta <cathy>

Suman_182 <PnP Cathy?!>

Saba_Rocks <?!?>

Nit@Insta <yea>

R0chelle <sounds legit>

Suman_182 <No pod? She's doing the full 9?>

Nit@Insta <yea,,, that's what Cathy sez>

Saba_Rocks <Wow. That hasn't happened in...>

R0chelle <unholy 10-p>

Saba_Rocks <Hah! I knew she was a slacker.>

R0chelle <we do all the work>

Suman_182 <Then Tanvi hates on it.>

Nit@Insta <she gonna lose productivity points lulz,,,>

Saba_Rocks <She's already getting fat in her holosnaps. Check out the double chin.>

Saba_Rocks has posted a link: insta.snap/tanvinair/holosnap_12917_n_2993885

Click here to report this link as offensive.

R0chelle <only gonna get worse>
<unpopularity alert>

Saba_Rocks <Low Social Points. Low Productivity. 9 months later...>
<Fired!>

Nit@Insta <lulz,,, fired AND downgraded..>

Saba_Rocks <DEPORTED... dun dun dun>

R0chelle <hype-tastic>

Saba_Rocks <Tanvi Nair. A seventy percenter.>

Suman_182 <Tanvi Nair...an analoggg>

Nit@Insta <no electricity no running water paper money,,,>

R0chelle <no personal stylist>

Saba_Rocks <Fat Tanvi Nair!>

Nit@Insta <fat analog tanvi nair>

ROchelle is typing...

Mrs Kapadia swelled like a pustule. She waved her hand and sent the Analog servant working on her nails scurrying.

She hadn't been comfortable having the girl around since the latest advisory had gone into circulation from the Policy and Governance Division, but there was no mani-pedi-bot out there who left her cuticles as glossy as the girl did.

'I heard from Aksha, who heard from Nita Kumari. You know, that girl who works for Tanvi?'

'The skinny one with the pouty face?' she asked.

'She's telling everyone at InstaSnap.'

Mrs Kapadia's face contorted with suppressed rage.

Her eldest daughter quailed. Bad things happened to bearers of bad news in her family.

'What do we do with her, Gayu? It's true!' Mrs Kapadia took several deep breaths. 'She told me she doesn't *want* a PregaPod transfer, as if that's a legitimate choice in this day and age. I've raised an idiot! A selfish idiot.'

Gayatri inhaled slowly before suggesting a constructive course of action. 'Can't we talk to Arjun, Mama?'

'That poor boy. When she married him, I thought they'd be properly settled. You know what a great Social Persona he has. His Productivity has won so many awards at Bell Corp…'

'Yes, Mama, he's wonderful.'

Mrs Kapadia began to hyperventilate. 'Your sister, though. As stubborn as – as…' she dropped her voice, 'as an Analog.'

'I know.'

'I thought I'd raised you girls right. You were both Pod babies.

You don't feel like you were cheated of my parenting as a foetus, *do you*?' She glowered at her daughter.

'No, Mama. You're the best mother in the world.'

Mrs Kapadia erupted. 'I don't know what we did wrong. Daddy's going mad with worry. The last old-fashioned birth in the family was my great-grandmother. That's over a hundred years ago!'

'I know, Mama –'

'There's *no control* over the child's genes with a natural birth. Did you know that? We *cannot* afford to be the talk of the town because someone in our family produced a vile-looking infant.'

'I'll talk to her, Mama.'

'I hope she's following the diet I sent her. She's piling on the pounds – everyone's talking about her latest holosnaps.'

'It's only temporary, Mama –'

'Vegan, but with protein and iron supplements. I had the entire plan shipped to her off FreshGoodz. And the personal trainer for aerial yoga?'

'I'm not sure, Mama –'

'I hope she called him. After a point you can't help the weight gain, but you can control it. At least that's what the witch doctors in the olden days believed.'

She glared at her daughter's holographic person hovering over the glass screen of her OmniPort.

'I had to find *books* to look up how a person stays pregnant for nine months. *Books*.'

'You're a very supportive mother, Mama.'

Mrs Kapadia tapped on the holosnap of the aerial yoga trainer she'd booked.

'I've been reading. There's no way anyone can go back to work and be instantly Productive after an old-fashioned birth. Did you know that? *Does she?*'

Her voice rose again. 'Maybe I'll send her some *books*! That'll teach her. Books!'

Mrs Kapadia took a deep breath to rein in her anger, and failed.

'And she just got promoted. The fool! Does she know how hard it is to stay at the top of the Curve, especially after a promotion? All her targets will have been recalibrated by now – the minute she stops earning her place in society, she'll be deported.'

'Mama…'

'They'll send her back to us in a titanium box.'

'Come now –'

'I'll be stuck raising an ill-begotten child! Poor Arjun. He must be mortified. I'd better call him –'

Mrs Kapadia swiped to check if the services of the aerial yoga trainer had been availed of.

'Harvest your sister, Gayu. She hasn't had a single session with my yoga instructor.'

'I've told you already, Mr Nair. Tanvi signed a waiver a few days ago, taking on all responsibility for an in-utero birth.'

Arjun watched the doctor gesture towards the screen. He had a 360-degree view of her office from within the concave shell of his VirtuoPod. The gentle curve of the Bell Corp insignia was barely visible, etched onto its glass screen.

She pulled up a copy of a digitally signed form bearing his wife's signature.

'See this? Page three. Take a close look. It says she is willing to bear all risks of a nine-month in-utero pregnancy, including compromises to her physical well-being, its potential impact on her Virtual Citizen Report, and any unforeseen outcomes to her foetus's genetic composition, including its physical attributes. It's signed in triplicate.'

'Impossible! She…she didn't tell me.'

Arjun tried to take charge of the conversation using reason.

'Dr Binny, this is ridiculous. Your hospital failed to communicate this to me. I'm the father of this child. Don't I have a say in its future?'

Dr Binny looked Arjun in the eye. 'Legally speaking, she's well within her rights to make an independent decision, Mr Nair. *It is her body.*'

'But I had to hear about this from Tanvi's mother! *Her mother!*'

Dr Binny sighed. 'Mr Nair. Women tend to get attached to the foetus. We've seen it happen before.'

'This woman doesn't!' Arjun snapped before checking his emotions. He continued in what he hoped was a rational tone. 'We planned this together. She's always had her priorities straight. She just got promoted! We're twenty percenters, not degenerate Analogs –'

'You should talk to her about it.'

'*Talk to her about it?* She didn't even bother telling me she wanted an…an…' Arjun lowered his voice. 'An *old-fashioned* birth.'

Dr Binny frowned slightly. She seemed to be tapping on her holographic keyboard.

'What?'

Dr Binny dragged something into his view.

'Your Compatibility Score seems to be dropping. Take a look at the graph. There's a big drop on your Marital Bliss Tracker. Did you have a fight?'

'No.'

'Well, your score was stable. Up until now. We didn't call you about the waiver because we thought, *naturally*, that you were the kind of couple who'd come to these decisions mutually.'

Arjun bristled under her thinly veiled criticism.

'*Especially* because you're such a power couple. So evenly matched on your Productivity Points, your Social Personas and –'

'Dr Binny, I suppose there's a point you're trying to make?'

'Mr Nair, the attachment to a foetus during pregnancy brings about *changes*. Women tend to make irrational decisions. All those *hormones*, you know? It could put your marriage at risk.'

'What do you –'

'If I were you, I'd try and talk her back into a PregaPod transfer. Before it's too late.'

Arjun stayed mute.

Dr Binny leant forward. 'Talk to her. Maybe you'll get through. If you don't, I suggest you find a good lawyer.'

'Tanvi Nair just cancelled her PregaPod transfer.'

The pronouncement elicited a collective gasp from the otherwise dignified ladies at the table.

'The rumours are true, then. They've been doing the rounds all week!' Sheila Prakash cackled, clapping her hands in glee.

She signalled to a brand-new server-bot, who refilled her champagne glass unsteadily, its mechatronic limbs still getting accustomed to the action. It swiftly returned to the shadows.

She sighed.

She'd been forced to rid her bungalow of its staff of Analog servants. All sixty of them had been sent packing after the most recent advisory. It had seemed paranoid – the thought of those bottom feeders plotting a rebellion – but one could never be too careful. Especially if one was in a position of power.

There had been consequences. The jacarandas on her property were never brought to bloom in time. The holosphere that rayed cloudless blue skies over her estate – blocking the reality of Apex City's jagged skyline looming over its bucolic grounds – was misplaced each time the server-bots rotated their duties.

These luncheons had lost some of their charm, not in the least because the compliments regarding her estate had somewhat diminished in their frequency.

'I don't know why Tanvi would sabotage herself this way,' Aafreen Ahmed said officiously.

This was precisely the kind of gossip they needed to restore levity to their small contingent, comprising the top one percent of women entrepreneurs – or as she liked to refer to them, femme-trepreneurs – in Apex City.

'There's no practical reason to have an old-fashioned birth in this day and age.' Aafreen took a small sip of her champagne. 'My great-grandmother might have had children that way, but those were dark days.'

'Yes, women weren't very empowered back then.' Sheila nodded.

'That entire era was a farce. Equal-pay-for-equal-work issues. The glass ceiling…'

'Good thing we got rid of that.'

Rebecca Binny raised her glass, congratulating the three women of power around her.

'I certainly don't want to be spreading a rumour,' she continued. 'But –'

'Oh, we believe you, darling. Your partner is Tanvi's doctor, after all.'

Sheila Prakash surveyed her guests with approval. Her private luncheons were an invitation-only affair. They were exclusively catered by @SugarnSpice – the only private event in all the world to be able to afford the award-winning chef.

Sheila prized exclusivity. As the founder of FreshGoodz, she'd been the first woman to make it to the top one percent on the Curve. She'd set an example by shattering myths about feminine weakness and sentimentality. She had a clear business mind and was a ruthless negotiator. She had no use for women who didn't share her drive to get to the top and stay there.

Rebecca was still talking.

'– imagine what would have happened to SkinDeep Services if I'd taken months off to drop a baby.'

'We wouldn't have had access to your curated cosmetics deliveries,' Aafreen said. 'Imagine the state of our Social Personas without our make-up on. Your completely rational decision is the reason we're here.'

'Hear, hear.' Sara Mathias raised her glass.

'Her Productivity Points are going to drop if she goes on maternity leave,' Aafreen said darkly.

'You mean, *when* she goes on maternity leave.'

'You don't know that for sure, Sheila –' Sara began.

'I'm just saying,' Sheila said loudly. 'It's unprecedented. It's been a while since one of our cadre risked everything for an old-fashioned birth.'

'Clearly she's not one of our cadre.' Aafreen smirked.

'I had such high hopes for her.' Rebecca sighed.

'She has 1.7 million followers on InstaSnap. Does she know how irresponsible she's being? Imagine all those other women following suit…'

Sheila and Aafreen shared a significant look over their champagne flutes.

'She's got chubby in her recent holosnaps. Sara, you might want to consider this – it might help the greater good if she's out of the public eye,' Aafreen said.

Sara did not comment. As CEO of InstaSnap, she couldn't possibly rise to her employee's defence. Not after her employee had made such a questionable choice.

Besides, Aafreen had a valid point, and she was an expert on what it took to run a social media platform. Aafreen had founded Woofer in her twenties. The portal currently boasted thirty million unique users each day, and patented Hyper Reality–enhancing holovid technology.

'I'd fire @Trishalicious if she even attempted to do this to SkinDeep Services,' Rebecca said flatly. 'As one of our biggest influencers, I wouldn't want her reaching out to people and encouraging these backward ideas. This is going to be bad for InstaSnap's brand image, Sara.'

'Sara, what do you think –'

'She'll probably be deported once she lets herself go,' Aafreen interrupted.

'She should think of the fate of that poor child,' Sheila said.

'Imagine raising it in the Analog world.' Aafreen nodded.

'No vacations,' said Rebecca.

'No HoloTech,' said Sheila.

'No rights,' echoed Aafreen.

'Does she have the scores to afford this?' Sheila asked. 'Productivity Points, Persona –'

'I really can't divulge that information. It's company policy to keep employee information confidential.'

'Oh, come now, Sara. We're all friends here.'

'I'm really sorry, but –'

'All right, all right. Keep your big data a secret.' Aafreen winked.

Sara wasn't sure if she should accept this show of camaraderie at face value. Woofer was *InstaSnap's* biggest rival, after all.

'Tanvi is being selfish, if you ask me,' Aafreen continued. 'I'd fire any employee who takes the company for granted. Wouldn't you, Sara?'

'Well, InstaSnap has a gender-equality policy and –'

'You can't fire her for being pregnant.' Sheila smiled ruefully.

'I'd fire her *after* she returned from her inevitable vacation. If I were you, Sara, I'd extend her a humane three months to get back up to speed. I'd watch her struggle. Then I'd put her on a Productivity Improvement Programme. She'd fail. I'd pull the plug and teach her a lesson. A reward for selfishness.' Aafreen's tone was ruthless. It was the kind of businesswoman she was.

'She's not just selfish, she's positively ungrateful,' Rebecca stated. 'We didn't win our war against the glass ceiling so women like her could regress into the dark ages.'

'Or behave like Analogs,' Aafreen said.

'Like bottom feeders,' Sheila spat.

Sara excused herself.

'You'd better be calling me on a Sunday with good reason, Sara.'

'Tanvi Nair cancelled her PregaPod transfer, Mark.'

'What?'

Mark Morris looked away from the holo-ray streaming onto his wall. CinderElle and the Warrior Princesses were suffering some first-round setbacks in this week's League of Champions game. Sara's news was an unwelcome interruption.

'She's our new Director of Persona Curation, Mark.' Sara tried to keep her impatience in check.

'I know who she is. Wasn't she just promoted? Now she wants to have a baby the…the *old-fashioned* way?'

CinderElle took some heavy damage to her side and was knocked off her feet.

'So it seems.'

There was a long silence.

'Mark?'

Mark signed out of his League of Champions viewership account with a scowl.

'I thought you'd picked the right person, Sara.' The Vice President of Bell Corp's Investments Division looked at Sara in disapproval. 'She was only promoted five months ago. On *your* recommendation. The timing couldn't be worse. Bell's Best and Brightest Awards are just around the corner!'

Sara's face was impassive. 'I don't need to remind you that her Productivity Points were stellar, Mark. If I recall, you were blown away by what an impressive power-user she was. You said there was no one better suited to the job.' She paused. 'We agreed on giving her this promotion. *Together.*'

Mark waved his hand, acknowledging her point. 'Where does the husband work, again?'

'He works for you. Bell Corp's Infrastructure Division. Arjun Nair.'

'There's no way he'd endorse this. He knows how important Productivity is. Bell Corp *hand-picks* its employees based on their commitment to our agenda of building a sustainable meritocratic technarchy. Our employees conform to and prioritize the Meritocratic Manifesto above all else, striving to belong to the upper sections of society. Our employees *do not behave like Analogs*.'

Sara sighed.

'There is no room on the Virtual side of the city for bottom feeders. Bell Corp makes this clear to its employees. I thought InstaSnap would too.'

Sara tolerated his stuffy monologue.

'The Director of Persona Curation is InstaSnap's most coveted role,' Mark said, returning to the problem at hand. 'Who else is going to set trends for the millions of Virtuals who access the portal to latch onto?'

His voice began to rise. 'And what about the nominees for the awards? Who'll curate those?'

'She has a backup team of five –'

'Impeccable taste can't be determined by democracy.'

Sara agreed.

'Can we demote her? Better yet, fire her?' Mark drummed his fingers on the table in agitation.

Sara ignored the sound.

'We can't fire her for wanting an old-fashioned birth. InstaSnap has a gender-equality policy and we don't punish women for –'

Mark Morris held up his hand. 'We invested in PregaPods to prevent this sort of thing, Sara. In the old days, women could screw corporations over by getting pregnant and going on maternity leave. They built their own glass ceiling. Smart women wanted to shatter it. We built PregaPods and solved the problem. This world is equal-opportunity in every possible way.

'Tanvi Nair is going to rebuild the ceiling all by herself. Wait until she goes on maternity leave. Harvest me, that's three whole months! When do we start the awards process, again?'

Sara forced herself to remain calm. 'She hasn't applied for it, yet.'

Mark ignored her.

'Do you know how many Shares-per-Follower she has? What is her Direct-Engagement-to-End-User-Outreach metric?'

'Over 1.7 million Uniques per day.'

'Do you know how many will follow her example? Women like this are anti-empowerment. Before you know it, all of Bell Corp's female employees will go on a rampage. Maternity leave for all!'

Sara rose to Tanvi's defence. 'Mark, we can ask her to keep it on the down-low –'

'Demote her. Downgrade her. Fire her. I have no time for this kind of ingratitude.'

'We can't –'

'Yes, yes. Gender equality. I know. She'll need to hit the ground running as soon as she's back, then.'

'I'll tell her so –'

'No excuses on the basis of hormones. If I see her Productivity drop before she goes on leave, she's fired. If her Tags-to-Trending conversion rate drops, she's fired. If her Engagers-to-Lurkers ratio drops, she's fired. If she talks about being on maternity leave, she's fired. If she screws up on the award nominees, she's fired.'

Mark took a deep breath. 'And you'll do the firing.'

'What did you do this time, Mark?'

Mark Morris scowled at the legal adviser to Bell Corp's Investments Division. Her face wore a smirk like a piece of twisted, expensive jewellery.

'InstaSnap's Director of Persona Curation – Tanvi Nair – is having her baby the old-fashioned way. No PregaPod.'

'So?'

'So? *So!* InstaSnap's entire image is built on her work. We can't afford for her to slack off like this. We're InstaSnap's biggest investors!'

'Ah. That's a problem.'

'She has an Outreach of 1.7 million followers. This could put dangerous ideas in their heads. It establishes a precedent for other lazy women. We need to do something about it. About her.'

'Your hands are tied, Mark.'

'I'm sure *you* can think of something, Jessica…' Mark wheedled.

'I'm looking up the Bell Charter on Reproductive Rights.'

'Thank you, Jessica.' Mark exhaled in gratitude, then proceeded to drum his fingers in agitation.

'*Concerning Analogs: Bell Corporation will not tender medical assistance to Analog citizens who intend to bear children. We discourage them from propagating their kind. Offspring will be registered at Birth. They will receive skill-based education towards occupying pre-assigned roles –*'

'Jessica, she's our Director of Persona Curation. Not our window-washer.'

'Mark.' Jessica's tone implied warning.

'*Seventy percenters: Bell Corporation deems it mandatory for each seventy percenter to donate ova or sperm towards the fulfilment of its Malthusian Manifesto. Offspring will be conceived and developed within Bell Corporation's ZygoCells. Offspring will be raised as Wards of* – Is she a seventy percenter?'

'What do you think?'

'All right. *Twenty percenters: Bell Corporation-approved twenty percenters who intend to bear children –*'

'Get to the point.'

'Calm down. *Bell Corporation recommends the use of a PregaPod transfer in order to safeguard a woman's Virtual Citizen Report, inclusive of her Productivity Points, Social Persona* – you know the list. *However, should a woman choose to bear a child in-utero, she may do so, against the recommendation of the technarchy.*'

'How is this useful?'

Jessica smiled superciliously. 'Twenty percenters have privileges, Mark. That doesn't mean she's unaccountable, but you'll have to rely on the system to deliver the consequences. Once she starts failing to meet her targets, the Curve will adjust her position and downgrade her. At the moment, though…'

'So we wait, then?'

'We wait.'

Mark passed a hand over his face.

'What aren't you telling me, Mark?'

'Jessica…'

'Spit it out.'

'The child. It's mine.'

Jessica Swanson pored over the contract Mark Morris had shared with her.

It outlined the details of a confidential Bell Corp-funded project run by the Genome Preservation and Propagation Division.

She rubbed her tired eyes, irritated that this was so top-secret she couldn't delegate the reading to an associate at the firm. She scowled at the thought that it had been so top-secret that Mark hadn't shared it with her, or consulted her before digitally signing the harvesting document on *every page*.

She cursed.

The story between the lines was such a cliché.

Mark and Tanvi had been chosen to genetically contribute their DNA towards the construction of the perfect offspring. The Genome

Preservation and Propagation Division had chosen to blend his financial wizardry with her creative genius to create a super-baby.

If the experiment proved successful, the child would grow up with a pre-assigned genetic capability towards a chosen field – perhaps finance, or art, or entrepreneurship – depending upon the projected requirements of the workforce when the child completed its education.

Tanvi was expected to raise the child as if it were her own. Her husband, Arjun, would never be let in on the secret.

It was an *honour* to be chosen for this.

Tanvi could be the solution to one of Apex City's most pressing problems.

Every year, when the bottom ten percent was culled from society, Bell Corp's Malthusian Manifesto ensured that there were sufficient replacements to join the workforce, employing seventy percenters from the Repopulation Wards or twenty-percenter children. Unfortunately, they couldn't always ensure that the skill sets of the incumbents matched the open requirements.

The city was then forced to look for expertise from the Outside, an arduous and expensive task that involved screening thousands of immigrant applications, interviewing shortlisted candidates and then realigning their generally dated ideologies into the acceptance of meritocracy.

Immigrants from Aqua-Socs, Agro-Socs, ONG-Socs and the like were used to cooperative societies, egalitarian forms of governance… Admittedly, the price of failure in an Agro-Soc was the failure of the Agro-Soc and the death of a few hundred thousands. The price of failure in any Bell Corp–governed city was the collapse of the technology that permitted the post-nation world to operate seamlessly. Millions of lives could be lost if a single citizen shirked their duties.

There was no room for error, here in Apex City.

Tanvi Nair held the power to minimize this risk for the entire human race.

Jessica couldn't understand the foolishness of any woman who wanted to turn the opportunity down. Or put it at risk, for that matter.

The foetus will be transferred to a PregaPod within 90 days of its development. The contributors of the sperm and ova will be present, but will not oversee the selection, manipulation and/or modification of the genetic construction of their offspring...

Jessica sighed.

There was no plausible penalty for failing to carry out a transfer. The contract simply assumed that both parties would comply – there was no reason for an in-utero birth in the modern age, after all. Tanvi had chosen to exercise her free will, an unforeseen outcome in any experiment conducted by Bell Corp. They hadn't accounted for such an extreme deviation from their expectations – it was a high-risk endeavour to face the consequences of the system, a fool's errand. And yet, here they were.

She'd been over the fine print thrice.

She could argue that Tanvi was in breach of contract. Then again, it would take weeks – maybe months – to call for a hearing for such a top-secret initiative. These matters weren't argued in Bell Corp's Adjudications Division. A special hearing would have to be convened, its arbitrators sworn to secrecy. The baby would be born by then, deformities, imperfections, dubious skill sets and all.

Jessica would need to rely on coercion. An ugly tactic for a lawyer of such finesse.

She choked down her pride.

'We've spent 67.5 million BellCoin on this project. It cannot fail,' Dr Ramamurthy stated. 'It took us years to harvest data from every single medical test conducted in Bell Corp's cities around the world. Our computers analysed billions of outcomes over half a decade –

adapting each time a new test result came in – before choosing to pair these parent genes. The future of Bell Corp's complete independence from the Outside – indeed, the future of the Outside itself – could very well rest upon the outcome of our experiment.'

'I get it –'

'Tanvi,' Sara interrupted. 'Be reasonable. You've just been promoted. The responsibilities you shoulder have never been more demanding. You can't afford to take the risk.'

'Or we'll fire you,' Mark snapped.

'Mark, play nice,' warned Jessica.

'I know, but –'

'Tanvi, look. I'm going to share a projection of your Virtual Citizen Report. This is where you are now…' Sara pulled up a holo-ray of a complicated curve. She indicated a point on the trend line.

'All green, all healthy. An impressive spike in your career graph with the recent promotion.' She paused. 'But this is you one year later. A full-term pregnancy, maternity leave, no PregaPod transfer, and you'll spiral downward. Straight into the seventy percenters.'

'Yes, that's why –'

'And we'll fire you,' Mark added. 'Bell Corp does not entertain slackers.'

'Mr Morris –'

'Tanvi, be reasonable,' Dr Ramamurthy soothed. 'Think of the role you're playing in the future of science. *You* will have carried the first genetically optimized baby in the world. *You* will be the reason Bell Corp no longer has to spend millions of BellCoin on *Outsiders* each time there's a shortfall in a specific skill requirement. We'll be able to hone the offspring's abilities from the wide array that you and Mark bring to the table, right at the foetal stage. We can guarantee a specific talent by the time your child achieves majority. Think of how this could play out in the future, at every deportation cycle, should our experiment prove successful. Think of the risks that arise from

Outside labour that we could minimize. You'll give women fresh purpose, renewed ambitions. You'll be an influencer for the greater good of science, and not just for pretty clothes or make-up or any of the other stuff –'

'Hang on,' Sara interjected. 'InstaSnap's not just about pretty things. Don't trivialize her role on the project and her contributions to the world of entertainment –'

'Ms Mathias, surely DIY holiday craft is less significant than the future of the human race.'

'We've spent over a billion BellCoin on that holiday craft, *Doctor*,' Mark snapped. 'It's worth a lot more than your toy test-tube set.'

'Mr Morris! Dr Ramamurthy said angrily. 'We hand-picked you for your skill with numbers, but we didn't realize you had such a nasty attitude.'

He addressed Tanvi. 'This is why we need the foetus in its PregaPod, Tanvi. So we can weed genetic predispositions to a nasty temper out of its gene pool –'

'Oh, you think I have a nasty temper?' Mark raised his voice. 'You haven't seen anything yet.'

'Mark!' Jessica hissed.

'I wish you wouldn't put genetic science on such a pedestal. Tanvi's baby is important to all of us. If she has a PregaPod transfer, we'll be able to keep millions of Virtual citizens happy and focused on their Bell Corp–driven objectives,' Sara said pointedly.

'We'll still be profitable,' Mark added. 'We'll have massive savings in the long run. Imagine the upper hand we'll gain in our trade negotiations with the Outsiders. Outside Socs usually pay for our technology with skilled employees at our request. Think of the full extent of our purchasing power when we no longer have to rely on them to fill our shortfall.'

'And we'll have a perfect super-baby to show the world. One more step towards the empowerment of women, to the power of their genes and their contributions as embryonic caretakers,' Dr Ramamurthy said magnanimously.

'Yes, Tanvi. You're one of Bell Corp's most prized assets. You stand for every single one of our core values. You've been such a shining embodiment of them so far…' Mark said.

'Tanvi, think of all the systems that rely on you. Come now, be rational about your choice.' Sara smiled reassuringly.

'Tanvi, the future of our civilization –'

'STOP.' Tanvi shot to her feet. 'Everybody stop. Listen.' She took a deep breath. 'I've… I'm no longer carrying the child.'

'Excellent, you've seen reason!' Dr Ramamurthy exclaimed.

'Good show, Tanvi.' Sara beamed.

'Well don –'

'NO!' Tanvi glowered at the other people on the conference call. 'If only you'd listen, we'd have saved us all this pointless conversation.'

'Tanvi, is everything all right?'

'I've changed my mind. I no longer want to be a mother… I've terminated the pregnancy.'

Several moments passed in silence. Mark Morris was the first to erupt.

'What kind of twenty percenter can't even deliver on her biological obligation to Bell Corp!'

'Mark –'

InstaB!tchezz <3

Nit@Insta <u wont believe this,,,>

Suman_182 <Wut>

Saba_Rocks <Tell us.>

Nit@Insta <tanvi nair terminated her pregnancy...>

R0chelle <no way>

Suman_182 <srsly??>

Nit@Insta <yep,,,>

Saba_Rocks <Well I'll be harvested!>

ROchelle <size o humanitarian score>
Saba_Rocks <Cold.>
Nit@Insta <yea>
Saba_Rocks <I want a new manager.>
Suman_182 <ikr>
Nit@Insta <what a heartless bitch>

ROchelle is typing...

Tyranny's foe is community.
We will not break.

– The Suzerain Rasae,
on the Eve of the Inauguration of the Museum of Analog History
(anecdotal)

A PARABLE FROM THE HEART OF THE SEA

THE ANALOGS CAME BEARING their decorations for the Amethyst Tree. They had achieved so much as a community. Together, they had built the Jewel Forest.

Anatronica blared from speakers set up around the tree. Teenagers bounced to the beat, bobbing their heads to the distinctive synth sound. A number of carts stood around the perimeter, their proprietors having moved from their usual spots in Market Square to sell handheld electric fans and loosely bound notebooks to the throng.

Representatives from every tribe except the Atae – excluded, as usual, for being beholden to the Virtuals in their Pleasure Domes – scrambled up the ladders set up at each of the tree's seven branches. They carried their gifts with care. A carefully cut-out set of paper stars fluttered from a branch, made by children under the supervision of the Mahae tribe who reared them. Scavenged hub-caps, painted over in bright colours, were bolted in place by the Tatae craftsmiths who volunteered their offerings. A line of bright green bottles hung suspended, a lump of metal between them striking each one to create an eerie music. The thieves of the Sutae tribe had filched these over the years from the bar cabinets of the Virtual elite.

The branches had begun to fill out.

The Rasae warriors offered ornamental weapons sheaths, the Vitae scavengers came bearing odds and ends of shiny plastic and metal.

Bashir Rehan, the Keeper of the Lore, prepared himself to make a benefaction of his own. It would not glitter from between the branches of the tree, but perhaps it would kindle a light of an entirely different sort.

All men and women are given a choice – to be the hero of the tale or its teller.

Bashir Rehan was content with being the latter. He'd often been told that he should run for office, that he would make a formidable Suzerain of one of the tribes. He'd never held this desire himself.

He'd found that his fulfilment was derived from an audience that hung onto his every word. He preferred for those words to be fictions rooted in the moment, not promises for a better tomorrow.

When the last branch was decorated with a stream of tattered ribbons, Bashir limped up onto a set of crates at the base of the tree. His cane snagged upon a wooden board but he wrenched it free, careful to display no discomfort.

His shoulders straightened as he contemplated the tale he was prepared to tell upon this occasion, his twenty-fourth and last story dedicated to the founding of the Jewel Forest.

The crowd stilled and the anatronica faded to static.

'I invite you to journey with me to a time fathomless to us all, to the very beginnings of the world itself. I invite you into the heart of the sea.'

The Keeper of the Lore cast his net.

'The ocean was vast and empty. An endless expanse of blue, it flung itself far and wide to cover the world. Its waves crashed upon each other with awesome violence, crushing everything in their path and dragging them down to its depths.

'All things fell before its power and might. None dared challenge its will.

'The ocean laughed at the fragility of all that lay before it. Each laugh rolled like thunder, shaking and churning the world all the way to its heart. The ocean believed itself unconquerable.

'Deep down in the cold reaches of its soul stirred a bubble of heat. The ocean paid this no heed. The bubble of heat poured out through a small crack, in a crag long since swallowed by the ocean's fury.

'The little molten pool frothed and bubbled, and what started as a solitary spark struggling to find its way to the surface slowly grew into a steady stream.

'And it was slow. Achingly slow. That is the manner of all acts of resistance.

'The ocean didn't notice. It had swallowed so much of the world that it was used to strange rumblings in its belly. Its being was intent on consuming everything in sight, feeding the endless need that had grown to fill its core.

'And so the stream flourished, molten and raging hot, rising its way over hundreds of years to the ocean's surface.

'When the first sparks felt the fresh, cool air upon their faces for the first time in centuries, they laughed and danced. When the first sparks heard the sounds and silences of the world above, they were filled with wonder.

'Atom by atom, an endless river of lava plunged through the cold darkness that had smothered their heat and fire. Their blazing rage began to simmer at first, then to cool. Always, new sparks of fire joined them. And always, they bided their time, hardening and thickening as they stood side by side.

'The ocean had set its sights too far and wide to notice.

'A molecule of bright green moss discovered an oasis of rock within the raging ocean. It clung to it. A molecule of grass soon followed and began to fan out, spreading its blades across the barren land. Flung out over millions of miles by the wind and waves, these were joined by a sudden flowering of sandwort and sea rocket.

'Both hardening rock and fresh lava welcomed them alike.

'Before too long, the first gull appeared on the island. It was large and black-backed, and soon hurried to summon all the other gulls to this thriving little rock in what was otherwise a watery wasteland.

'The ocean had finally sensed that something was wrong. It turned its gaze to this strange being that had formed in its midst.

'It experienced a sharp burst of agony, which quickly turned into fury. It rushed to the island and battered against it with all its power. This was unacceptable – who dared stand in the way of the absolute will of the ocean?

'Upon the island, the gulls and other birds huddled beneath the rocks as a torrential rain poured down upon them. Over the years, the winds had carried a few seeds that had plunged their way through the soil and were now young, strong saplings. They dug deep with their roots, holding as much of the island together as possible as the ocean threatened to rip it apart.

'For a hundred years, the ocean shattered itself upon the island in wave after wave. Pieces of the island broke away and were swallowed into its gaping maw, but the steady stream of fire from within the ocean's depths continued to flow. The island continued to hold, firm and unbreakable.

'In time, the ocean gave up. It fled to nurse the doubts that had begun to gnaw away at it. Could it be that it was not as all-powerful as it had imagined?

'The island was cracked and weathered. It had lost many of its young trees and wildlife, but it had survived the ocean's ire. It continued to grow, aided by a steady flow of sparks and lava from one little crack deep on the ocean floor. And, as it grew, a world began to thrive upon it.

'The ocean does not forget. It continues to return to the island. It rages and crashes and attempts to submerge it with the full force of its fury. But still the island stands.'

Bashir paused.

'Still the island stands.'

Power has its price. Pay it or perish.

– Aafreen Ahmed, *An Influencer's Guide to Power*, Chapter 3

AVATARS

FHWUPP.

Fhwupp.

Fhwupp.

Fhwupp. Fhwupp.

Fhwupp. Fhwupp. Fhwupp.

CinderElle whipped the Flaming Flail over her head as she stalked towards her enemy.

She liked to take her time, watching the fear build in her opponent's eyes.

Sometimes their eyes blazed with defiance. She liked that even better. It was more satisfying to bludgeon the fight out of someone.

This one, however –

The shaggy Ox_Beast cowered before her. She'd injured it with a flurry of crossbow bolts. It was about to breathe its last.

She'd pierce its heart and get it done with, if CinderElle were a warrior of mercy.

She wasn't.

Besides, the crowd wanted a spectacle and she wasn't about to disappoint.

A notification popped up in the top-left corner of her scope. She dismissed it with a push of her mind.

Who's managed to get through my Communications Fog?

She broke into a run towards her prey.

The crowd began to scream, chanting her name.

The Flaming Flail spun like a Ferris wheel of destruction.

She brought it down in a powerful arc, slamming it into Ox_Beast's neck.

The beast erupted into flames. Blood spurted from its wounds.

The crowd came untethered. The sound was deafening.

CinderElle plucked the pennant from its now undefended post. She'd captured the flag. Again. She'd conquered Alfhaven. Again.

The Warrior Princesses had won. Again.

They were this year's Heroes. After a rocky start to the season, they'd come back with a vengeance to dominate the League of Champions with sparkle and gore for the fifth year in a row.

Her team ran in towards her, thumping her on the back. The heat- and pressure-sensitive material of her Haptic-Hero suit relayed the warmth of their hugs as a welcome respite from the icy chill of Alfhaven's winds, which had knifed through her armour.

The notification popped up again, obscuring vision in her left retina. It was persistent.

She felt a knot of dread in her stomach.

The Warrior Princesses rode on their Triumph in a carriage drawn by flame-breathing skeletal unicorns. They wore their crowns of laurel studded with diamonds and moon dust. They waved out as thousands of fans flung virtual bouquets at their feet, clapping, stamping and cheering them on.

The notification popped up every three and a half minutes, much to CinderElle's chagrin.

There were interviews, signings, photographs, and then the evening was over.

CinderElle severed the link to the Alfhaven map. Notoriously dangerous for its highly adaptive environmental hazards, she was grateful that they'd trained extensively to handle its terrain. The Tactile Turf that surrounded the floor and walls of her home-arena blazed neon blue before dimming, no longer simulating the packed snowdrifts and treacherous glaciers of Alfhaven.

The world slowed down as her senses disconnected from Hyper Reality.

She rubbed her shoulder beneath her Haptic-Hero suit. She'd taken a terrible blow to it when the warrior DarkSyder had slowed time during their bout, swinging his sword down to try and sever her arm. There would be bruises tomorrow.

Ox_Beast had toppled her off her feet, crashing into her from the side. Her ribs ached.

She couldn't wait to take a hot shower and watch a replay of the Contest… She took her Haptic-Hero helmet off, wiping a towel across the sweat on her brow.

The notification popped again, this time on to her intel-lenses. CinderElle, now returned to her diminutive real-life avatar, groaned.

She opened the envelope dancing before her vision.

She recoiled.

It was an invitation.

To the Bell Corp Best and Brightest Awards.

Adrenaline ebbing, exhausted from the Contest, she slumped to the floor.

CinderElle might be a Hero, but *she* most certainly wasn't. CinderElle drew crowds like moths to her flame. *She* was a nobody.

And now her non-self had been nominated for Influencer of the Year.

This would not end well.

@Trishalicious was about to go live.

She pulled up her program to pick a face for today's Woofer episode. She'd designed the program herself, writing its code while paying the utmost attention to detail.

She flicked through a holo-ray of possible faces and zeroed in on one of her most popular ones.

Blonde hair, green eyes, a spatter of freckles across both cheeks.

When @Trishalicious looked in the reflecto-screen, the face rested as an overlay upon her own somewhat plainer face. It raised and widened her thin cheeks, opened up her eyes and lengthened her forehead seamlessly.

It was a better palette for make-up than her own face could ever be.

She ran through her list of quality checks.

She turned her head left and right, slowly at first and then faster. There was no lag. The face moved with hers.

She tilted her head up and down, then flipped her hair. The face's chin followed her movement. There was none of the double-chin effect that most facial-mapping technology suffered from.

Her hair moved naturally, each strand carefully animated to realism.

She smiled, and the face's oxbow lips parted, revealing perfect teeth. It was impossible to tell that it was a face-sync filter.

She hit record.

'Hey everyone, it's Trishalicious, and today is all about glamour.'

Her script scrolled up, built into the holo-prompt that rayed across the wall beside her mirror.

She flashed her virtual audience a grin.

'Of course, I'm going to teach you how to be glamorous with restraint. You don't want to look like an Analog, erm…' she paused dramatically, '*lady of the night*, hmm?'

She rolled her eyes, and giggled at her own joke. The face she wore was flattered by the action.

@Trishalicious began to walk her audience through the complex application of powder and paint required to achieve this desired effect.

Her mind rested on the perfection of the face in front of her. She'd picked it because it received the most traction across all of Bell Corp's cities. She used a different one for special episodes, though.

Once, she'd swapped three faces in a single episode, showing viewers how to buy the right foundation and colour-correction for darker shades of skin. There hadn't been a single glitch.

Her own face had been revealed for nanoseconds at a time at

transition points; suffice to say, only her followers with sophisticated holovid decryption and freeze-frame tech would have caught a glimpse of her true self.

She'd also created several vids on eyeshadow techniques for phoenix eyes, downturned eyes and hooded eyes. In each episode, she'd worn a different face. Her eye-mapping overlays had been accurate.

No. Flawless.

These episodes were great for spikes in viewership, but the blonde diva she'd designed was reliable for consistent ratings.

@Trishalicious tittered as she accidentally smudged her lipstick.

'Oh, this happens to me *all the time*!'

That was a lie. Her hand had slipped because her mind was distracted.

'But never fear, unicorns! Let me show you the perfect technique for dealing with some smudginess.'

She hated this. Going off script, improvising.

She proceeded to use a cue-tip to erase the smudges. Her heart juddered as the seconds crawled past. She was so close to the end.

Her face perfect, she blew a kiss at the audience.

'Thank you so much for watching, rainbow sparklers! Until next time, ciao!'

She paused, ended the recording, hit post, and gazed at her pixelated magnification in the reflecto-screen.

The make-up was a mess on her face since she hadn't applied it along her own lines and curves.

'Ugh.'

She reached for the make-up remover, applied it liberally onto cotton pads and swiped across her skin with a vengeance.

Plain and make-up free, @Trishalicious arranged her brushes with care. She ordered them by function, and then sorted them by size. Each category had its own tray in its own drawer.

There were rules. The brushes couldn't touch each other, once they were put away.

Foundation, powder, lipstick.

Crease-line, eyelid, under-eye, blending.

Sculpting, bronzing, highlight, blush…

A notification rang noisily through the silence of her bedroom.

'Ten percent!' she swore when she dropped her tray of brushes. She scrambled after them while reaching for her OmniPort, lying somewhere on the table.

Her nerves jangled as she watched an envelope dancing above its surface.

She opened it. Read it.

It was an invitation to the Bell Corp Best and Brightest Awards.

She screamed.

She had been nominated for Influencer of the Year.

Make-up had saved her life. Now, it was about to ruin it for good.

@SugarnSpice basked in the radiance of her oven.

She gave it a few moments to let the hot air escape, then reached in with her sunflower-patterned gloves, pulling out a tray of freshly baked cupcakes.

She took a deep breath, letting the scent of sugar and lemons wash over her.

@SugarnSpice was in her element.

She left the tray to cool on the rack, then pulled off her mittens. She began to stretch the muscles of her back as she entered her living room, pausing midway to kiss her partner on the cheek.

'Are you done, honey?' @EyeCandy asked.

'Soon. I just need to decorate them. I'm calling this batch "Sunshine of Your Love".'

'Oh my! Do you expect brownie points for that one?'

'Admit it, I'm winning.'

@EyeCandy raised their camera and took a holosnap before @SugarnSpice could protest.

'Stop! You know I hate pictures –'

'Hmm. Smug does become you.'

'Delete that.'

'I'm keeping it for myself.'

'Now!'

'Don't you have cupcakes to decorate?'

@SugarnSpice shot them a disapproving look before returning to the kitchen.

'Tell me when you're done, love. Or do you want to share holosnaps of the process, today?' @EyeCandy rose from the couch and stepped into the kitchen.

@SugarnSpice felt them wrap their arms around her waist, and leant into them momentarily.

'Don't distract me while I'm decorating.'

'You distract me all the time.'

'Out.'

She picked up the piping bag, and held it gingerly over the first cupcake.

'Out. Seriously. I need elbow room.'

'You're always so serious,' she heard @EyeCandy sigh behind her.

@SugarnSpice pictured her significant other rolling their eyes skyward and smiled.

'Let me take some photographs. Please.'

'No, my work speaks for itself.'

'Come on, you can't hide behind your pastries forever! You're a beautiful woman –'

'Yes, I know. I don't want that to bias public perception of my work.'

@SugarnSpice moved on to the second cupcake.

'That's the stupidest thing I've ever heard.'

'All right, love. Then why don't you take a holosnap of yourself and share it right now?'

'I'm a photographer. My place is behind the lens –'

'And I'm a baker. My place is behind my cupcakes.'

@SugarnSpice, now having mastered how to pipe the consistency of this batch of icing, sped up and finished three cupcakes in quick succession.

'Such a bore,' @EyeCandy muttered.

'Such a nag,' @SugarnSpice tossed back.

Her holo-watch vibrated with such violence that her hand shook, upsetting the perfection of the swirl of icing on the last cupcake.

'Ugh! Bottom feeder!'

@SugarnSpice finished repairing the damage to the cupcake. She tapped on her watch, deciding to view the cause of the disturbance before adding her fondant sunflowers and bumblebees.

No more slip-ups.

An envelope danced into view, opening itself with an elaborate flourish.

Her jaw dropped.

@EyeCandy laughed. 'Oh, this is good. This is brilliant!'

'No!' @SugarnSpice smacked their arm, but not hard enough for it to hurt.

'Face it, A –, you're about to be unmasked! Haha!' @EyeCandy doubled up with laughter.

'Z –, this is disastrous!'

'Aw, come here, babe.' @EyeCandy wrapped her up in a hug. 'I'm so proud of you. And just think of all the followers you'll have once they see you're a beautiful woman who bakes like a goddess!'

'That's the problem, don't you see?'

She'd been invited to the Bell Corp Best and Brightest Awards. She'd been nominated for the Influencer of the Year.

This had never been the plan.

Her cakes would now be overshadowed by the gorgeous face attached to them.

'N –, we absolutely must make an appearance.'

'Absolutely not.'

'To ignore a nomination like this is career suicide!' Selma lowered her voice. 'Besides, they've been cracking down on any hint of anti-Bell sentiment, and you don't –'

'I will not go. They can't persecute me for not wanting to reveal the face behind CinderElle.'

CinderElle sat curled up in her chair. She sipped on her green tea, fighting a battle with her publicist.

This was the only kind of battle she was prone to lose.

'You've worked all your life for this.'

'No, I haven't,' she snapped. 'I've worked all my life to master a Hyper Reality video game. That's it. I never wanted a public image to follow.'

Selma, her publicist, tapped her perfectly manicured bottle-blue nails on the table. 'Did you really expect that you wouldn't be nominated one of these years?'

CinderElle scowled. It was unbecoming on her small face, the knot of her eyebrows accentuated by her thick square glasses.

'You're a Hero! You've inspired millions of people to watch League of Champions. You've inspired millions of *women* to revolt against the male-dominated Hyper Reality space!'

'Yes, and I know what they say about me too. *CinderElle is an Amazon – if I had muscles like that I'd never get laid.* Or, *What cup size do you think is behind those ivory breastplates?* Or –'

'Every public figure has naysayers.'

'I don't want to be a public figure. I decided to be a League of Champions athlete because it's a *Hyper Reality game*. I have an *avatar*.

I'm a stereotype who *obviously* hated socializing and took to playing video games. Don't tell me you don't know this by now, Selma!'

'Well, if it makes you feel better, you don't look anything like your CinderElle avatar.' Selma smiled. It was meant as a kindness. It was not meant to make CinderElle snap.

CinderElle snapped. 'And you think that isn't a problem?'

She leapt up from her chair. 'Look at me, Selma! Look at me!'

Selma looked.

'I'm a skinny girl in glasses. I'm barely over five feet tall. I have dull brown hair. I look like a mouse. I can't be a mouse warrior!' She waved her teacup, sloshing hot water over the sides.

Selma winced.

'I drink green tea, not that Carnatic Ale of Heroes rubbish that I endorse as CinderElle! I – would you…just take a look – I mean, would you take a look at her already? She's over six feet tall! She's has deep brown skin, not my sallow, sun-deprived complexion. And she's built like a tank. Do you see my muscle? No? *That's because it isn't there!*'

'You've got muscle, N –'

'Not the kind that makes CinderElle. Just enough to get through each Contest when I'm using my weapons and spell-casts right –'

'Calm down, N –'

'What'll they say when they see me for what I am? I'll be the laughing stock of the Championship! Nobody will take me seriously again. I'll lose all my psychological edge.'

'You've made public appearances before, dear.'

'Through my VirtuoPod!' CinderElle nearly shrieked. 'Never. In. Person.'

'All right, all right. I'll see what we can do.'

CinderElle took a deep breath. 'What do you mean?'

'It's a smart new world, honey. We can take care of this.'

'What do you mean, Selma?' CinderElle looked at her publicist uncertainly.

A feeling of unease swept over her. It was not for nothing.

'We're very proud of you, honey.'

'Th-thanks, Dad.'

'You will be attending the ceremony, won't you?' He raised an eyebrow.

'A-a-about that, D-dad…'

He plunged his fork into his dinner, skewering a piece of chicken on its end.

@Trishalicious winced. 'I d-d-don't k-know if…if th-that's necessary.'

'I know it'll be hard, but you should put a brave face forward, don't you think?'

@Trishalicious swallowed, even though she hadn't touched her dinner. 'I – I'm –'

'Scared? Nervous? That's normal, don't worry. Why, when I was nominated for the Productivity Champion of the Year, I was terrified, but then –'

@Trishalicious zoned out as her father launched into one of his favourite long-winded stories. She looked down at her plate where she'd carved her chicken into two-dozen pieces of equal size. To the right was her salad, arranged so that it wouldn't touch her meat.

She forced herself to stab a piece of chicken.

She forced herself to eat her greens.

She felt sick.

Dinner tonight seemed endless.

When she was done, she quickly cleared away the plates and excused herself, retiring to her room.

She felt faint.

Make-up. Everything had gone wrong until make-up.

She'd been a fourteen-year-old genius – acing tests, being fast-tracked to Apex City University's Genius Incubator Programme.

The university had felt like an escape in those early days. Tucked away in her en-suite lab on the ninety-seventh floor, she'd experienced the endless potential of infinity with panoramic views of the vast sky. She'd looked out the windows over the tops of rain trees, all the way out to Bell Corp's twenty-six towers, their mushroom-cap crests housing exotic biomes for their employees' recreation.

She'd proposed convoluted theorems and solved compound problems while dreaming of one day earning her place at the topmost window of Bell Tower A.

Her mind had raced ahead faster than her body could keep up. Her mind was always racing, problem-solving, perceiving patterns and stitching them together.

That's when she'd had her first meltdown.

She'd been dropped from the programme.

Oh, she could still solve complex problems and write composite equations.

She just couldn't do the other thing any more.

Show them to people. Listen to people. Talk to people. People.

She'd been sent home, doomed to be deported to the Analog world as soon as she turned eighteen.

Her parents had spoken to strangers in hushed voices, exploring illegal avenues through which they could send her to the Outside as a refugee. Once they'd even tried to convince her of the peace she would find leading an obscure life as a rice farmer, in the drought-plagued Krishna–Godavari Agro-Soc.

She'd thrown a tantrum.

Her parents had bought her colouring books to soothe her nerves.

'It's all she can handle,' Mrs Naidu, her therapist, had told them.

And she'd discovered light and colour and shadow.

She'd discovered make-up.

It had helped her crawl out of her shell.

She'd built her face-mapping, face-puppeteering algorithm. She'd started her Woofer stream. She'd found a way to be around people, again, without ever having to see them.

And now this.

I'd be forced to talk to them.

Imagine their horror when perfect, pretty @Trishalicious opened her mouth and out came a stutter.

Imagine their disdain when they looked down at her nails, only to see that she'd bitten them down, had pulled at the skin around her cuticles.

She'd seen other people with crippling anxiety be torn to shreds by the twenty-percent club.

Her own father had ignored her for years – she'd been the source of his burning shame. Her mother had taken to travelling the world – shopping in Crown City, business ventures in Crest, an affair in Pinnacle, anything to escape from her problem child.

Then @Trishalicious had shot into the public eye.

The only reason she was here was because she could hide behind all the faces she had invented.

What would they do to her when the mask dropped? How would they view her when her true face was revealed?

@EyeCandy wouldn't shut up about the nomination, and it was causing @SugarnSpice's nerves to fray.

@SugarnSpice had one big reason to operate out of secrecy.

She'd never once posted a holosnap of herself, but as she examined her face in the mirror – she hated the 360-degree pixel-perfect clarity of the reflecto-screen – she couldn't strictly say that it was unattractive.

It was because of this very fact that she'd chosen to keep it hidden.

She was beautiful, in the way every woman who has ever looked at the cover of a fashion magazine has, at some point in their lives, aspired to be.

She was full-figured, wearing her curves with pride. Each time she walked into a party, heads snapped to attention, unable to tear their eyes away.

Where, then, would there be room for her baking?

She recalled every comment on every holosnap she'd ever seen that featured food and its maker.

The maker was always the biggest distraction.

With food like that, no wonder she's fat.

Thank god for that macaroon tower – the remainder of this photograph is just ten-percent ugly.

Looks good, but she's so skinny, so I wonder if her food ever tastes as good, lulz.

It was folly to pay attention to the comments, no doubt.

She was beautiful, so she had nothing to worry about – except, perhaps, overtly sexual comments and unseemly propositions.

But her food – her food would be overshadowed.

She'd be the hot chef, the babe baker, the bootylicious cook… and that would be the end of things.

Who would pay attention to her pastries any more? Who would judge them for what they were worth, independent of the value of the face attached to them?

Her anonymity gave her work its true measure.

She couldn't sacrifice that, just to – possibly – accept an award.

'– zoning out again, my love,' @EyeCandy snapped.

'That's because you won't stop talking about the awards ceremony.'

'That's because you're dreading it so much.'

@EyeCandy softened at the look of worry on their partner's face. 'I'm just teasing, you know.'

'I know.' @SugarnSpice sighed. 'I'm just – you know, I've seen it happen tons of times. People disregard pretty women because they believe there's nothing more to them. And then –'

'I've heard this tons of times. And then their work is devalued, blah blah. You know what? If you're so damned worried about this, why don't you just go hidden in a cake?'

@SugarnSpice slapped her hand to her forehead. 'Of course!'

'What?'

'I'll hide in a cake!'

'No, wait, I was kidding –'

'It's the perfect solution.'

'Come to bed, darling. It's been a tiring day.'

'You're a genius!' @SugarnSpice turned, placed her hands on either side of @EyeCandy's face, and drew them in for a long kiss.

'You're not serious are you? I was – was just kidding –'

@SugarnSpice turned out the light.

The Custom-Ordered Simulacrum arrived the night before the ceremony.

CinderElle cut her training regime short so that she could accept the delivery.

Selma buzzed herself in just moments afterward.

They unpacked it together, and CinderElle felt a chill run up her spine as they regarded their solution.

It was the splitting image of her avatar, with some concessions made to reality.

It towered above them at five feet and nine inches.

It wore CinderElle's signature ivory breastplate and iron-spiked epaulettes, her sleek leather leggings, with her throwing knives in the left boot. Her flail was demurely tucked into a sheath in her leather cummerbund, and twin swords were crossed at her back.

CinderElle began to laugh. Selma joined her.

'Isn't it a bit much?' she gasped between giggles of relief.

'I don't – don't think they'll let weapons into the Holofield Theatre!'

CinderElle stripped the C.O.S. of its weaponry.

'How do we animate it?'

Selma and CinderElle looked at each other helplessly.

They found a switch concealed on the side of its body, beneath its armour. There was a low drone as it powered to life.

The C.O.S. extended a hand. 'Pleased to meet you. I'm CinderElle.'

The real CinderElle and Selma jumped backwards at the familiar tone of voice. It was set to the exact pitch of her League of Champions voice-mod.

'It worked!' CinderElle said.

Selma grinned.

The C.O.S. strolled around the apartment, taking it all in.

'Not much of a home for a warrior,' it said, turning its nose up at the indoor plants and the floral-patterned couch.

'Opinionated, aren't you?' said CinderElle.

'A bit of a disappointment, you are,' said the C.O.S., regarding her curiously.

CinderElle drew herself up to her full height. 'Who do you think you're talking to? You wouldn't exist without me!'

'Enough!' The C.O.S. slammed its hand into the glass coffee table, causing a web of cracks to spread outward from the point of impact. 'You will now bring me a meal worthy of a warrior princess.'

'Ah, no,' said CinderElle. 'House rules. One: stop ruining my furniture. Two: you're a silicone body with a personality borrowed from stored data on the Nebula. You don't eat.'

'No one refuses CinderElle.'

'How do we turn this harvesting thing off?' The real CinderElle frowned at Selma.

'I am not a thing. I am a warrior.'

'You know, I'm not so sure about sending this in to the awards tomorrow. It seems pretty one-dimensional.'

'Is that an insult?' The C.O.S. tilted its head, scrutinizing CinderElle.

'You bet it is.'

The C.O.S. leapt across the room, covering an alarming distance and knocking over the sofa.

'Selma…' CinderElle's voice trembled. 'What personality-mod did you choose for it to be programmed with?'

'I –' Selma was backed up against the front door. 'I picked your CinderElle avatar, N –'

'You mean it has violent tendencies?' CinderElle's voice emerged as a squeak.

The C.O.S. lifted the flail from where CinderElle had dropped it on the floor.

It began to whip it over its head in a signature move.

'Selma?'

'N –'

'Run.'

@Trishalicious had worked three straight nights to develop her latest FaceWear program.

It was the morning of the awards ceremony, and she was nearly ready.

She flipped through a sequence of faces, puzzling over which one to wear.

If she chose her most popular face, she'd likely be accused of being one-dimensional. If she chose her favourite face, however, the one with phoenix eyes and galaxy hair that shimmered in all the colours of a nebula, she'd be criticized for being inauthentic. She might even alienate portions of her audience by being too edgy.

She scrutinized a face with a dark, rich skin tone. If anything, she'd be applauded for subverting the notion that only light skin could be beautiful.

She mapped it onto her face from the tiny nodes she'd implanted beneath her skin via nanobot surgery.

No dark circles, no limp hair.

Instead, a glossy sheen of perfect skin, a full pair of lips and waves of ringlets all the way down to her shoulders gazed back at her from the reflecto-screen.

Her face was flawless.

She looked down.

Her hands were flawless.

She ran the program through its tests.

'Welcome, @Trishalicious! It's such a pleasure to meet you.'

'Thank you, it's a pleasure to be here.'

The program responded to key words and phrases, engaged the appropriate response, and delivered it in a voice that was a perfect imitation of @Trishalicious's own.

She wouldn't have to say a word today.

She picked at the skin on her nails, but when she glanced downward, she couldn't see the breaks on the skin on her hands.

She set to choosing her make-up filters from the extensive database of looks she'd already created for the face she wore. She even managed a genuine smile.

All would be well tonight.

@EyeCandy laughed themselves hysterical when @SugarnSpice rolled out an enormous, five-tiered cake.

It comprised several cakes arranged around a central hollow sphere, complete with slits for visibility and breathing.

'I can't believe you've spent the whole week working on this.' They rolled their eyes.

It was decorated in delicate pastels, with lilies and violets topping it, bougainvillea winding around it – an enormous garden made from batter and spun sugar.

'Help me inside,' said @SugarnSpice with grim determination.

'You're wearing *this*?' @EyeCandy looked at their partner's batter-splattered apron disapprovingly. 'Take it off! You've got to be presentable – what if the cake gets eaten?'

@SugarnSpice complied, grinning when @EyeCandy whistled at the shimmering gold dress she had on underneath.

'You look stunning! Wouldn't you rather go like this? Take the cake as a bribe for the jury…' @EyeCandy suggested.

'We've been over this before –'

'Fine.' @EyeCandy huffed. 'Do as you wish.'

They eyed the five-tier cake. 'How will you move?'

'I'll walk. It's open at the bottom,' @SugarnSpice said.

@EyeCandy sniffed when they spotted their partner's shoes.

'No?' @SugarnSpice followed their gaze. 'They're so comfy, though.'

@EyeCandy simply glowered at the offending pair of sneakers.

'The gold heels, then?' @SugarnSpice asked meekly.

@EyeCandy sighed in exasperation. 'I pity the fool who'll have to sit next to you!'

@SugarnSpice grinned and blew them a kiss.

The evening began without a hitch.

Several interviews were given on the red carpet. The most elite of the twenty percent made physical appearances, for this was an event at which one had to be seen and heard in person.

The Holofield Theatre was a resplendent structure, built into the hollow remains of an ornately carved dome that had once been the seat of governance, back when the city of Bangalore still belonged to a bigger nation. Its former name was lost to history textbooks, seldom discovered by even the most enthusiastic historians.

Tonight, it sparkled like a solitaire set in a crown bejewelled, surrounded by pools of lilies and extravagant fountains. Thousands of glittering lights led the way up the red carpet and through its doors. A fine spray of jasmine-scented mist lingered in the air, settling like crystals on gowns designed by Bijou, Sierra and Elizabeth Eton. Sharp jackets featuring Brunieri's signature angular collars were extensively admired.

The event was live-streamed on HoloTube, where every single Virtual who hadn't merited an invitation tuned in to feel like they were a part of the glitz and glamour.

Long speeches were made. Significant others were thanked profusely. One winner even thanked his Hyper Reality pet kitten for its unconditional love.

David Kuruvilla, the world-renowned Virtuoso, enraptured his high-society audience with a fine selection of neo-Acousta pieces arranged for the grand piano.

Things started to go wrong when the committee at the Bell Corp Best and Brightest Awards were informed that CinderElle would be unavailable for the evening, owing to legal implications arising from a rogue impersonator that was said to be terrorizing the streets.

John Alvares, Head of Policy and Governance in Apex City, rose from his banquet table at the announcement, politely excusing himself. He made calls to the Seditious Activities Unit and to the Securities and Enforcement Division. When they reported no excessive anti-Bell activity, he made another call to a number so top-secret that he was one of three people in the world who had access to it. He requested Bell Corp's Security, Subterfuge and Espionage Network to get in touch with their asset. He took care not to upset the other patrons at the venue, returning to his place with a beaming smile and a few jokes about Hyper Reality golf.

The eloquence of @Trishalicious charmed everyone who met her.

She always said the right thing at the right time with a laugh that bubbled like champagne. Sadly, her presence was overshadowed by a growing sense of mystery in the room. An outsized apparition made from spun sugar was doing the rounds at the banquet hall, piquing the curiosity of even the most jaded members of high society.

The audience was aghast when the winner of the Influencer of the Year rose to accept the award. No speech was given by the five-layered confection in gold heels. The award teetered amid its sugared lily blossoms as it trundled off-stage, relegated to an existence as a gaudy cake-topper.

We are the unseen.
Shh – you didn't hear that.

– Motto of Bell Corp's Security, Subterfuge and Espionage Network (anecdotal)

POCKETS

'WE'RE NOT MAD THAT you're a spy. We're offering you a choice, a chance to come work with us.

'There's good news and bad news. Good news first?

'Everything you know is a lie. You have proof. A picture's worth a thousand –'

She runs a hand over the folder in her pocket. She's put it away in a hurry after examining its contents.

Grey skies.

A child runs down the track, away from her parents' cottage. They stand at the door, laughing. She's chasing butterflies and they lead her down a rough path made of stones and into the woods.

She doesn't look back.

In the years that follow, she'll wish she had.

'– the bad news: If you refuse to work with us, we'll still know you're a spy. And that won't make you a very good one, will it? And if you do work with us, and if we lose, they'll probably harvest you with the rest of us. But that might happen anyway, since we know you're a spy.

'Take your pick. You're the one in charge.'

'Why?' she states simply.

A figure stands apart from her, lurking in the shadows and observing her in silence. Its face is cast in darkness.

She's hated their kind for sixteen years, ever since she was informed that they burnt down her home in a vicious attack.

She was raised in a specialized Repop ward, her education decidedly different from that of the other teenagers there – embryonically grown and harvested in PregaPods, trained to fulfil specific roles by Bell Corp.

Her entire existence has been off the record. She's been taught to write code, play music and engage in basic hand-to-hand combat, but not with ambitions of being the next CTO of Woofer or dreams of becoming a demi-Virtuoso or a League of Champions hero.

There is only purpose.

She'd accepted the assignment so that she could inch closer to her goal. Infiltrate the Analog city, where surveillance is near-impossible. Gain access to Analog secrets. Earn their trust, one conversation at a time. Report everything.

She has a photographic memory. She can recall the most infinitesimal detail, but she has scant recollection of her life before.

Photographs.

'Why?' she repeats, running a hand over her forehead and through her short, spiky hair.

'They opposed a highly profitable trade treaty. Well, profitable to Bell Corp, at least. Bell Corp felt that it was best that they were... *removed* from society.'

From the timbre of the voice, she infers that it is a man speaking.

'I don't remember –'

'That's how they remake the best of you.' He nods. 'I'd know.'

'What do you mean?'

He waves his hand. 'Immaterial. This is about your lost origins, not mine.'

'What gave me away?' she asks.

'You're the only person to ever openly accost Marie and demand an opportunity to write Sentient+.' He smirks. 'There were other markers, but this was a dead giveaway.'

'What markers?'

He ignores her. She frowns.

Fish, they'd laughed. *Lost at sea.*

Swim, they'd said, with every intention of letting her drown.

The Analog world had not been a welcoming place. The dust was suffocating. The heat was oppressive. The filth that accompanied living in a sewer – even an abandoned one as arid as the shifting sands on the surface – was odious.

The Analogs themselves were suspicious of everyone, especially exiled Virtuals who'd been thrust upon their doorstep.

She adapted. She learnt to curb her enthusiasm. She learnt to be monosyllabic in most of her responses. She tried to be their friend, to earn their trust.

She masked her hatred beneath a veneer of indifference. Sadness, even, ever since she'd begun to come into her false identity. She posed as an InstaSnap developer, downgraded for a lack of social acceptability.

As easy as breathing. If only the dust weren't so stifling. If only the Analogs weren't so closed off. If only everything she'd ever known wasn't unravelling…

Deep in the pockets of her outsized tunic nestles the docket. She runs a finger over its edge and gasps at a sudden stab of pain. Hurriedly pulling her hand free, she nurses the cut. It stings like the contents of the envelope.

'How do you have this information?' she asks uncertainly. 'Where'd you get the photographs?'

'I have my sources.' He shrugs. 'I can't tell you more until I'm sure you're on our side.'

'Let me guess. You have access to PanoptiCam footage, thanks to a team of hackers adept at breaking the Nebula's security algorithms written in Sentient+.'

'Maybe.' His tone is non-committal. 'I'd have thought the contents of the envelope mattered more than how we got our hands on them.'

'I won't be fooled again.' Her voice is hard. 'If I was fooled at all, in the first place.'

Barely visible in the dense vegetation around the cottage are a group of men in suits. Three droids armed with LasTech guns take careful aim at the space that has been a void in her heart ever since.

They are evidently not Analogs.

She still remembers the acrid stench of burning overpowering the smell of wet earth as she was bundled up in a blanket and removed from the scene.

'Analog filth,' the first responder-bot had sworn as it carried her away.

'The Analogs don't attack the Outsiders,' the man says patiently. 'Never have, never will. We had no reason to attack someone in as remote a place as the Nagarhole Eco-Soc. In fact, you were probably an aberration in their plan, an unexpected one that they used to their advantage.'

'You're telling me the Virtuals killed my parents, pinned it on the Analogs, and then used that to manipulate me into working for them?'

'Yes.'

'That sounds an awful lot like a conspiracy theory…'

'And it would be,' he concedes, splaying his hands out, palms upward. 'If we hadn't just handed you photographic evidence that proves every word we've just said.'

Within her pocket, her hand clenches into a fist.

The smell of burning brick and wood… The antiseptic cold white light of her pod in the Repop ward…

'So now you think you have the right to use me, just like they did – allegedly, of course – because you've shown me the truth?' Anger flares within her.

'Nope,' the man says. He sighs. 'Listen, we'll be fine carrying on without your services, but we thought you'd want the chance to –'

'What, get even?' She laughs.

'To see your parents again.'

Her stomach feels lined with lead. 'That's not funny,' she snaps.

'And it wasn't meant to be,' he says gently.

'They…they survived?' The words come out as a sharp hiss. She is embarrassed of herself already. Her handler would be deeply disappointed in the way she has conducted herself.

She forces her hands to stay still as they stray towards the documents concealed in her robes. She's been trained to answer interrogations impassively. Even this slight act of emotion unsettles her – one doesn't easily forget jolts administered from hundreds of electrodes, or the blinding headaches and nausea from infrasound exposure.

She empties her mind, clears her face of all expression.

'This is blackmail,' she says archly. 'You're no better than they are.'

'This is an act of good faith.'

He takes three sudden steps forward, towards her. She flinches but stands her ground.

He hands her another envelope, then quickly retreats.

Her knees go weak as she slides out a glossy photograph.

They look older, more careworn. Her father's hair is greying, and her mother has wrinkles at the corners of her eyes, but their smiles are unmistakable. A daughter would know.

The truth is as clear as the photographs she holds in her hands.

They're alive.

'Wh-when?' she chokes.

'Two weeks ago. I tracked them down.'

'I hope you didn't –' she begins, but he interrupts.

'I didn't tell them that you were alive. I wasn't sure if you'd even make this meeting.'

She feels the rage coursing through her ebb.

'Thank you,' she says, and she means it.

'Of course.'

'How did they survive?' She struggles to keep her voice steady.

'They went looking for you in the forest. When they returned, their cottage was burning and they fled. They're holed up on the Outside, at the Kodagu Agro-Soc now.'

'Why are you telling me this? I haven't said I'll join your cause yet.'

'Like I said, it's an act of good faith.'

She looks down at the photograph of her parents.

The betrayal cuts sharp as a knife.

They lied to me.

She looks back up at the man in the shadows. 'Care to tell me who I'm working with, then?'

'Tariq,' comes the response.

'Rohini.' She extends a hand. 'My friends call me Ro.'

'Welcome to the resistance, Ro,' he says, reaching forward to clasp it and give it a firm shake.

'So what do you need me to do?'

Adopt at your own risk.
No guarantees, no returns.

– Signboard over the door of the Analog Orphan Adoption Home

ÉTUDES

'HAPPY BIRTHDAY, IT!'

I stare at the birthday card in front of me in horror.

I shouldn't have opened it. Not here, in front of them. Not ever, if I'd known what the inside read.

I flip it wide open and turn it towards my best friend, Mae.

I hate that word.

'It.'

'It will need to earn its place in Virtual society.'

I sit on a leather stool in front of the Home's creaky upright piano. I look down at the keys.

I've just played Barthöven's Sonatina 23 in alt-F Minor.

I've made four obvious mistakes, I fumbled three runs. Including the opening section.

I hope I'm still worthy.

These two strangers could change their minds at any moment.

I glance up at them. They seem to be studying me.

I look back down, staring really, really hard at the black keys in between F, G, A and B, just to the right of middle C.

Mrs D'Souza's voice fills the silence.

'It's toilet-trained and reports excellent personal hygiene. It reads at an average pace and has done fairly well on our psychological tests. No tendencies towards violence, no delusions of grandeur.'

The strangers say nothing.

Mrs D'Souza continues. 'Mr and Mrs Anand, we assure you that you will have no trouble with this one. We only let the very best Analog wards get to this stage of the adoption process. The less competent ones remain at the Institute until they become employable or drop out. The defective ones are sent straight to the vegetable farm.

'You could always change your mind about taking it home, of course. But it's one of our very best.'

I turn my head and see her beaming at me.

'We wouldn't let distinguished twenty percenters such as yourselves take home a flawed child.'

Mrs D'Souza talks about me as if I'm not in the room. I'm used to it.

One of the strangers smiles at me. The man.

I stare at him.

'We do have some guidelines, however. It is in your best interest to follow them. We dissuade you from developing a strong personal attachment to the ward, despite being its adoptive parents. You may give it a name – this one is biologically female, and is approximately twelve years old.'

The woman frowns at this.

I wonder if I've done something wrong.

'We recommend that you don't permit it to refer to either of you on the basis of your filial relationship. First names are better than Mum and Dad. It leads to an easier separation should the child fail to qualify as a Virtual Citizen.'

'We'd like the child to feel accepted,' the man says.

Mrs D'Souza sighs. 'These decisions are left to your discretion, of course. The Home will assess the child annually to assess if it is appropriate for Virtual society.'

'Yes, we've read the fine print.' The woman's tone is sharp.

'Psychologists have found that Analog wards with a lower sense of personal identity are more Productive. They're more eager to please if they perceive identity markers as rewards for good behaviour. We recommend that it be placed in impersonal surroundings. The fewer preferences it has, the easier it will find readjustment should it need to be returned to the Analog world, though we will not take it back in –'

'Why are you certain they're going to fail?'

'Can we stop calling them "it"?'

The man and woman speak together, and they sound angry.

I've been told to keep a smile on my face, but I frown at that.

If I'm not 'it', what am I?

'– it's – I mean she's done really well for herself, all things considered.'

His smug voice brings me back to the present.

Mae is staring him down in a look of distilled hatred.

'It's only taken her ten years.'

Dear Nina of the Future,

I'm literally the only living person, this century, to have owned a journal. I hope you never forget where you've come from once you're a Virtuoso.

Haha.

That's wishful thinking.

Here I am, stuck at my birthday party, when I should be practising Bracht and Rodriguez for my upcoming demi-Virtuoso Examination. It's only ten days away and it's ONLY the opportunity of a lifetime to get into the Apex City School of neo-Acousta Performance Studies.

But who cares about the opportunity of a lifetime, right?

'What are you writing in that journal, anyway?' he says, reaching out for it.

I slam it shut.

'Touchy.' He grins. 'Now where was I?'

He returns to his captive audience. They're supposed to be my friends. And he certainly isn't.

'Right. So I was talking about my first time. There I was, right? Never having played before… I remember looking down at those keys. Completely blank.'

Everyone leans in to listen to what Andrew Sommers has to say. Everyone except Mae, who mimes strangling him from where she stands behind him, taking care not to spill her strawberry shake.

I twirl a straw around my glass of carrot–cucumber juice.

'But then, the GlimmerKeys kicked in and began to highlight the score for me. I don't know why people even bother with sheet music any more. It took me through the entire song, with my InEars keeping perfect tempo for me.'

Niraj and Anushka are hanging on to every word.

Andrew Sommers is the best-known musician at our school. He has an official HoloTube account, with a following in the hundreds of thousands in Bell Corp cities across the world.

How long has he been learning?

Eighteen months.

How long have I been learning?

Ten years.

What's the difference between us?

DreamMusician.

I'm surprised he even showed up at my party, considering we aren't friends. When I say that, I don't mean that we don't have any classes together, or that we've never given recitals together.

We just haven't made eye contact. Ever.

We've never spoken a word to each other outside of a practice.

And yet here he is, celebrating another year of my life going by.

Why?

'You must be at a real disadvantage, Nina.'

'What?' I scowl.

'It must be so hard for you. Learning the *Analog* way.'

I don't like the way he emphasizes the word 'Analog'. I hear it all the time but I'll never get used to it. I look down at the birthday card, and the word 'it' glares back up at me.

I don't want to get into a fight. I can't afford to. So I shrug instead.

'I mean, how do you keep time? Do you count in your head?' Andrew smirks.

'It's more than you can do. Count, that is,' Mae mutters loud enough for everyone to hear.

Niraj's laugh sounds like a strangled bark.

'And what about the dynamics? Do you just bang away at the keys until you get the proper tone?'

I realize that I've begun to shred the edges of the card.

'Seriously. I'm curious.' He winks.

I really can't afford to get into a fight. Not with the Citizenship test so close. I begin to focus all my attention on my breathing.

'Don't get me wrong, you're not bad at all. You just lack. . .*precision*.'

I feel heat spreading through my cheeks.

'Anyway, I should be leaving. My parents don't like it when I hang out at *the Mall* too long.' He gives our surroundings a significant look.

'Yeah, The Strip is way cooler.' Niraj grins.

Sycophant.

Andrew gets to his feet. 'Good luck, Nina. I expect you'll be playing at the demi-Virtuoso Examination too.'

Too?

Did he just say, TOO?

Does that mean Andrew Sommers is part of the competition?

'Don't be upset when they pass you over. It's not your fault you don't have precision. It must suck to have been born an Analog,' he says nastily and leaves.

Mae looks at me with concern, but I drop my gaze and take a sip of my juice.

Niraj and Anushka head over to examine a coin-operated arcade machine with interest.

Yes, I said coin-operated. You push physical tokens into a slot and then play a game with 3D graphics on a flat-screen monitor.

'Do you guys want to head to the Strip?' Anushka asks. She's looking around as if she expects a dodgy Analog to jump her any minute.

'Umm, guys.' I look at the table. 'No chip, no intel-glasses, no Hyper Reality experiences, remember?'

Anushka opens her mouth as if to argue.

'If you guys want to head there, though, carry on...'

'What! Nooo!' Anushka forces brightness into her voice. 'It's your birthday! We want to hang out with you!'

Sure.

The giant, squat structure rests at the edge of an abandoned airstrip. The relics of long-forgotten passenger aircraft litter vacant tracts of land outside. Rumour has it that at one point, the Analogs used to mount raids to strip them of fuel and scrap metal.

The Mall is made from rusty metal appropriated from former aircraft parking bays, old strips of steel and tin bolted together and painted over in depressingly bright colours. It houses seven floors of twentieth-century gaming technology, flat-screen movie-watching experiences, and clothing stores where you have to physically try on an outfit before buying it.

It's the only place where I can find entertainment that isn't gated on HoloTech privileges I don't have.

Compared to the Hyper Reality at the Strip, this must feel like a trip to the poorhouse.

My poorhouse.

Welcome to the last century, guys.

This is where I live. All the time.

'Did you have a good birthday, honey?'

Mum plants a kiss on my cheek as she ladles a generous helping of mac and cheese on to my plate.

'Um, sure,' I say tonelessly.

Dad gives me a look, and suddenly grins. 'You know what? I think we need to liven things up a bit. It isn't every day that our only daughter turns seventeen!'

'What do you have in mind, Madhu?' Mum's tone is unnecessarily bright.

'Oh, I don't know... It needs to be special.' Dad waggles his eyebrows excitedly. 'I think we need to give Nina her first sip of wine.'

'Of all the clichéd coming-of-age rituals, Madhu...' Mum says, exasperated.

'Come on,' Dad says. 'She'll remember this moment with her parents for the rest of her life!'

He heads to his impressive bar, and hovers at the wine rack indecisively.

'It needs to be a really fine one to mark the occasion,' he mutters.

'Dinner's getting cold, love.' Mum rolls her eyes.

'We're building a new tradition,' Dad says. 'One that we can add to our birthday mac and cheese dinner.'

I feel small. I've eaten half my mac and cheese. I can't eat any more. It's delicious, though.

I wonder if I should tell her. The woman.

'What names do you like, kiddo?' The man smiles at me.

I don't know. I don't say that out loud.

'Do you feel like a boy's name or a girl's?' the woman asks.

I don't answer. Girl, I think, but I don't want to get it wrong.

'Shaila! No, you don't look like you own that name.'

'Anuja. Does she look like an Anuja to you?'

'I'm not sure. Let's ask her what she'd like to go by?'

They look at me over the dinner table.

I only know me as D2721, Performer Class. It.

They didn't give me a name at the Home.

'You play the piano beautifully,' the woman says.

I smile and nod, my gaze fixed on the hand-carved patterns along the border of the table.

'Do you have a favourite musician?' the man asks.

I shake my head. I wasn't permitted to like things at the Home.

'Would you like to listen to some music? Maybe you'll find a name you like.' The woman smiles.

'Thank you,' I say nervously.

They let me pick a record – it's glossy black and very shiny. It's so light that I'm scared I'll break it.

They show me how to put it on the player, and how to make it work.

It's amazing. The sound is clean and pure.

I've only listened to cassettes on a tape player. The hiss of the record makes it less alien, more familiar.

'They're nearly two hundred years old, vinyl records. But nothing has ever managed to beat them for sound quality,' the man explains.

'This one is Pierre Bolling. I don't suppose you could be a Pierre. It's usually a boy's name, though don't let that stop you!' The woman smiles again.

The music is beautiful.

They change the record.

'Have you heard this one? It's Frida Szeltsmann.'

The music sounds happy, like a memory of chocolate.

I've eaten chocolate a few times before. We were allowed a square each time we behaved well at the Home.

They put another record on.

'Give this a try. It's called Wanderer of the Air. *It's by Nina Rodriguez.'*

The music is quiet. I can tell that it means many things without saying any of them.

'I like this.'

I say it out loud. I shouldn't have said it out loud.

I look at the floor.

'I love this,' the woman says.

'It's like you,' the man says. 'Quiet, but mysterious.' He's smiling at me.

'I like it very much,' I whisper.

'Do you know about the composer?'

I shake my head, no.

'Nina Rodriguez was the first woman to become a neo-Acousta Virtuoso. She was a brilliant pianist and composer. And she was blind.'

'Wow.'

'She learnt by listening, without reading a single sheet of music. She wrote many wonderful pieces of music, and taught demi-Virtuosos at the Apex City School for years.'

'Does she inspire you?' the woman asks.

'I don't know what that means.'

'Does she make you feel like you're unbeatable? Like you can do anything your heart wants to?'

I think about it for a minute. I imagine being blind. I imagine playing perfect music without being able to read the notes. It sounds difficult. She must have been really clever.

'I would like to be like her.'

I burst into tears. I don't know why.

The woman hugs me until I stop crying. I stop crying quickly. They didn't like us crying at the Home.

'So...Nina, for now?' the man asks. He's grinning.

Nina.

I say it in my head. I feel it.

Nina.

I look up at them.

'Okay,' I say slowly. 'My name is Nina.'

I feel it on my tongue for the first time. It tastes like hope.

'To Nina!' Dad pronounces, holding up a glass of wine.

He nudges another one across the table towards me. I notice that it's only half as full as his own.

'Go on, now. A drop of alcohol won't poison you.' He winks.

'Go easy,' Mum warns.

I grin. I can't help it.

'To me!' I giggle, raising my glass.

'To Nina!' they say together.

I take a sip and try not to spit it out. It tastes terrible.

Mum and Dad burst into peals of laughter, and after a moment, I can't help but join in.

Dear Nina of the Future,

I'm sitting in history class, and it sucks to be me at school.

I'm the only person in the room with a textbook. On printed paper.

Everyone else is watching a Hyper Reality holovid on their intel-glasses. Meanwhile, I'm reading about the pre-Bell history of Apex City, comprising the early stages of the Start-Up Revolution in Bangalore.

Reading.

It's so much slower.

Well, sucks to be me, right? No Bell Biochip, no intel-glasses, no HoloTech. Not until I pass my Virtual Citizenship test. I have to prove myself worthy of their technology, just because I was born an Analog.

~~It isn't as if I can blow up the school with a holo watch.~~

Stuff like that is dangerous to write. Especially for an Analog-born.

It's so anti-Bell that they could deport me for saying it.

And so the cycle continues... I'm perpetually falling behind in class because I don't get information beamed straight into my brain, or Hyper Real worlds where I can explore ancient maps of Apex City, or

'Nina, are you having trouble catching up again?' Magistra VX81 flashes a pixelated scowl.

I hide my journal under my printed textbook. The rest of the class is staring at me.

I look at my desk. 'I need a few more minutes to get through the chapter, Magistra.'

She sighs. In her electronic voice, it sounds like the scrape of sandpaper over a tin can. 'Go on.'

I feel the eyes of the entire class on me. I skim over the page as quickly as I can.

What I wouldn't give to have intel-glasses right now.

'The rest of you can start putting forth arguments in favour of or against the Ceasefire Treaty.'

The Ceasefire Treaty ended competitive advertising on social media, I read. I balk when I look at the sea of text that forms a detailed analysis of the agreement.

'It's not our fault she's slow,' someone mutters.

'Are you sure you learnt how to read at the orphanage?' Someone else sniggers. 'We. Speak. English. Not. Trad.'

'Enough, class.' Magistra VX81's voice is firm.

Someone says something unintelligible to me.

'I don't speak the traditional dialect,' I snap.

The class bursts into giggles.

'Enough!' Magistra snaps. 'Nina, I'd like you to stop disrupting my class.'

My ears are hot. The words on the page start to blur, so I slam the book shut and look up.

'I'm done.'

'Good.' Magistra VX81 smiles at me. 'What were the consequences of the Ceasefire Treaty?'

I swallow.

I skipped that paragraph.

'Um…'

'She's so slow that she's practically a time traveller. Into the past.'

I ignore the taunting and take a deep breath.

'Nina, come on. The rest of the class is waiting on you. We can't do this every day.'

'Slooo-ooow,' says someone in a sing-song voice.

'What happened after the Ceasefire Treaty?'

I rattle off facts while my brain races to fabricate a plausible answer.

'The Population Catastrophe saw the collapse of nationalism. Large-scale governments could to longer meet the escalating demands for resources from their citizens. When they tried to go to war with each other, the Woke Wave Uprising – armed forces and citizens alike – rebelled against them in the Great Nuclear Boycott.'

I flub, recapping basic history, buying myself more time.

'Resource distribution became riddled with allegations of corruption. States seceded from parent countries, cities established independence. It occurred worldwide within the span of a decade. This led to the rise of multiple systems of micro-governance, formed on the basis of trade in natural resources.'

I fidget with the spine of my journal.

'Bell Corp emerged as a conglomerate in erstwhile Singapore, now called Premier City. When promising technological communities emerged around the world, Bell Corp invested in them and helped them self-organize into sustainable meritocracies.'

'Get to the point, Nina,' Magistra drones.

'London was transformed into Crown City, Berlin became Pinnacle, San Francisco is called Crest, and Bangalore joined the big leagues during the Bell Takeover, rebranding itself Apex City…'

'Nina!' Magistra snaps.

Someone behind me sniggers.

'When Bell Corp began its investment in Bangalore, the city was divided along traditional communal and cultural identities, but was a thriving start-up hub. The city had escaped the worst of the effects of the Population Catastrophe owing to its high economic stability…'

The class has lost interest. Whispers break out all around me.

'Yes, Nina, very good.' Magistra VX81 jerkily brings her mechanical appendages together, mimicking applause. 'You remember your third grade history lessons. Admirable.'

I roll my pencil across my desk.

'What happened next? What was the outcome of the Ceasefire Treaty?' she fires.

'Bangalore's start-ups…competed on social media for pride of place, eating into each other's potential market share? The Ceasefire Treaty ended competition on social media, and…and Bell Corp swooped in and saved the day?'

Magistra VX81 gives me a look. It looks hilarious on her pixelated LED face but I've seen it before. It isn't meant to be funny.

'Homework. I want a two-thousand-word paper on the Bell Takeover, from the consequences of the Ceasefire Treaty onward.'

'Please Magistra –'

'I want it on my desk, Monday morning.'

'Psst, Nina,' someone whispers. 'She wants it in English.'

'I'll translate,' someone else sniggers. Her voice lapses into gibberish.

My head spins and I take several deep breaths, trying not to let the laughter in the room overwhelm me.

'Is she an Outsider?'

'I think she's an Analog.'

'Not even a Repop kid?'

'Nope.'

'Wow, our school's standards are dropping.'

'I hear the Analogs don't speak English.'

'I hear that they can't read or write. I wonder how she got into our school.'

'Shh! Her parents are the Anands. They're the twenty percenters who own the Apex City League of Champions.'

'Oh! Those Anands.'

'Yeah, those.'

'Why would they ever let a freak like this into their home?'

'Guilt, probably. Who knows what they've done to the Analogs.'

'Ha ha, are you telling me your parents have never used the Analogs?'

'Come on, who hasn't?'

'Maybe she has a special talent.'

'What, like being ugly?'

I keep my head down. I don't look around me.

They've been whispering all day. All week.

Everyone is eating but I'm too scared to unwrap my lunch. What if they make fun of my sandwich?

They won't make fun of my sandwich. My parents – adoptive parents – are important twenty percenters. It's a tasty sandwich.

I've never seen so many twenty percenters. They're scary. They're all well dressed. They look intelligent. One girl even has blonde highlights in her hair. Another one has a FantasyLights backpack – it keeps flashing beautiful patterns.

I'm wearing nice clothes too. They're new and clean.

The woman let me pick the colour. I was really scared to, but then I chose a pale blue dress. She even combed my hair into a braid.

I look like them, but I don't feel like me.

'What do they make you do?'

A girl stands across from me. She's smiling at me.

'N-nothing,' I say.

'Harvest-shit. You must have some value. Do you clean the floors? The bathrooms?'

Another girl joins her. The one with the FantasyLights backpack. 'I'm sure the Anands can afford a server-bot, Sneha,' she drawls. 'She must have other uses.'

She reaches forward. It's sudden.

She grabs the front of my dress and rips it. Buttons fly everywhere.

My cheeks flush. Everyone's looking at us and laughing.

She looks at the training bra under my dress.

'Nope. Clearly there are no other uses.'

Something snaps. I'm on her, pulling her hair. The back of my hand makes contact with her face.

She screams. Somebody pulls me off her.

I look down and notice that my fingers are curled around the edge of my desk. My knuckles strain white against my skin.

'Sit down, Nina,' Magistra VX81 says.

They're still laughing. She hasn't intervened.

They laugh all the way until the bell rings to signal the end of the day, and it seems like the longest five minutes of my life.

I slam my textbook shut. I rush out of the school's corridors and get into Mum's self-driving car, slamming the door shut behind me. She has to pick me up every day since I'm not allowed to use the teleportals.

'Something wrong, honey?' she asks.

She speaks an address to the computer and it drives us away.

'Nope.'

'I'm not your mother for nothing. Did you get into trouble at school?'

'NO!' I say angrily. 'I – it's been years since I retaliated.'

'Let's call your dad and we can talk about it,' she soothes.

I look at the city. It's a blur as we rush past it.

'Nina,' the woman begins.

'You shouldn't have hit that girl,' the man says.

I look at the floor. It has a carpet.

'I'm sorry.'

'Why did you hit her?'

I'm silent.

'You can tell us.'

'She ripped my dress open. She said mean things.'

The woman looks at the man. 'I thought as much, Madhu. I knew the principal wasn't telling us everything.'

'Yes, but she should know better than to lash out at them.' He sounds angry. 'You know it's going to be hard for her to become a Virtual Citizen.'

'Yes, but I think she's too young to understand this.'

'I think we should tell her. Luckily, we convinced the school to keep this off her permanent record.'

'Good thing we padded our BellCoin stacks before the meeting, yes.' The woman's eyes flash angry. 'Building donation, indeed!'

'Anya, there will always be eyes on her. She needs to be careful.'

I slide my shoes under the carpet.

'Nina, what did the girl say to you?'

I don't answer.

'You have to tell us, Nina.' The man's voice is stern. 'We don't want to have to punish you.'

I feel my eyes sting. 'She said you're going to make me work for you. Cleaning things. And other things.' My voice begins to shake. 'Because I'm an…an…Analog.'

The words tumble out of me before I can help myself.

'I know I'm an Analog, but please don't send me back to the Home because I hit her. I didn't mean to. I can be good. I'll be useful – you've been so kind, not making me do any work at home, but I know how it works. I'll clean up – I'm good with a broom, I can mop the floor and I can't really cook, but you could teach me and then I could do that too. Just please don't take me back to the Home…'

I can't bear to look at them.

'Nina, that's ridiculous!' the man exclaims. 'Our home is your home now.'

'We're not going to make you work for us,' the woman says.

'She said that's why you bought me.' My voice comes out as a squeak.

The woman's eyes glitter with something that looks like anger and sadness.

'Who's that odious little girl? It's Sheila's daughter, isn't it? I'm going to have a word with her mother…'

'Yes, you should, love,' the man says to her.

Then he looks at me. 'Nina. Let me establish this, once and for all. We adopted you. We didn't buy you. We always wanted to have children, but we couldn't. You're the child we've always hoped for. You might be an Analog by birth, but that doesn't mean you're not a wonderful human being.'

I take a deep breath.

'And we will never, never make you work for us,' he finishes angrily.

The woman turns and looks me over.

I'm glad I'm not crying this time.

'Nina, you're our daughter. I think it's time you started calling us Mum and Dad.'

'Nina,' Dad says, his likeness holo-rayed across the backseat of our self-driving car. 'I hear you had a bad day, kiddo.'

'Meh,' I reply.

'We're very proud of you for keeping your cool,' he says.

'Hmm.'

'We're so proud that you've managed to get such good grades, in spite of being disadvantaged by your lack of HoloTech,' he continues, beaming.

'Hmph.'

'And that's going to end soon!' Mum chimes in brightly. 'Your Citizenship test is just around the corner!'

That knocks me out of my sulk. 'What?'

'We got the email just this morning. It's in two weeks' time.'

My stomach does a few backflips.

If I become a Virtual Citizen, it'll mean access to intel-glasses. I'll be able to hang out at the Strip and experience Hyper Reality.

I won't be *different* from everyone else in school. I won't be that *special kid* every class has to put up with, while she *reads* her way through a textbook.

If I become a Virtual Citizen, I'll be able to get my InEars, wired straight through to my Bell Biochip and synced to the Sonic Highway. I'll have unlimited access to every piece of music ever written – a library hundreds of years old, all up on the Nebula – that'll stream directly into my consciousness with a single thought. No more having to manually trawl through hundreds of vinyls to find a song. No more having to fast-forward and rewind cassettes to listen on my Walkman. I'll have unlimited access to everything.

The thing that I'm most excited about – the one thing I've wanted for years, that I've never been allowed to have is –

'*DreamMusician.*'

Mum and Dad look at me in surprise.

'That's what I want. As soon as I pass the test, I'm going to sign up.'

'Are you sure you want that? Isn't it more fun to learn from Mr Kuruvilla?'

I stare at the both of them like they're crazy.

'Sure. Yes, he's a great teacher. But I want to learn real precision. I want perfection. It's the only way I'll make it into the demi-Virtuoso programme next year.'

'Next year?' Mum looks confused.

'Aren't you taking the examination this year?' Dad frowns.

I sigh. 'Yes, of course, Dad.'

He looks at me expectantly.

'Let's face it. There's no way I'll make the grade.'

His expression is blank.

'All my competition is DreamMusician-trained!' I say impatiently.

He smiles in understanding. 'I know it must be intimidating. But you underestimate yourself, Nina.'

I exhale in exasperation. 'No, Dad. Look. I'm being realistic. All of them have trained with InEars. They have a Metronome feed directly into their heads. They haven't had to learn to read sheet music; they just use GlimmerKeys and the piano tells them what to do. Their command over dynamics –'

Dad holds up his hand. 'I get it, Nina. I really do. They're trained to play like machines.'

'Exactly!'

'But here's where you're different, kiddo.' Mum grins. 'You play with your heart.'

I groan inwardly. I don't know how they do it, but it feels like my parents really do finish each other's sentences.

'You'll be the most unique sound they hear!' Dad snaps his fingers, and grins. 'There, now don't you feel better? What's a bad day at school compared to all the great ones to come.'

I groan at his positivity.

'Dad, this means that I now have my Citizenship test *and* my demi-Virtuoso exam within days of each other.'

'When it glitches it fries, eh? Don't worry, you'll ace both.'

He glances at his holo-watch.

'I'm running late for a meeting. See you at home, kiddo. Love you both!'

I do feel better, but as I stare out the window a tiny flip-flop of something cold and unpleasant crawls around in my stomach.

I'd better get to work.

The price of failure is deportation.

'Nina.'

Mum drums her elegant fingers on my notebook.

'Stop studying. Don't you need to practise for your demi-Virtuoso exam?'

I roll my eyes.

'Mum, the Citizenship test is way more important.'

'And you know everything you need to pass it already. You're burning yourself out. Go play the piano! It's something you love…'

I sigh.

I get up from the coffee table and head into the living room.

I set myself down on the piano bench and carefully lift the lid. I place my fingers over the keys and begin to run through the trickiest sections of *Wanderer of the Air*, or Op. 9 No. 1, Ballet in supra-B-Flat-Major by Nina Rodriguez. It's still about fifteen minutes before my piano teacher arrives, and I'm making the most of this opportunity to not run through finger drills.

It isn't like the one at the Home. That was off-key half the time.

I only had a one-hour slot to play it, every week.

Here, I can play the piano all the time. Except when I'm at school, of course.

Sometimes it's scary to sit at it. It stands all by itself in our large living room.

It's magnificent and glossy black. The name Manuela Alvares is embossed in a beautiful gold loop along its front. I wonder who she was. Maybe she was a famous musician.

At the Home, we had one grand piano that we would play when we gave performances. Most of the time, it was to raise money for the Home. Otherwise, we practised on a creaky upright with missing felts.

All the songs I know sound wrong. Maybe because this piano can be properly tuned to the alt and supra scales. Maybe because none of the keys get stuck when I play them.

The Anands – Mum and Dad, as I've started to think of them – get me some sheet music. I can read it and I do my very best to learn it right.

They're looking for a teacher. I thought it would be easier to find a teacher on this side of the world. They are twenty percenters, after all.

Maybe all the Virtuosos are too busy being famous, travelling the world and giving performances.

I'm practising one of my new pieces when Mum knocks on the door.

'Honey, we think we might have found you a teacher.'

I stop playing. I can't believe it!

'He wants to meet you and hear you play. Do you think you're ready?'

'N-now?' My hands shake a little.

'Yes, unless you'd rather not. I understand if it's a bit sudden –'

No. This is so exciting. 'No. I can play.'

A tall man with long dark hair steps into the room.

'David, this is Nina. Nina, this is Mr Kuruvilla.'

I stand, nearly tripping over the stool.

'What have you learnt so far, Nina?' His voice is low.

'Br – Brächt. Barthöven. Some preludes and sonatinas.'

'Okay, can you play me some music?'

My hands are shaking. I fumble for my sheet music, turn the page, and begin.

The keys feel like they're listening to my every touch.

I start off right. Nice and soft. I get through the opening section and into the trills without a fault.

My fingers stumble over the last trill.

Hold it together, Nina.

I enter into the next part of the piece, building it up to its eventual crescendo.

Three bad notes.

My hands are shaking now.

Hold it together, Nina.

The crescendo is perfect, but I think I've pedalled inaccurately.

A rest.

I pause. Collect my thoughts in a second.

The piece descends back into its opening bars. I play this part well.

It diminishes, and ends on a dramatic flourish, played forte, and I hit the notes right.

I sit back. I breathe. I hope I've done enough.

The room is quiet.

'That's not bad at all, Nina.' Mr Kuruvilla smiles at me. 'Some obvious mistakes – but practice and the right technique can iron those out.'

'Th-thank you.'

'You read sheet music? Who taught you?'

'I learnt…at the Home.'

'And you've never been trained virtually?'

'What's that?'

'DreamMusician?'

'I don't know what that is.'

I wonder if I'm failing this test. I look at my feet, still resting on the pedals.

He turns to my Mum. 'You say she won't have access to any Virtual music aids?'

'She won't be allowed to use any until she passes her Virtual Citizenship test.'

He nods slowly.

'I won't lie to you, Anya. It'll be difficult, very difficult. She'll have to internalize rhythm and timing. She'll need to learn each piece by rote, by reading through the sheet music. Tone, dynamics – she'll have to find her way around through feel, work on her musicality the old-fashioned way.'

'I'm sure she can –'

'Anya, it's like teaching the blind to paint.'

Mum stands up. 'Thanks, David. I understand. Don't worry about it, we'll find someone else –'

'Hang on.' Mr Kuruvilla grins. 'I didn't say I wouldn't teach her. She's got instinct. I can provide direction.'

He looks at me. 'If you really want to learn – if you're serious about the piano – then know this. It will be hard. It will be harder for you than for anyone else I've known in a long, long time. I can show you how to become a Virtuoso, but you will have to put in hours and hours of practice to do it. Do you want to do that?'

I hold my breath.

Does this mean he'll teach me?

'I only teach the very best, Nina. Would you like me to teach you?'

I exhale.

'I would like that. Very much.'

'Focus, Nina.'

My hands stop abruptly.

I didn't even notice him enter the room.

'Your mind isn't here, today.' He frowns. 'It needs to be here, every day. You need to be present. *At the keys*. Remember, neo-Acousta is only created when precision meets emotion in perfect aural union.'

I grimace. I fumbled a cadenza on its descent.

'The cadenza is one of the most prized performance skills in any Virtuoso's oeuvre. It demonstrates absolute control over the instrument. Rodriguez herself would use these sections to improvise in her live performances.'

'I know. I'm sorry.'

'You don't need to stick to the time signature of the piece, but the descent still has to sound musical. Which means that you must deviate from perfect timing with intent. Symmetry is a big part of Rodriguez's music. You aren't playing Wyschnegradsky here.'

I sigh.

'It's a bit late in the day for this, but I think you need to make a conscious effort with your timing.'

He picks up the metronome that sits at the top of the piano. It's antiquated – it isn't holographic, there's no touch interface, and its construction is a geometric curiosity. At the base of its pyramid structure is a small knob. Mr Kuruvilla winds this, then releases the pendulum from its casing. He shifts a weight on it and sets the tempo at *moderato*.

He replaces it at the top of the piano.

The pendulum sways back and forth.

Tick…tock… Tick…tock… Tick…tock…

I play.

I have to recalibrate the movement of my fingers to match the slower timing. Usually, this section is played with a gradual increase in tempo, until it becomes a sonorous flurry of notes.

I can feel Mr Kuruvilla's eyes on the backs of my hands.

It's hard to calm my nerves. It's not as if I have a Bell Biochip to regulate my adrenaline and suppress my anxiety. I don't even know how I'm expected to perform at this level without one. My fingers go rigid from the strain of sticking to the timing, they begin to cramp from my obvious distress.

'Light fingers, Nina,' Mr Kuruvilla chastises.

I grit my teeth and begin again.

Mr Kuruvilla talks over my repetitive practice of the cadenza.

'You know, normally Analog metronomes are saved for – no, you're half a beat behind, start again – what was I saying? It's only after you're an accepted Virtuoso that you get to use the liberties of a physical metronome. You'll never develop the same degree of precision without InEars in your formative years of study – stop, you're losing it. Begin again…'

I try to drown him out and focus on my accuracy.

It's hard to be perfect without InEars. I'm listening externally and trying to attune myself to the metronome's rhythm, instead of having a tempo beamed directly to my brain.

Not that Mr Kuruvilla seems to have any sympathy for me.

'You're losing sound clarity each time your little finger plays a note. I wish you'd played this for me last week. We have only days to go to your examination.'

It's almost impossible to be dynamically en pointe without DreamMusician. I'm trying to manually exert different degrees of pressure on the keys to evoke emotion. I don't think I'll ever be spot on.

'Any chance you'll get your InEars before the exam?' He's stopped me again, recalibrating the metronome to slow it down further.

'No, my test is two days after.'

He doesn't make eye contact.

'You'll do fine. Don't worry.'

'How?' I snap. I didn't mean to.

'I'm sorry?'

I try to check my temper and fail.

'*How* will I do fine? I haven't learnt any of this with InEars. My dynamics are all by feel, I don't even know if they make sense. Sure, I'm following the sheet music, but I'm not following it using carefully calibrated Tactile+ on DreamMusician. Everyone else is going to sound *perfect*.'

'I'm going to stop you right there.'

I pause.

'Yes, everyone else is going to sound perfect. But you are going to sound genuine. All this – neo-Acousta – is about the purity of sound. And you create that experience because you play with purity of heart.'

'A good heart has never got someone into this programme,' I grumble.

'Okay, enough for the day.'

'Are you kidding? The examination is in five days!'

'I'll come back tomorrow. You take the day to clear your head.'

'Mr Kuruvilla, I'll practise. Really, let's go.'

I reach for the metronome.

'Up.'

My shoulders sag. I rise to my feet.

'Why did you choose this piece, Nina?'

I know why, but I don't want to tell him.

'What does it mean to you?'

I say nothing.

'You're not going to tell me. I get it.' He sighs. 'It means a lot to you. It's a very personal choice, I gather.'

I nod.

'You know how I chose my piece for my examination? I picked it for its complexity. I picked it because it would demonstrate my technical superiority.'

'Did it work?'

'Of course it did. That's how it's been done, for years and years.'

'Great, thanks. I'm going to fail.'

'Listen, kid. You'll be the only person there playing music that comes from the soul.'

'Good for me.'

'Not so fast. The jury will connect with that. In its pursuit of perfection, neo-Acousta has ignored the expression of the soul for far too long. You'll remind them of this.'

I roll my eyes.

'Homework. Think of what this piece means to you. What is its story? Write it down for me.'

'Really?'

'Yes, really. We'll reconvene tomorrow.'

Why does everyone keep making me write things down?

Dear Nina of the Future,

Have you made it yet? I hope you're world famous by now.

I've been practising non-stop for my demi-Virtuoso Examination, and I'm sure I'm going to fail miserably because try as I might, I can't nail down this cadenza, even after working on the story of the piece and showing it to Mr Kuruvilla.

He loved it.

I love it too, but that's not the same as playing it perfectly, is it?

'Are you stressed about the exam again?'

I look up from my journal.

Mae is staring at me, her brows furrowed in concern.

I slam my notebook shut. 'No. Nooo. I'm fine. *Fine.*'

She arches her eyebrows, and I can tell she doesn't believe me.

Niraj and Anushka look over from where they've been arguing over whether almond milk or soy milk is better for their weight-loss diets.

'Is Andrew Sommers going to be playing at that thing?' Niraj sounds enthusiastic.

'Ooh, will you get to watch?' Anushka squeals.

Mae shoots her a filthy look.

'What, he's dreamy!' She pouts.

'Don't worry, Nina,' Mae says, touching my arm gently. 'We'll all be there to cheer you on.'

'Will they let us listen to everyone's performances?' Anushka asks brightly, then quickly adds, 'I mean, we'll be there for you, but it wouldn't hurt to check out the competition.'

She blushes before quickly absorbing herself in the pile of greens on her lunch tray.

'You haven't touched your lunch,' Mae mutters.

'Not hungry,' I mumble.

'What?'

I glare at her.

'I've had enough,' she says, getting to her feet. 'Let's go.'

'Go where?' Niraj says, shocked.

'What do we have after lunch?'

'Double psychohistory,' Niraj says promptly.

'Yeah, Nina and I are skipping that.'

'We are?' I start.

'We are. You guys let Magistra know that we had a…erm…what could have gone wrong? A…*a female emergency*.'

Niraj chokes on his chicken salad.

'You'd better cover for us.' Mae glowers.

'Mae, I dunno… I've got my Citizenship test round the corner too. What if this counts against me?' I say uncertainly.

'Suddenly getting your period? I'd like to see them try!' she huffs.

'I'm not on my period.' My cheeks flush.

'And they'll never know because you don't have a chip. Ha. Haha,' she laughs sarcastically. 'Nina. Up.'

She's bossy. It's impossible for me to ignore her, even at the best of times.

I spring to my feet, pushing my untouched lunch aside and grabbing my journal. I scurry after her as she strides out of the lunchroom.

'Where…where exactly are we going?'

She doesn't meet my gaze. Instead, she marches me straight through a pair of bright green gates that mark the end of the school campus.

We stand on the sidewalk under the shadow of a tree, as far from the school's visible PanoptiCam lenses as possible. I look around guiltily, hoping that the school doesn't have any hidden cameras, and even though Mae does a great job masking it, I can tell she's twitchy.

Behind us, the enormous grey stone buildings and red-tiled roofs of our school glower ominously down upon us. Skipping out could have consequences; being able to socialize and learn in a physical schooling institute, instead of being distance-educated, is a privilege that only the twenty percenters can claim.

I glance nervously up the school's driveway for signs of the patrol-droids. I fervently hope that we don't run into a Magistra, or worse, the Principal on her rounds.

I heave a sigh of relief when an empty self-driving cab rolls up within three minutes.

'Meridian Gate, please,' Mae announces to the computer, pulling me in after her.

We ride together in silence. I knot the tassels on my jacket sleeve and Mae types away furiously on her OmniPort.

I don't know why she's taking me back. I haven't been near the other side since that horrible train ride I'd been forced to go on.

'Welcome aboard! This is Maglev Adventures's Mission Analog!' the tour guide says, beaming at our class.

I ignore the class when they all give me pointed looks and giggle at the word 'Analog'.

Magistra AB43 sits up front with the tour guide watching us all, recording our behaviour. Mum and Dad warned me that she'll be paying careful attention to me, live-streaming my every reaction onto the Nebula so that the people at the Home can check how I respond to being back in the Analog world.

'It's a test,' they'd said. They'd looked worried.

I know I need to pass.

I stare blankly ahead, keeping a straight face all through the tour guide's announcements and instructions. When the train departs, I don't join in when some of my classmates begin to shriek and cry. Instead, I wave to my parents who are waiting on the station platform.

'We're going to visit your real home,' Anastasia Prakash mocks, flicking a wad of paper at me.

'Do you have servants?' Sneha giggles beside her. 'Oh wait, you are servants.'

The rows behind me take up the giggle.

I ignore them, staring straight ahead. I don't even gasp when the big blue shield opens itself up and lets us through.

The girl sitting beside me is new. That's probably why she chose to sit next to me – most people avoid coming near me. She hasn't said a word to me. She must be learning.

The train zooms into a pod-house and I flinch. I can't believe we're entering someone's home uninvited. We'd never have dared, when I was being raised at the Home.

The house is filthy. I wonder why. We were much cleaner at the Home.

'Did you live in a box like this?' Anastasia says loudly.

'No wonder you're so scared all the time,' Sneha adds. 'You're not used to seeing daylight, are you?'

I'm about to snap at them, but I feel Magistra's gaze on me and ignore them.

Magistra addresses the class. 'Why don't the Analogs have any privileges?'

'Because they're bad citizens,' the class recites. I chime in the loudest.

We're going past the vegetable farm now.

'Is this why you're an orphan?' Sneha whispers. 'Do you carry your parents around in a little box in your backpack?'

Everyone except the girl sitting beside me giggles, even though they all look terrified at the thought.

When the tour guide points out the nutro-shakes and protein porridge that I was raised eating, I cringe at the memory of their taste.

'She's never eaten real food before,' Anastasia gasps.

'That explains the brain damage,' Sneha says cruelly.

More laughter.

For the first time, the girl sitting next to me turns around and glares at them.

'What are the principles of the Bell Curve, class?' Magistra asks.

We recite the Rhyme of the Percentiles that we've been taught. It's written on the first page of all our textbooks. I chant it louder than anyone else, especially the last verse.

'Bottom ten
deport, forget,
Mice, not men
must live in regret.'

When we arrive in Market Square, I begin to wonder if I'm going to fail my test. I look at all the shops around me and wonder if I'll be sent back to work in one of them. When the tour guide plays anatronica over the speakers, I bob along to the beat of it before realizing that everyone's staring at me.

'You call this music, Nina?' Anastasia hisses.

'I thought you were a pianist.' Sneha smirks.

'A pianist!' Anastasia laughs. 'What sort of pianist would ever enjoy this garbage? I'll tell you – a fake one. I'll bet you my allowance for the year that she's deported before the end of term.'

I focus on the glass of the train window. I stare through it, barely registering a word that the tour guide is saying. If I stare at it hard enough, maybe it'll break and the Analogs will attack and Anastasia will finally shut up.

The girl sitting beside me whips her head around.

'You're on.'

'And who in all the Analogged world are you?'

'Mae. Mae Ling. I just transferred from Premier.'

'Hmm… Mae Ling, let me tell you how it works. There are some of us who belong here, and there are those of us who don't. Who would you rather be?' Anastasia whispers fiercely.

'Human,' Mae Ling says coolly, turning her back on her. 'Nina, it's

so cool to finally meet you. I heard you play at the recital the other day – you're supra-brilliant…'

I think I've just made a friend.

'You're a brilliant pianist, my friend, but you've got the attention span of a fly,' Mae says, clearly annoyed.

I snap out of my daze.

'What? Sorry, Mae, what were you saying?'

'I was ravishing you with compliments, but I guess you'll never hear them now.' She grins.

The baobab-shaped structures of Bell Towers F and G cast their scattered net of shadows upon the city streets. We pass through the Arboretum, driving close to an overturned statue lying on its side. She's covered in moss and vegetation, though her plaque still proudly names her 'Vic'.

'Look,' Mae commands.

'At Vic?'

'At the shield.'

We are at the edge of the Carnatic Meridian. The car rolls to a stop.

Mae passes her hand over a holoscanner to pay for the ride, another thing I can't do. We step outside.

'Look through it. Look beyond, to the other side.'

'No thanks,' I say hurriedly, turning away.

'Look,' she insists, grabbing my shoulder and shaking me slightly.

I look. All I can make out through the shimmering blue haze are the skull-like silhouettes of pod-houses reaching into the sky, a tightly packed warren of dust paths weaving their way through them into infinite black.

'Why are we here again?'

She waves at the world beyond the Meridian, the world that was my life before I was Nina.

'You might have come from over there, you might have spent your childhood on the other side. You might want to prove yourself to the world. But here's the thing… You've got nothing to prove. Not to me, not to your parents, not to Mr Kuruvilla. Do you understand me?'

'I need to prove to myself that I'm worth it,' I say flatly.

'You are worth it,' she says simply.

'I don't want to disappoint everyone –'

'Nina, we want you to succeed. We want you to make it. That is the deepest wish of everyone who loves you. It's a wish, that's all. It's not an expectation. We'll love you, no matter how things turn out.'

I look through the Meridian. I look at Mae. Her words are heavy, and several seconds pass before I burst into a sudden fit of giggles.

'All right, good talk.'

'That's the most serious conversation we've ever had.' I laugh.

'Ugh,' Mae says. 'Talk about getting sentimental.'

'If I get deported, you'll come visit?'

'You won't get deported,' she says with finality.

Dear Nina of the Future,

I've handed in my essay to Magistra VX81.

I've studied for my Virtual Citizenship test.

Now I just have to nail my examination.

Here I am.

I haven't seen the jury yet. I'm in the waiting room with all the other demi-Virtuoso hopefuls. I don't know what pieces they've chosen to play. The room vibrates with an air of secrecy. We aren't allowed to listen to each other's auditions.

Andrew Sommers is here –

And he hasn't even looked at me.

Anushka keeps whipping her hair back, tossing him sidelong glances, but he's ignoring her. He has a contented look on his face, nodding his head to the music that's probably filtering straight into his mind through his InEars. Niraj nearly went up to him to wish him luck, but Mae quelled him with one of her death glares.

My friends and family talk in hushed voices around me, while I listen to my piece one last time before I play it.

I feel every inch the Analog with my Walkman and my over-the-ear headphones.

There are pianists here who have holo-pianos. They're Hyper Reality simulations of the instrument, complete with weighted keys and pedal units. They're practising on them and appear completely immersed.

One of the pianists plays with tons of flourish. Clearly she'll have the upper hand on the drama quotient.

Someone appears at the door.

'Nina Anand,' she announces.

'Good luck, kiddo.' Dad thumps me on the back.

'Go for it, honey.' Mum hugs me.

Mae squeezes my hand, and Niraj and Anushka toss me a thumbs-up sign and a heart sign.

My legs feel like jelly. I'm wobbly all over.

Andrew Sommers doesn't even look in my direction.

I step through the door and enter a dark room with the loudest silence I've ever heard.

Five jurors sit at a dais, and the room is empty but for a grand piano.

'Name, please.'

'Nina Anand.'

'And your piece?'

'*Wanderer of the Air*, or Opus 9 No. 1, Ballet in supra-B-Flat Major by Nina Rodriguez.'

'What can you tell us about Nina Rodriguez?'

'She was blind. She learnt to play music by ear. Her pieces are about underlying symmetry and simplicity, disguised by technical complexity and flourish.'

'And why did you pick this piece?'

I panic. I don't know how to answer. The reason – this piece – is so much bigger than me. It dwarfs everything that comes within its reach. It contains me, and all I can do when I play it is wander the halls of its melodies, lost within a magic unlike any other.

I stop my train of thought and settle for a predictable, unemotional response.

'It – it embodies the spirit of neo-Acousta. It's pure and elevated, outward-looking but deeply personal.'

The jurors don't react.

'You may begin,' one of them says.

I sit at the piano. I adjust the bench.

I place my hands over the keys and take a deep breath.

I don't have a Bell Biochip to soothe my nerves by inducing adrenaline suppressors.

I don't have InEars to guide my rhythm.

I don't have GlimmerKeys or Tactile+ to help me create an artistically designed atmosphere.

I only have my soul.

I play my story.

Dear Nina of the Future,

I'm hoping to hear from the demi-Virtuoso Examination today. I hope I get to finish my Citizenship test first, though. The disappointment of failure would be a crushing blow, and I'll probably be deported because I underperformed.

I'm sitting in another waiting room – why is my life a story of waiting on other people's approval? – and I feel grateful for my parents. I look around at the other Analog adoptees. I've never seen another one in my life, and they...

They break my heart.

They don't look like they come from loving homes. Or like their lives are filled with opportunity. They look terrible, as if they've never been able to escape the other side.

I don't know why, but I've understood over the years that not all adoptive parents are as nice as mine. Some of them are downright awful.

'Nina Anand.'

I feel like I'm always being summoned.

I step into the room. It's bare. It has a single desk within it.

I sit at the desk. I'm handed a holo-questionnaire and a stylus by a patrol-droid that's monitoring my performance.

I gasp at how unfair this is. Most of the Analog children here may have never seen this technology. They'll probably be intimidated by the droid.

I'm one of the lucky few who saw it at school all the time, whose parents showed me how to use it.

I look down at my test. I blitz through it. I know I've aced it.

I'm led by a patrol-droid through a door made of reinforced steel. I sense another adopted child take their place at the seat I just left, and hope they do well, before I refocus and enter the next room.

This is the part where my parents warned me not to lose my temper.

They call it the *Character Evaluation*.

A wood-panelled table runs the length of the room. Behind it sits a pair of women, both staring at me indifferently.

'Ms Anand. How long have you been in the Virtual world?'

'Five years,' I say immediately, and then cautiously add, 'Madam.'

'Explain the Bell Curve to me.'

'The Bell Curve is an algorithm that takes into account several factors.' I rattle off an explanation of all its points systems. I know this like the back of my hand.

'And where do you see yourself on this Curve, young lady?'

'At the top twenty percent. Madam.'

The women are silent.

'Why do you think you'll make it there?'

One of them lifts her intel-glasses off the bridge of her nose, sceptically.

'I'm an extraordinary pianist,' I say, with more confidence than I feel.

The women laugh.

'*You're* an extraordinary pianist despite your lack of tech? Come on, Ms Anand. Don't delude yourself.'

'It's true,' I stick to my guns politely, like my parents said I should.

Apparently the jurors like what they call Alpha-Behaviour Characteristics. It proves to them that I'm not a browbeaten Analog likely to crumble under pressure.

'Who's your teacher?'

'David Kuruvilla, the well-known Virtuoso.'

'We don't pass liars.'

'I'm not lying. You can verify this.'

I tilt my nose upwards, putting on my best twenty-percenter air.

One of them runs a check on a holo-device I can't see.

'It's true.'

'Very well. So you want to be a Virtual Citizen?'

'Yes, please.'

I'm extra polite, now that I've made my point.

'Why do you deserve it?'

'I've assimilated the culture and philosophy of merit that is propagated on this side of the world. I understand how it works. I work hard, I'm Productive. I have friends at school, despite not being able to share in their tech experiences. Imagine all I could be once I have access to HoloTech?

'I impressed the jurors in my demi-Virtuoso examination, despite never having used DreamMusician. Do you know how far I could go once I have music-learning aids?'

'That's all well and good, but how do we know you're still not an Analog at heart?'

My heart sinks.

One of the women leans forward.

'Any links to them? Do you listen to anatronica? Do you find yourself longing for home?'

'Yes,' the other woman adds. 'Do you ever visit? Pass them information about us?'

'This is my home,' I say boldly. 'The Analogs are filthy. They're slackers and lowlifes. They are the bottom ten percent. I wouldn't go back, not for any reason in the world.'

I say it with a conviction that I'm not sure I feel.

'You believe you're superior to them? You were born of them.'

'An unfortunate accident that was beyond my control.' I grimace.

The women nod.

'You will hear from us shortly.'

And just like that, I'm dismissed.

Dear Nina of the Future,

We made it.

We're a Virtual Citizen.

We heard from the demi-Virtuoso Examination too, and I came in second. That means I'm eligible to join the programme, straight after school.

Now there's no looking back.

If you ever happen to look back, though, don't forget that you're more than what the world tells you you can be. That you're loved, no matter what you achieve. Your life might be wrapped up in your music, but you're also so much more...

My Bell Biochip itches a little. I guess I'm getting used to having an implant behind my ear.

It distracts me from the piece that I'm playing, but I ignore it and carry on.

Mr Kuruvilla is making me work harder than ever, now that I'm about to make it to the big leagues.

I'm not using DreamMusician yet. I checked it out but it was way too distracting. It's like constant background noise.

The GlimmerKeys confused me, and the InEar Metronome plug-in gave me a headache. I found Tactile+ far too restrictive. It felt like a straitjacket.

I get to use intel-glasses at school, and Hyper Reality blows my mind. I can finally talk to Dad without needing Mum around to sign me in on her OmniPort. I've discovered HoloTube, where my piano videos are steadily accumulating followers…

'Stop,' Mr Kuruvilla barks. 'You're rushing into playing this forte. I want you to build up to it. Try again.'

I begin again.

'Stop. See, here? That's the exact note. It's such an abrupt transition.'

I begin again.

'Better. Keep going.'

To everything turn, turn, turn.

– **Ancient Proverb**

ANATOMY OF A NEW WORLD ORDER

We challenge the prevailing algorithm of our times.

We do not want power, we want reform.

The Bell Curve divides our civilization along the lines of institutionalized markers of merit.

- Why should Productivity be defined by a singular set of criteria?
- Why should Social Personas be aligned towards an external valuation?
- Why should Core Skills lend themselves to the greater good?

Who determines that these are values?

The Bell Curve divides our civilization into those with privileges (the Virtuals) and those without (the Analogs).

- We don't want a bigger piece of the pie. We want a seat at the table.
- We don't want war. We want discourse.
- We don't want unification. We want to be able to celebrate differences.

Why are we punished for purported dissent?

The Bell Curve –

Numair stopped reading. He began to separate the pages of the pamphlet from their string binding.

'Wh-what are you doing?' the boy asked.

Numair ignored him, hoping he'd go away. He placed the metal pipe that functioned as his walking stick upon the ground. He sat upon the dust, holding the papers of the pamphlet to his chest. Standing for long periods of time tired him these days.

'If you're not interested, you could just give it back,' the boy snapped.

'It became mine when you handed it to me freely,' Numair said gruffly.

He began to fold a sheet of paper in half, pressing the line down gently along its diagonal.

'That's the property of the resistance,' the boy said.

'What resistance?' Numair asked absently.

His fingers felt stiff against the paper. Bending them at the joints was hard work.

'*The* resistance. Against the corpse-climbers on the other side,' the boy said. 'Well, we don't mind the average Virtual but we take issue with Bell Corp and their manifesto.'

'Indeed,' Numair said dismissively, pressing his thumb along a fresh line in the sheet.

'Listen, old man. We're uniting against them. Against their mistreatment of us.'

'Mmm.'

'We want a more relevant set of rules to govern this world. Rules that are meant to be inclusive of different perspectives, that don't punish people for wanting to be different.'

'I see. And how do you intend to implement these rules?'

'We…we –'

Numair embarked upon an intricate series of folds in the paper.

'Read the pamphlet,' the boy said hurriedly. 'We've laid it all out.'

'Did you write it?' Numair looked up at the boy, noticing him for the first time. He was in his late teens. His hair fell in an unruly mop of curls around a strong jawline that would, in time, be construed as arrogant. At the moment, it was covered in a fine burst of acne.

'I – no, not directly, at least.'

'Contributed your incendiary ideas to it, then.'

'Well – yes. Listen. I don't have time for this.' The boy made to leave.

'The Karthiks' boy, aren't you? Varun, Sharan – I forget your name.'

'It's Arun. You know my parents?'

'All old-timers know each other,' Numair said. 'Especially on this side of the world.'

Numair felt the boy's gaze upon him, flat and unwavering with all the misguided judgement of youth.

'If – if you read the pamphlet instead of desecrating it like that, you'll know that we intend to put an end to the whole idea of there being two sides to the world.'

'Ah,' said Numair. 'Then you'll do what no civilization has managed to in thousands of years of human history.'

'Nobody has tried hard enough,' Arun said angrily. 'When you have the right intentions, the willpower to see it through –'

'This resistance fascinates me,' Numair interrupted. 'They've been feeding you a lot of strong motivation.'

'You're jaded in your old age, *sir*,' Arun said.

The intonation was not lost on Numair's keen ear. He began to pursue a neat series of pleats in the paper, ruing the fact that his hands slipped and several of them weren't as crisp as he desired.

'Tell me, young sir,' Numair said. 'When you win this war –'

'We don't want war. We want dialogue. We might have to fight for a seat at the table, but we don't seek power once we have it.'

'Noble. When you win this war, what do you intend to do?'

'Read the pamphlet and you'll know.'

'Humour an old man, Arun,' Numair said, without looking up.

'We intend to reform the world. We want a cooperative society, not a competitive one. We want equal rights and privileges for all – HoloTech, access to basic amenities, a say in our policymaking...'

'So you want to be a Virtual, except one with moral superiority.'

Numair began to gently tear the page along the folds he'd made.

'No – yes, maybe – but not really,' Arun stumbled.

Numair sighed.

'Before Bell Corp, the world was a terrible place too,' he said. 'At least, that's what we infer from the histories. Life was chaotic and fragmented. Caste, class, religion, race, nation – these were ideals that shattered reality. The Bell Curve tried to repair historic divisions with a system of meritocracy, just as communist philosophy tried to solve the class divide and the Woke Wave tried to end social prejudices –'

'What's your point, sir?' Arun said impatiently.

'My point is that you will do your best, like all those who went before you, and you will fail, just as they did.'

'We're not bad people,' Arun snapped.

Numair held his creation up before him. He studied the cut-out concentric circles he'd fashioned as the boy strode away.

'You don't have to be.'

We invest in the wisdom of experience, insofar as that investment continues to yield results.

– from the Meritocratic Manifesto,
'Concerning Geriatric Supervision and Ministration', Article III (c)

TIME

'REMEMBER, REMEMBER...WHAT WAS it called? You know the one, Ravi. The bitter drink from the morning?'

'Coffee.'

'That's right. Coffee.'

'Hmm.'

'I sure miss the taste.'

'Hmm.'

And so goes a morning like any other.

Krishnan pulls a face at the nootropean proto-blast in his white mug. Ravi swills it around three times – counterclockwise – before swallowing it in a single gulp.

Warden B613 presses a button.

The large bio-glass windows that mark the bounds of the cafeteria pull apart along the eastern wall. A doorway appears, its path leading to bright green grass and potted palms beyond.

Ravi, Krishnan and the eighteen other Breathers who live in Ward B file out to take their morning exercise.

They walk through the gardens of the Geriatric Custody and Supervision Centre in pairs. Their neat line passes the line from Ward A on the lawns. Polite nods and smiles are exchanged. Ward C is encountered upon Pebble Shore, on the borders of the recently reconstructed Lake Timeless. More smiles, a few waves.

Their exchanges are monitored by the Warden. Shards glimmer in the sky as the patrol-drones keep their distance. The facility is humane – they try not to scare the inmates here.

The morning is spent working. Ravi and Krishnan have their consultancies to run, mentoring young business owners who have been funded by Bell Corp. They do this from their VirtuoPods set up in the Conference Chamber, a great oblong hallway with plush carpeting and arcs of curved glass that fragment its spaciousness into individually functioning territories.

Ravi advises an emerging technology project that's focused on ushering in a cutting-edge form of communication. Krishnan auditions up-and-coming HoloTube programmes.

All is as it's always been.

In the afternoon, they lunch on nootropean capsules and farm-fresh organics.

It is nap time when Ravi and Krishnan part outside the doors of their rooms.

When they wake, it is time for Inter-Ward Socialization.

'Amar.' Ravi and Krishnan acknowledge the familiar face from Ward C as he takes his place at their table.

'Jugs.' All three of them greet him. The fourth joins their table.

Krishnan shuffles the cards in an elaborate display of dexterity.

'This is the Ephemera, the most complex card-shuffling technique known to magic,' he explains.

Everyone nods politely. They do this every day.

'I shot to fame after I invented it. I even toured with the great Cadabra and his partner Skellige. That was before the tremors kicked in…'

'The Analogs are being too quiet these days,' Jugs says abruptly.

Cards fly like a flock of birds between Krishnan's trembling hands.

'No matter what card you call out, it'll always appear at the top of the deck,' Krishnan says valiantly in an attempt to reclaim their attention.

The deck is in perpetual motion, being flicked between right palm and left. Fanning, flipping.

'I don't trust them.' Amar scowls. 'Violent lot.'

'Queen of Hearts,' says Jugs.

Krishnan stills the deck and flips the first card over. It does not disappoint.

'They aren't violent,' Krishnan says. 'They're oppressed.'

The cards fan out again, spinning together and coming apart.

'Shush,' says Ravi. 'They're looking for sympathists, and you don't want to make the list. The most recent line of the Policy and Governance Division is ruthless.'

'Two of diamonds,' calls Amar.

Krishnan deftly flips the first card over.

The trick is repeated a few times before everyone loses interest. Krishnan deals a game of CardSnatch and lapses into silence, his magician's banter replaced by an air of gloom.

'Remember, remember…what was it called, Ravi?'

'Hype music.'

'Yes, Hype. It was a lot more…upbeat, wasn't it?'

'Yeah, this music is several decibels too calm.' Jugs smiles, revealing his pearly white dentures.

'Guess it keeps our heart rates down.' Ravi shrugs.

'Yes. I suppose so.'

'It's neo-Acousta. It's the purest form of sound known to humankind, you philistines.' Amar smirks. 'Or it would be, if these kids weren't so terrible.'

In the centre of the room, students from the Apex City School of neo-Acousta Performance Studies play a soothing concerto for piano and acou-violin. The faces change every year. The music does not.

The game is left incomplete, as it always is. Inter-Ward Socialization is only slotted for an hour, and everyone knows that a game of CardSnatch takes at least four hours to complete. They play it anyway. A new game every day, as the hygieno-bots clean up the space after them.

The Breathers at Ward B now prove their usefulness to the wider community by splitting up into groups of four for Coordinated Activities.

Ravi and Krishnan sit side by side, knitting. They belong to the Purls. The sweaters they're working on right now will be given to children seeded and raised to be seventy percenters in the Repop wards. The group beside theirs is grading final-term assignments for Repop children. They're called Skill's Angels.

Beyond them are the SongCatchers, who train youth musicians, currently debating the winter choral; the BenchMarkers, who raise funding for Bell-sponsored children's programmes, currently arguing over what performances will bring in top BellCoin from wealthy patrons; and the Springlings, who take care of the gardens, agreeably incorporating every opinion on the floral arrangements for the concert.

It's a happy little home.

'I keep losing count, knitting be harvested…' Krishnan mutters under his breath.

'Quiet, now,' says Ravi.

'I wish I were a BenchMarker. I would raise the standard for children's HoloTube programmes.'

'Not so loud,' says Ravi.

'The current ones are getting stale. Season 9 of *Clash of Empires* just doesn't make sense.'

'Krishnan, it isn't a children's –'

'In my day, we had higher standards for television.'

'They're listening, Krishnan,' Ravi warns. '*Clash of Empires* is a historic drama. It instils a sense of pride about our origins in the youth –'

'Let them listen,' Krishnan raises his voice. 'All I'm saying is that we need some Analog representation. Start them young. It'll prevent things like potential rebellions –'

'You're a sympathist,' Ravi chides. 'You always have been. But this could turn out to be a real problem.'

'You know my problem, Ravi? Knitting. Counting.'

'Hmm.'

'Remember, remember…what was that music called again?'

'Hype.'

'Yes, Hype.'

'What's this aural sedative they're playing, eh?'

Soon, it's a dinner of nootropean pills and garden-fresh salads. Then it's lights out, and all is still in the Geriatric Custody and Supervision Centre.

'Remember, remember…'

'Coffee.'

'Right. Coffee. I miss coffee. It woke me up.'

Krishnan scowls at the nootropean proto-blast in his white mug. Ravi swills it around three times – counterclockwise – before swallowing it in a single gulp.

Warden B613 presses a button.

The Breathers of Ward B file outdoors for their morning cardio.

They walk through the garden in pairs. Their neat line passes Breathers from Ward A on the lawns. Both lines converge upon each other in bobbing heads and smiles. On Pebble Shore, Ward C makes its presence known and polite heads nod like dandelions in the light of dawn.

Nobody calls out to each other, just like the plants in the garden.

The Warden hovers a few feet off the ground, propelling forward and keeping its gaze steady. Patrol-drones twinkle like stars in the day sky.

Ravi and Krishnan take their places in their pre-assigned VirtuoPods. The hallway is climate-controlled, and nootropic uppers are served every half hour.

Ravi has an intense discussion with a project lead on non-verbal experience design.

In the pod across from him, Krishnan waves his hands animatedly at someone across the virtual table. He rises to his feet, gesturing violently in the confined space, his face a mask of fury. A soothe-sentient is assigned to his pod.

It gently takes him by the arm, and leads him out of the hallway.

Krishnan misses his lunch of nootropean capsules and organic-fresh ingredients. He must be napping early.

At Inter-Ward Socialization, the usual greetings are exchanged.

'Amar.' Ravi acknowledges his friend from Ward C.

'Jugs.' Ravi nods towards the familiar face.

'Where's Krishnan?'

'Napping.'

'Oh.'

'Meltdown?' asks Jugs, concerned.

'He was taken away by a soothe-sentient.' Ravi shrugs.

'Oh.'

'Hmm…' Jugs says. 'I guess we can't play CardSnatch without our fourth.'

'What do we do?' asks Amar.

'Play ThreeHand?' suggests Ravi.

'I rather like this music,' Jugs says as he deals the cards.

'You would,' sneers Amar. 'It's uncouth and populist.'

'You'd know, would you?' snaps Jugs.

'I would. That pianist girl there? She's been trained by David Kuruvilla.' He points her out, barely disguising his contempt.

'Who?' asks Ravi.

'How do you know?' asks Jugs.

'A charlatan. My one-time protégé. It's evident from the way she plays. She's using all my tricks and techniques, but playing his questionable tastes. That thief.'

'Game time,' Jugs says, abruptly changing the subject.

They get through five rounds of ThreeHand. It's a much shorter game than CardSnatch, and the slotted hour gives them plenty of time to play. The hygieno-bots clean up the space after them.

The Breathers at Ward B gather for Coordinated Activities.

Ravi knits with the other Purls, none of them acknowledging the empty space left by their fourth member. Skill's Angels read.

The SongCatchers harmonize in mellow tones over sheet music. The BenchMarkers pore over their list of charities. The Springlings have flower samples in their laps.

It's a quiet little home.

Soon, it's dinner time and lights out.

Ravi remembers the taste of coffee as he swills his nootropean protoblast around three times – counterclockwise – before swallowing it in a single gulp.

Warden B613 presses a button.

The Breathers of Ward B file outdoors.

They walk through the garden in pairs. Except for Ravi. Ravi is alone.

Their neat line passes Breathers from Ward A on the lawns and Breathers from Ward C on Pebble Shore.

There's a deeper silence today.

The Warden hovers a few feet off the ground, focusing most of its attention on Ravi. Patrol-drones are flying in formation. They're armed with sedatives today, in anticipation of an outburst.

Ravi takes his place in his VirtuoPod. Krishnan's is unoccupied.

Ravi has an intense discussion with the project lead on the importance of clear, easy-to-discern graphics.

A soothe-sentient is prepped to attend to Ravi, should he react to Krishnan's absence.

Ravi eats his lunch, made from nootropean capsules and organic-fresh ingredients. He takes a nap.

At Inter-Ward Socialization, the usual greetings are exchanged.

'Amar.'

'Jugs.'

'Still no Krishnan?'

'No.'

'Oh.'

'That's serious,' says Jugs.

'He shouldn't have expressed so many opinions.' Ravi shrugs.

Amar nods.

'So ThreeHand?' Jugs asks.

'Deal,' says Ravi.

'The pianist girl is back,' Jugs observes.

Amar scowls. 'She'll never make it,' he declares.

'That's harsh,' says Ravi.

'It's the truth,' Amar states flatly. 'The only reason David Kuruvilla got famous is because he stole *my* Symphony in sub-E-Minor-alt-E-Flat-Major, also called *Battle Hymn for the Plastic Flowers*.'

'You wrote that?' Ravi raises an eyebrow.

'I discussed the entire concept with him.' Amar shrugs. 'He ripped it off and became a world-famous Virtuoso. I got stuck playing neo-Acousta at office retirement parties.'

'I didn't even know you played,' Ravi says.

'Once.' Amar holds out his shaking hands. 'Never again, I'm afraid.'

They get through four rounds of ThreeHand today. The hygienobots clean up the space after them.

It's time for Coordinated Activities in Ward B.

Ravi knits in silence.

After dinner, the lights go out.

'D'Costa.' The man extends his hand. 'I'm your new neighbour.'

'Ravi,' he says, closing the handshake.

'You're my buddy, says the Warden.'

'Nice to meet you.'

'Likewise.'

'So? Where do I start?'

'You just retired, right?'

'Yep, and everyone told me that this was the place to be.'

'It is. And you'll be mentoring…?'

'New investments in Bell Corp's portfolio.'

'Ah, we might get to collaborate.' Ravi nods. 'I'm mentoring an up-and-coming project too. A graphic communication venture.'

'I look forward to it.' D'Costa smiles.

He takes a sip of his nootropean proto-blast and makes a face.

'You'll learn to love it,' Ravi says tonelessly.

'I don't think I'll ever get over coffee.' D'Costa shakes his head.

'I believe you will,' says Ravi. 'At the very least, you're going to want to try.'

Warden B613 presses a button.

The Breathers of Ward B file outdoors for their morning exercise.

Analogs, Analogs, all the same,
Unproductive, filled with shame.
Anti-Social, Anti-Bell,
If you kiss one, do not tell.

– Virtual Child's Playground Rhyme

The Rasae fight for equal rights.
The Tatae craft our tools.
The Atae walk the streets at night.
The Vitae are brave, not cruel.
The Mahae teach us how to read.
The Sutae steal to live.
My tribe fulfils my every need.
To mine, my life I give.

– Analog Child's Tribe Initiation Pledge

THE TINDERBOX

THE SUZERAIN RASAE ACCEPTED the titanium box without glancing at it. It weighed little in the palm of her hand.

The Courier lingered, eyes downcast.

Waiting for a reaction to fuel some gossip, no doubt.

The Suzerain wielded silence, cold as the edge of the blade at her waist.

The Courier glanced at her, then bowed hurriedly, sensing his dismissal. Eyes fixed on the dusty floor, he backed away from her Receiving Hall.

She waited.

His footsteps receded from the inner chamber of the Old Temple.

She looked down at the package in her hand for several moments.

Someone coughed.

Her eyes flicked upwards. Her Inner Circle had arrived.

'We have a delivery from the vegetable farm.' She held up the box. 'This is all that remains of our First Lieutenant. She has been harvested, *in totalis*.'

Sunlight filtered through ancient carven windows. It was insufficient to light the faces of her courtiers, but an ill wind of murmurs carried through the gloom.

'Madame Suzerain.' The Secretary stepped into a pool of light. 'I received her last letter.'

He pulled a scrap of paper from his tunic.

'*They know*,' the Secretary read. '*They are coming*.'

The Suzerain held her hand out to receive the note.

The Secretary lowered his gaze.

There was a clamour of voices.

'I will avenge her, High Suzerain!'

'And I!'

'I will lay down my life for you, High Suzerain!'

'I –'

'Enough!' the Suzerain snapped.

The Inner Circle fell silent.

She rose to her feet.

'As you are well aware, we have laid a trap to further the cause of the resistance. The loss of our First Lieutenant is an unfortunate one, but we must remain focused on seeing our plan through. We will strike back in due time but –'

'Ahem.'

'What is it, Mr Secretary?'

'I – some of us within the Inner Circle, madame – we call into question the support of the…*resistance*. We believe that matters of the tribe must come first.'

He looked around at the assembly.

'As your Inner Circle, I believe it is only fair that we are allowed to weigh in on this decision –'

She silenced him with her gaze. Her eyes glittered in the dim light.

'As my Inner Circle, Secretary Rasae, you are encouraged to voice your opinions, but in the matter of decision-making, I shall continue to spare you the burden.'

'With all due respect, madame –'

'Suzerain! Suzerain Rasae!'

A Scout raced into the Receiving Hall. A cloud of dust puffed into the air as she fell to her knees.

The Suzerain Rasae reached for the shotgun slung across her back. She hated interruptions.

'Speak! Make it fast. Three. Two –'

'*They are coming*,' the Scout gasped. 'They are coming. They are coming.'

Her chest heaved. Tears streamed down her cheeks.

The Suzerain Rasae stepped forward, her shotgun held at the ready.

'The Virtuals. They're coming for the Temple.'

The Suzerain Rasae stilled.

She exhaled slowly. Then she smiled. Everything was going according to plan.

The Inner Circle had begun to shout.

'The Temple!'

'We cannot sacrifice that.'

'They dare not –'

'We will fight them to the death!'

The Suzerain raised her fist. The clamour died to a rustle of unease.

She focused all her attention on the Scout. 'You are certain of this?'

'I saw them. Th-through the Carnatic M-meridian. They're boarding a Maglev train as we speak. Toter-bots and dismantler-droids. Un-cementers. Sculpt shifters. Forty Virtuals and their patrol-droids. A contingent of drones. I ran here. As fast as I could...'

The Suzerain Rasae made a slew of swift decisions.

'Leave!' she snapped at the Scout. 'Get out of my sight.'

The Scout scurried away, her sobs carrying into the gloom.

Her Inner Circle rushed to make its views known.

'I will rouse the troops.'

'We will make our last stand here. For honour, for glory –'

'Enough, you fools!' the Suzerain bellowed. 'Enough!'

The Receiving Hall fell silent.

'All rebellions demand sacrifice. Are you so vain that you refuse to give up the Temple to support the cause of the entire Analog people?'

'But, madame –'

The Suzerain silenced the speaker with a glare.

'The Temple is bait, nothing more. It is a trap. We will stand by and see it sprung. We will not intervene, no matter the cost,' she hissed. 'Besides, you're trained warriors. Use your military brains, or have your years of training been for nothing? We are *outnumbered*. The Virtuals are armed to the teeth with LasTech weaponry. We have shotguns and blades. They're prepared to annihilate an Analog uprising.'

'Madame Suzerain –'

She might have imagined the march of heavy machinery in the distance.

'Now deploy our traps. Our defences will take care of the Virtuals. The resistance will do the rest.'

They brought out the bodies.

The Suzerain Rasae looked on impassively.

She'd pitched a tent among her tribesmen, lost in the maze of their canvas city.

Her tribespeople had managed to activate the Temple's intricate array of booby traps. Hopefully, they'd survived them on their way out the escape passage. The Suzerain hadn't heard from them in two days, but at least the time and resources spent in the defence of the Old Temple seemed to be paying off.

Digger-droids were sent in after the first wave of deaths. The eastern side of the temple had collapsed. Ten Virtuals had been killed, including a noted anthropologist.

'This is all going according to plan,' the Suzerain smirked.

'It was easy to turn their operative.' Tariq stood by her side. 'This is the problem when you manipulate someone based on extreme circumstances.'

The Suzerain nodded. 'The Virtuals have no subtlety.'

'None,' Tariq agreed.

'A noble cause,' the Suzerain muttered. 'Her parents must be brave.'

'Noble deeds can get you killed in a world like this.' Tariq grimaced.

'How did they survive?'

'Sheer dumb luck. They left to go looking for her, worried about a storm warning. Didn't get to Rohini before the Virtuals did, though.'

'Harvest those heart-eaters,' the Suzerain swore.

'But our misinformation has clearly sent the Virtuals scrambling. Rohini must have been very convincing about the weapon we're building in the Temple.'

The Suzerain snorted in laughter.

The dusty roads outside the Temple had turned into a site of chaos.

It was certainly buying the resistance time as their Jewel Forest scraped every Virtual device on their territory for its credentials. And the Suzerain had to admit that she relished the body count. Death was to be celebrated, especially when the losses were one-sided.

The only problem was getting close enough – breaking through the circle of armed droids – to relieve the dead Virtuals of their technology. Many thieves of the Sutae tribe had volunteered, but it was no mean task to stand up to the threat of LasTech fire.

Twisted and deformed heaps of metal were routinely removed from the Temple gates. The surviving Virtual overseers had withdrawn into a tight circle beneath a ClimaTech tent. It was probably air-conditioned, something the Analogs had never experienced on this side of the city. The Virtuals had probably never experienced real weather.

Unknown to them, the Sapphire and Topaz Trees towering above them transmitted every signal beamed by their OmniPorts and holo-watches, registering InstaSnap activity, BellCoin transactions and vid-mails alike.

They emerged several hours later. They recalled their most skilled machines.

And then they sent in the Analogs.

'No,' Tariq gasped.

'Corpse-climbers,' the Suzerain growled.

A steady parade of their hirelings – those directly employed by Bell Corp – entered the Temple gates and were never seen again.

The Suzerain observed the proceedings through a pair of binoculars. Screams of terror rang out over the city of dust. She winced inwardly at the needless loss of Analog life.

'I'd hoped it wouldn't come to this,' the Suzerain said.

'Worst-case scenarios have a way of playing themselves out,' a voice whispered. 'We must wait and watch.'

The Suzerain turned to where the scrape of a voice had emerged from. Deep within the shadows of a tent, the Ten-Percent Thief stood with her back to them, her hood drawn low.

'Like the Temple itself,' the Suzerain Rasae agreed.

The Old Temple shook upon its foundations, but it remained standing, as if a symbol of how she would need to lead this resistance.

'They're spilling the blood of innocents,' Tariq said.

'It is the price of rebellion,' Nāyaka said quietly.

'We cannot retaliate,' the Suzerain agreed. 'We don't have the firepower. Not yet. The craftsmiths are still assembling the canons –'

'We can't just stand idly by!' Tariq snapped.

'The Temple has been my home since I was a child,' the Suzerain said calmly. 'I hate to watch it being desecrated like this, but this is a war we fight. An ill-timed skirmish will not win it for us.'

The Temple had been the seat of Rasae power since she'd been initiated into the tribe. Analog-born and raised, she'd worked her way up the ranks until leadership was thrust upon her young shoulders.

Nobody knew of the Temple's origins and cultural significance in the erstwhile city of Bangalore. The stories behind the detailed murals on the ceilings had cracked and faded over time, and the intricate sculptures on the walls crumbled to dust, taking all memory with them. A broken signboard lay caked in grime at the base of its facade. It proclaimed a single word, 'CON'.

In spite of its mysteries, the Old Temple was the last monument left standing on this side of the Meridian. South of Market Square, practically at the heart of Analog territory, it was an imposing echo of the past on an otherwise barren landscape. Bell Corp had viciously relocated every other scrap of erstwhile splendour, including those constructed to honour Analog memory. They had stripped the Analogs of all identity and history, denying them a reason to look skyward and training their eyes to the contemplation of dust and ruin.

It hurt her physically to watch it under assault, to have her hands tied by the lofty goals of the resistance.

Let Nāyaka talk of peace and rebuilding the world. For me, this is a war we hope to win.

'We must act. The loss of innocent life –'

'Tariq, we will act when the time is right,' Nāyaka said.

Digger-droids emerged with another batch of bodies.

The humans dead. The droids in various states of dismemberment and charring.

The Suzerain lowered her binoculars. 'What do you propose we do, Tariq?'

'We take the fight to them, madame.'

'It's a suicide mission,' the Suzerain responded flatly.

'There is honour in death, madame. Isn't that what the Rasae is founded upon? Isn't that why we formed the resistance?'

'Dying is easy, Tariq.'

'Those are our people in there! Members of the resistance – innocent bystanders – are being killed, as we speak.'

'I'm not Rasae, please! I don't own the Temple… Y-you c-can't make m-m-me go in th-there!'

'You will do as you are told.'

A pair of patrol-droids forced a ragged Analog man up the steps and through the doorway. There were several seconds of silence. Then, a staccato of gunfire.

The Suzerain swore. There would be retribution from every tribe that had been affected over the last two days. The affairs of the resistance would be discussed in the open. The people would point to them and demand compensation. Worse still, they might blame the Rasae, whose very purpose was to defend them against threats from Bell Corp, for their silence. They wouldn't be happy about their people being used as trap-fodder to fuel a cause, no matter how noble.

'Madame Suzerain, the tribes will be unhappy about the deaths of their own –'

'When you have information that I am unaware of, Tariq, then do enlighten me.'

'My apologies, madame.'

A woman was dragged before the temple doors, sobbing.

'I'm Atae, I'm not a labourer! I'm a skilled LoveMaker. Please! I work in the Pleasure Domes!'

'Consider this your new assignment.'

She was forcibly thrown into the temple. A hideous shriek pierced the cacophony of the streets.

A procession of men and women continued to be led to the Temple door. All of them screamed their tribe allegiances as if that absolved them of their singular crime of being Analogs. The Suzerain pitied them; if only they knew that the Virtuals saw them all as the same. Dispensable, filthy and degraded, justifiable sacrifices.

The bottom ten percent.

A crowd of Analog onlookers surged towards their loved ones as they were marched into the Temple.

'Let them go!'

'Release her!'

'She's only seventeen!'

There was a sudden shout.

Someone had broken through the phalanx of patrol-droids and was racing towards the line at the Temple steps. There was the shrill whistle of LasTech fire.

The crowd erupted.

A crush of human bodies surged towards the patrol-droids.

Laser sabres sliced through Analog flesh. Noxious vapours from tear grenades brought several to their knees. The patrol-droids fired indiscriminately, their Virtual overseers retreating to their climate-controlled tent.

Suzerain Rasae winced at the crowd's stupidity. Armed droids could never be overcome without Hydro-Weapons. And yet, she felt a surge of hope. Perhaps this would stimulate the Analogs when the time for the final battle came.

'So many more will die,' Nāyaka said quietly.

'This is all my fault,' Tariq said sombrely. 'I invited them onto our doorstep.'

'We had no choice,' the Suzerain Rasae hissed. 'Wasn't it you who told me that the resistance needs access to live HoloTech? Devices that are still directly uplinked to the Nebula?'

'There's no way to get those unless we loot the newly dead,' Nāyaka said. 'Their credentials are disabled as soon as their deaths are reported.'

'And yet, how do we access them now?' Tariq grimaced. 'Our chances were slim before, but now, with a full-fledged riot on our hands –'

'I'm starting to think we should have attacked a Maglev like we'd proposed at the beginning,' the Suzerain said.

'To incur the wrath of the Virtuals for an unprovoked attack?' Nāyaka said with a hint of scorn. 'At least this looks like self-defence.'

'I will convene with the Rasae and we will form a strategy,' the Suzerain said. 'Our people will know that our losses have not been in vain.'

She counted the visible dead even as the dust settled in pools of blood. There would soon be a reckoning, for every single one.

ꟷ⊔⊓ꟷ

The Suzerain and her Inner Circle secured their headquarters in the ruins of a train station. The stench of oxidized metal lingered in the air, but it was a relief to be under a solid roof. Here, at least, they could guard their precious stores of paper and weaponry from the elements.

A dust storm shrieked outside. The tent city that comprised the holdings of the Rasae and Vitae tribes was torn from the earth and flung haphazardly about. The streets shifted and disappeared beneath its assault.

At least work on the munitions for their offensive would carry on. The Tatae craftsmiths worked exclusively underground, making use of the stormwater drains that had ceased to function when the Analogs stopped receiving running water.

In the days that had passed since the Analog riot, the Virtuals had retreated entirely to Atae territory, right at the edge of the Carnatic Meridian. Scouts reported that they'd been instated in one of the Pleasure Domes to rethink their strategy against the Old Temple.

The Temple itself was surrounded by patrol-droids carrying LasTech snipers and laser sabres. Patrol-drones hovered at its periphery, dive-bombing any Analog who got within ten feet of the perimeter with tear grenades.

Their tents had been torn apart in the dust storm. Most of her people languished under the unrelenting sun, gnawing on grimy crusts of bread.

'Get the Vitae scavengers to find some food in the Junkyard,' she snapped at her Chancellor. 'Trade our resources for nutro-shakes. Fix this!'

The death toll from this operation weighed heavily upon her conscience.

'How many arrested?'

'Ten.'

'Heart-eater,' the Suzerain swore.

'The sun scorches them, Suzerain. ClimaTech regulates their body heat, offering some respite.'

The Suzerain Rasae sighed.

'The Vitae and Tatae tribes have united with us, as expected. They send their sympathies at the death of our First Lieutenant, and the promise of their full support to the resistance.'

'Very well. I appreciate their loyalty,' the Suzerain said.

The Secretary nodded.

'The Tatae will need to prepare the canons.'

'I took the liberty of communicating the same. A Courier has already been dispatched.'

'What of the other tribes?'

'The Mahae will not participate openly, but you are free to carry out what actions you will on their land. Upon one condition.'

'Which is?'

'The children must be unharmed, and cannot be involved. There can be no links from the resistance back to the Institute, or to the Adoption Home. Should we fail, it will strip them of their futures.'

The Suzerain nodded. This was a fair request from the child-rearing tribe.

'The Atae condemn this.'

'Of course they do.' The Suzerain smirked. 'They have everything to lose. What is a lapdog if it stops receiving scraps from its master's table?'

'We can coerce them, Suzerain…'

'No. We have no need of their alliance. I don't need their whores whispering our every move to the Virtuals.'

'Yes, madame.'

'And, Secretary, send a courier to Nāyaka. We must send in the technologists – they'll know what to look for. We will strike tonight.'

The Suzerain Rasae slid between gusts of grit and sand streaming through the air. She'd chosen to lead her troops into the most violent night of the storm.

She dodged the blinding flurry of shingles as if she were participating in an intimate dance with the elements, zig-zagging and spinning away.

The Rasae underwent extensive training in the Sand Arts so they could battle through any weather conditions, but the Suzerain proved that she was worthy of leading the tribe as she navigated the sandstorm with skill. Her warriors crept behind her, not all of them possessive of her grace, some of them dragging heavy Hydro-Weaponry into the shifting dunes.

They fanned out in a wide circle as they surrounded the Pleasure Domes, moving like a dark shadow upon the ground towards the structure at the very centre.

The Suzerain's personal Scout had reported that the Virtual overseers were holed up in the Dome of Dancing Water Birds and, sure enough, the Suzerain could detect the heat signatures of the secure-droids stationed along its periphery. Visibility through the storm was at four feet, and she was grateful to the Tatae craftsmiths for dedicating a good part of their expertise over the years to therma-sense goggles.

She signalled near-imperceptibly for her warriors to slow down. Only years of training exercises had enabled them to read her every gesture through their scopes.

Patrol-droids stood guard every ten feet around the dome, revolving around its periphery like a deadly disc.

The Suzerain shifted uncomfortably in her ClimaTech gear. Nāyaka's representatives had assured her that this was military-grade; they'd stolen it from right under the noses of the Security and Enforcement Division on the southern side of Apex City. It would deaden their heat signatures to near-nothing for a distance of up to forty metres. The Suzerain Rasae had had every single component tested. She only hoped they held up tonight. The Electro-HydroCanons had a range of forty-two metres. They'd be cutting it close.

Crouched in the sand, the Suzerain surveyed the scene before her.

The streets were deserted. The Atae – given their love for pleasure and the finer things in life – were nowhere in sight in the midst of the gale. The Dome of Celestial Pleasures and the Dome of Feral Fantasies lay twinkling in the distance to her left and right.

The Suzerain signalled again for her troops to move forward, an obscure sign that was immediately obeyed amid the shifting sands.

Stillness is death, her mentor's voice echoed in her head. *Keep your face to the wind and keep moving.*

Sixty metres away now.

The patrol-droids showed up more clearly on the Suzerain's scope.

She was transported back to the night of her first raid, when she was only thirteen. They had crossed through the Carnatic Meridian, into Virtual territory in an armed attack at the unveiling of the restored Holofield Theatre.

That night had ended in massacre.

In retaliation, the Virtuals had rounded up Analogs indiscriminately, consigning them to being harvested *in totalis*. The Analog population had dwindled by close to a hundred thousand…

You're getting old, Chandrika. The Suzerain smirked as she addressed herself by her true name. *Stop reminiscing, keep moving.*

Fifty metres now.

She had been thrust into power after the massacre, leading a struggling tribe in a world filled with violence and uncertainty. She'd toiled with the newly anointed Suzerains from the other tribes to raise the morale of their people, broken and destroyed in the aftermath of the event.

The Virtuals had stayed silent for all those years. Until now.

I cannot watch them break my people. Not again.

The Suzerain clenched her fist.

I might have invited them onto our doorstep, but I didn't give them permission to slaughter our kind.

The Suzerain grinned savagely.

Blood. Blood is the price they will pay.

Forty-five metres.

The Suzerain made a sign and her troops slowed down. They closed in around the Dome of Dancing Water Birds, compressing the spaces between their bodies and slipping together to form a tight net around the structure.

The Suzerain raised her fist.

Her troops stilled before rushing into a burst of hushed activity.

The Electro-HydroCanons were set up with clockwork precision. Each carried a hundred gallons of water, bought from the Analogs' water ration and paid for with the limited resources of the resistance. A slender nozzle was fitted to the mouth of each cannon, along with a compact chamber filled with corundum, known for its abrasiveness and acquired at high cost from the Junkyard.

The motors began to turn. A shrill whine cut through the air, drowned by the howling winds.

The patrol-droids would perceive a change in the sound waves in the air any moment now. There was no time to spare.

The Suzerain threw her hand to the ground.

The canons erupted.

The motors crescendoed in a high-pitched whine, pumping water into the mouth of each canon under high pressure. Razor-sharp shards of corundum emptied into the chamber, escaping through the thin nozzle as deadly shrapnel, traversing the forty metres to their targets at deathly velocity.

There was a rattle like a hailstorm as shrapnel crashed upon steel. The hiss of circuitry frying as water pulsed into every joint in their machinery. The shrieks of LasTech as the patrol-droids lost control over themselves and their weaponry, firing blindly into the dark.

'Move. *Move.* MOVE,' the Suzerain bellowed as she detected the sea of robots crashing into the earth.

The time for subtlety was over. The time for battle had arrived. Swirling like a tornado of finely tuned muscle and sinew, she plunged into the winds towards the Pleasure Domes, her sword felling all obstacles in her path.

It sank through flesh. She wrenched it free.

It crunched into bone and she hacked away, severing an opponent's arm at the shoulder.

She rolled to avoid gunfire, time slowing as she spied her enemy. She reached for the knife in her boot and flung it without a second glance, turning away by the time it had buried itself in the soft flesh of his neck.

Her Rasae warriors were equally adept, slaughtering everyone in their path. The satin cushions on the floor were drenched with blood. The intricate artwork on the walls featured fresh drizzles of red.

The massacre was complete.

It had taken minutes.

The Suzerain and her troops led a crew of hackers through the debris. They gathered every scrap of technology they set their eyes on, stripping bodies of holo-watches, intel-glasses and OmniPorts. In between the retching and heaving at the sight of all the blood, each of the OmniPorts was unlocked using the empty stares of the dead.

A ragtag army of developers and a proud phalanx of warriors left the building side by side.

If anyone had witnessed the event, it no longer mattered.

The wind howled at their backs. Nobody stopped the resistance.

The Suzerain Rasae placed the titanium box upon the plinth, visible for all to see.

She turned and addressed the members of her Inner Circle who had gathered at the edge of the Junkyard.

'The First Lieutenant stood for all the things that this tribe is built on – loyalty, sacrifice and pride. She gave her life to provide us with a better one. We now have an opportunity to rebuild ourselves, after the ravages of the dust storm and the loss of Analog life. But first, we will remember.'

She struck flint against steel in a rapid succession of strokes. A shower of sparks fell onto the box. The embers flared, igniting the titanium dust that coated it, dancing into flame.

The night was cool. Satellites winked at them from the clear skies.

'Tomorrow,' she said. 'Tomorrow we will go to war.'

'Revolutionary.'

– *The Bell Tech Review*

'A game-changer. We've never seen anything like it.'

– *Virtual City Magazine*

'The future of communications is now one BE-moji away.'

– *Mac and Muralidhar's Curated HoloTech List*

'No words.'

– *The Bell Bibliophile's Quarterly Journal*

THE BE-MOJI PROJECT

NOBODY LOOKS FORWARD TO Pitch Night at Bell Corp.

Sub-par cocktails. Hours spent pretending to like each other. Desperate presentations from unprofitable special-interest groups. It's a good thing they're forced to attend only once every quarter.

At this quarter's event, the bigwigs from Bell Corp's Investments Division, the Policy and Governance Division, and the Emerging Technologies Division are unmoved.

The usual suspects have turned up with their predictable asks.

The Analog Outreach Programme wants to extend grief counselling to the bottom ten percent of society. This, they reason, will help them cope with their mortality before they're taken to the vegetable farm.

They are politely shown the door. No questions are asked.

The ClimaTech Environmental Risks Division needs a sizeable investment of BellCoin to gather sufficient water reserves. Purifying those water reserves requires another generous loan.

There's a big drought coming, they say.

'We have water safeguards in place. Didn't we approve the Atmospheric Harvesting Programme a decade ago? That should supply us with enough water from the atmosphere to –'

'It's being implemented only in Apex City.'

'So?'

There is some dithering.

'We'd like to offer wider access to the technology.'

'The Analogs are not our concern.'

'Wider.' The presenter quails under the impassive gaze of the panel.

'How wide?'

'Outsiders,' he chokes.

A laugh booms out in the stillness. One of the panellists is wiping tears from his eyes.

The presenter smiles nervously.

'Why would we lose our upper hand in trade negotiations by giving the *Outsiders* tech solutions for free?'

'The aftermath of this disaster will affect all of us. Imagine the refugee crisis if Outside Socs can't sustain their cities.'

'We don't harbour refugees.'

'It will only be a matter of time before this impacts us in Apex City.'

'What sort of timeline are we looking at?'

'Forty years, best case, before the water in the atmosphere –'

'We'll deal with it in thirty-nine.'

Armed patrol-droids escort the contingent outdoors.

Planetary Wonders asks for a special allotment of skyscraper-free land. Their dream is to enable all the citizens of Apex City to drive out into the world to watch the stars.

They are laughed out the room.

Things are going badly.

An entrepreneur walks in without a holo-ray presentation, using paper charts instead of interactive graphs. One of the bigwigs has a severe reaction to a pill designed to simulate the taste of red-velvet cupcakes at a fraction of the calories. The reconstituted champagne in the PowerDrivers they're sipping doesn't meet the required rate of bubble effervescence.

Then a bright yellow sphere walks into the room.

'Is that a beach ball?' Mark Morris, Vice President of the Investments Division, asks.

'It has a face on it,' John Alvares, Head of the Policy and Governance Division, states observantly.

The face transforms its expression from a pleasant smile into a grin cracked wide open.

'What in the history of Bell Corp –' Anuradha Reddy, Chief Researcher in the Emerging Technologies Division, gasps.

'It's an emoji,' John says knowledgeably.

The grin changes to a laugh. It animates, opening and closing its mouth in a fixed loop.

'This must be a joke.'

The large sphere shakes its head vehemently from left to right.

'Is this a real pitch here?'

The beach ball speaks. 'This is the future of global communication.'

The emoji-head dissipates to reveal a woman's face behind it. 'We envision a world where the face you wear speaks for itself.'

She pauses. Smiles.

'I'm Suchitra Kashyap from Bell Corp's Language Development Cell. We work out of the Experimental Sciences Lab, in Apex City's Bell Tower W.

'Meet the BE-moji.

'The BE-moji is the singular true expression of your current state of mind. It is infallible in its honesty. It communicates on your behalf, even when you don't want it to.

'We believe that the world of communication is filled with friction. Even the simplest requests require long character strings to be vocalized. *Pass the salt*, or *Another PowerDriver, please*.

'No more.'

The BE-moji sweeps back over her face, radiating into a sphere from her neck upward.

It transforms into a salt cellar. It transfigures into a pint of beer, complete with a specific label for CarnaticLite. It morphs into a cupcake, a bottle of Sp@Home Moisturizer, a ticket to a League of Champions game.

The holographic projection shrinks, returning Suchitra's face to normal.

'Communication can now operate at the speed of thought, with never a word said. The last major breakthrough in the communications space arrived in the form of the OmniPort. Everyone uses one to call their friends and loved ones, to access the world around them, but we've reached a plateau with development. Face it. All our upgrades are based on updating pixel clarity and solving interplanetary video lag.

'This – the BE-moji – is a technological revolution.'

Suchitra looks at the trio of stunned faces. 'Unconvinced? Sceptical? Face the future and try it out.'

She hands out tiny lapel pins that magnetically snap on to each collar.

'These contain the smallest holo-ray devices ever developed. We've licensed the technology – it's completely above-board – from an independent developer right here in Apex City. She prefers to remain anonymous, but we will be paying her a royalty. Each device detects each face's unique dimensions and snaps the BE-moji on them as an overlay.'

John begins to laugh.

'Head to the BE-moji portal on your OmniPorts. It'll ask you for permission to sync with your Bell Biochip. As we all know, the implant monitors your heart-rate function, your hormone levels and your neurological matrices. The BE-moji analyses all this information, computes it within nanoseconds, and projects a second-by-second update of your every need.'

Mark chuckles. A yellow mass of pixels blossoms over his face, its mouth turned upward at an angle, eyes narrowed in a wicked smile.

Anuradha's line-drawn mouth opens in a pronounced 'O', her eyes growing to the size of saucers.

John's pixel-eyes reduce to slits, bright blue tears streaming down a face whose mouth is rapidly expanding into an exaggerated 'D'.

'This is genius.' Mark's head morphs into a stack of shining gold BellCoin.

'This is adorable.' Anuradha's eyes are replaced by popping hearts.

'I like it.' John's voice emerges from behind a larger-than-life thumbs-up.

'Using BE-mojis leads to a 12 per cent increase in Productivity. It's hard to focus on work when your subconscious mind is thinking about how to communicate your wants, needs and emotions to the people around you. We take this away, seamlessly integrating our technology with your Bell Biochip to relay instant messages. You will never have to say a word again.'

The investors in the room look at each other, their BE-mojis united in individual expressions of awe.

'This is excellent work.' Mark didn't have to say it. His BE-moji cycles rapidly through projecting a stack of BellCoin, a double thumbs-up, a face that wears a grin from ear to ear and a rainbow trailing sparkles.

'Consider us on board,' says Anuradha. 'Just when we thought Pitch Night was going to disappoint, yet again.' She didn't have to say it either. Her BE-moji tumbles through her reactions, including floating purple hearts, stacks of BellCoin, a unicorn streaming rainbows and a puppy bouncing on a trampoline.

John lets the BE-moji do the talking for him.

Bell Corp's Investments Division soundlessly and synchronously gives the BE-moji Project a triple thumbs-up.

The prototype has several glitches.

The see-through tech on the inside of the BE-moji – the side facing the wearer – needs a series of upgrades. It isn't transparent enough. This is leading to sensations of claustrophobia in user-testing. The smartest minds in the cities of Apex, Crest and Premier come together to solve the problem.

The mapping of emotional states mined from the Bell Biochip is fairly accurate, but the accompanying BE-moji art doesn't deliver deeper, more nuanced expressions. Research teams are hired to analyse papers on the James-Lange and Canon-Bard theories of emotion. They map facial feedback from hundreds of faces across the world, after presenting each one with a diverse range of stimuli.

Arguments are made in the form of holo-rayed presentations between the Lange-Fellows and the BomBardiers, as they come to name themselves.

The Lange-Fellows have an advantage – the developmental cycle based on their theory will be much shorter, thanks to its lessened complexity. The BomBardiers press forward with a hypothesis that their method will help predict human behaviour far more accurately and, in time, could even help manipulate it.

The outcome is top secret.

Meanwhile, Sentient Intelligence programs are designed and commissioned to produce BE-moji art featuring thousands of expressions. These are curated into clearly recognizable and relatable sets by the humans at the Grand Masters Society of Pixel Portraiture.

Ancient tablets with pictographic scripts from the Egyptian and Indus Valley civilizations are pored over by Grand Masters and Sentient Intelligence programs alike. The key to this new language, both man and machine agree, will lie in its graphic simplicity.

Many pictures are drawn.

Big brands line up to watch demos of their labels being featured on the BE-moji platform. It doesn't matter that the product is a long way from launch. They attend business meetings and interact with prototypes on a regular basis, even creating internal divisions dedicated to integrating their companies with the state-of-the-art world of graphic communication.

In addition to CarnaticLite and Sp@Home, the project receives commissions from the cupcake company Sugar 'n' Spice, the food- and produce-delivery service FreshGoodz, and social media platforms InstaSnap and Woofer.

The social media asks are the hardest to integrate.

There is no simple way to design graphics that communicate a person's need to use social media. BE-mojis cannot simply replicate company logos. It is argued that their emotional subtlety will be lost. It is pointed out that the idea isn't cutting-edge enough.

It becomes the BE-moji Project's highest priority to find a universally acceptable identity marker for each social media portal, and to devise a symbol for it.

The Language Development Cell is stumped.

The Sentient Intelligence programs devising art for the platform draw a blank.

The Grand Masters Society of Pixel Portraiture are thought leaders, not problem-solvers.

A competition is held across Bell Corp's cities to crowdsource solutions to this dilemma. The world population votes on the top ten entries.

The winning design for InstaSnap is a recently taken holosnap of a user with hearts dancing around its frame.

The winning design for Woofer is a happy dog. It barks.

Bell Corp congratulates itself on a job well done.

Its leaders watch the hitherto insignificant careers of the members of the Language Development Cell skyrocket into success.

The Bell Curve algorithm recognizes their Productivity Points and Social Persona ratings to be comparable to other twenty percenters on the Curve, elevating them to the premier reaches of society in Apex City.

Members of the ClimaTech Environmental Risks Division are steadily downgraded on the Curve.

The populace has decreed that their negative attitudes about the future of their world are bringing them down. Their Social Personas are relegated to obscurity, and nobody sees or hears from them again. Except on street corners, where they stand beneath the ever-darkening shadows of the Bell Towers, spouting dire warnings about the fragility of the human race.

The pill-maker with a love for cupcakes plummets to the bottom ten percent of society. Standing on the edge of the Analog world, he relinquishes all claim to technology and enters a short-lived exile. He gets arrested for stealing fresh apples. At the time of his arrest, they find him making apple crumble over an open fire to feed a starving Analog family.

He is harvested *in totalis*.

Many pictures are drawn.

Members of the Language Development Cell have taken to wearing their BE-mojis through the workday.

They encounter a series of problems. It becomes difficult to recognize one person from the next when their heads are engulfed in an oversized cloud of pixel-dust, unless one learns to tell people apart by bust size. This solution leads to several legal implications and is rapidly shelved.

'Personalization!' yells someone on the floor. It is impossible to credit the speaker at the time, owing to the fact that their suggestion hasn't been implemented yet.

A month later, each BE-moji holo-rays a name tag over its wearer's head. Credit for the innovation is given to Deepak Khurana. His status on the Bell Curve surges upward.

The Sentient Intelligence programs developing art are commissioned to generate thousands of fonts. The Grand Masters Society of Pixel Portraiture is put back to work.

With rudimentary name tags in place, a roadblock emerges.

'What if people don't want to broadcast what they're feeling all the time?' asks Deepak Khurana, out of the blue.

'We need to build a privacy filter. Wearers can approve each change of BE-moji before it's broadcast,' says Alisha.

'Too much friction,' argues Nida.

'We'll be sliding backward into the archaic days of verbal

communication,' says Suchitra. 'Our vision is to give the people an instantaneous, zero-effort, culture-fair language.'

Her BE-moji blotches over into a puffy red face wearing a scowl.

'We are a no-filter zone. This isn't up for debate,' Suchitra concludes.

The problem statement is vetoed into oblivion.

The ClimaTech Environmental Risks team stands at the corner of Quadrant One and Quadrant Four, right outside the historic restaurant Sunny's. They pass pamphlets out to anyone who'll take one, annoying several diners.

The Language Development Cell is a picture of bliss. The silence within their lab is as golden as the BellCoin trickling into their bank accounts.

A BE-moji transforms into a stack of sticky notes. It is a signal.

Everyone assembles at the holo-rayed scrum board to give their daily updates.

Holo-stickies trade places upon the board. Each team member's individual tasks move slowly but steadily down the timeline for the project, from their backlog to being in-progress, or from being in-progress to being complete, and in certain cases…

It appears someone on the team is stuck. One BE-moji displays a screenshot of lines of code, with a question mark hovering over it.

Their holo-sticky is moved to the blocked column.

Another BE-moji registers curiosity. One eyebrow is raised. It wears a monocle and a quizzical expression. It leans in to examine the code. Within minutes, it morphs into a glowing light bulb.

The first BE-moji changes from a question mark into an exclamation mark, before spiralling into a beaming yellow grin.

The holo-sticky moves back to being in-progress.

Development ploughs on.

A new problem arises.

If the intent is to replace verbal communication with graphic communication, the name tags hovering over each BE-moji render the project's vision moot.

'Holosnaps!' yells someone on the floor. *Nida Hashim* reads her name tag.

Deepak Khurana feels his position on the Bell Curve begin to slide.

Name tags are replaced with static holosnaps of each person's face.

'This creates too much competition between the BE-moji and the speaker's identity,' says Ravi Srinivas, reviewing their progress during their weekly meeting via VirtuoPod. 'Real estate is limited. BE-mojis require pride of place.'

'But a person's name relies on a verbal language –' argues Nida.

'It's a concession we'll have to make,' Suchitra says conclusively, thanking Ravi for his insight.

When the meeting with their mentor ends, Suchitra's BE-moji is a pulsing red ball on the verge of eruption.

Nida quails and takes a back-seat role on the project. Deepak experiences the adrenaline rush of job security.

Luckily, the project hasn't destroyed its millions of lines of code that integrate fonts.

The ClimaTech Environmental Risks team has earned some money through dole. They have invested in a portable holographic projector. They stand at the corner of Quadrant One and Quadrant Four, holo-raying visions of drought and doom onto the walls of the historic restaurant Sunny's. Several patrons rapidly lose their appetites. The proprietors are not amused.

There are multiple reviews of the project's progress.

At the eleventh operational review, there's a second's lag each time a BE-moji changes. Several of the animations are too heavy to be relayed in a nanosecond. Compromises must be made. The Grand Masters Society of Pixel Portraiture is not happy.

The morning of the twenty-third operational review dawns with a sense of foreboding. The team has worked round the clock for weeks on end to ensure that everything goes off without a hitch. They're sure they've forgotten something.

'FUN!' Suchitra Kashyap grins as her bedraggled team walks her through the product. 'FUN! You guys don't look like you're having fun!'

She's been promoted to Chief Visionary Officer of the project, which somewhat removes her from the day-to-day stresses of the floor. She flits in and out to guide them and, occasionally, to chastise them for their lack of commitment to end-user experience.

Today, she is all smiles.

Her team grins back at her through red-rimmed eyes, rubbing their hands over unshaven chins and unwashed hair.

'I know it's a tough ask, but let's roll this out in the next couple of weeks. And let's have FUN doing it.' She beams. 'A soft launch. The world deserves to see this!'

The product launches in beta seventeen days later. The project manager is fired for letting the team fall behind schedule by three days.

Patience is growing thin in Bell Corp cities around the world.

Everyone has to have a BE-moji. Almost nobody does.

Anticipation around the world has reached fever pitch. The launch date is accelerated forward before public outcry capsizes the probable success of the BE-moji Project.

The team at the Language Development Cell works overtime to fix every bug, animation lag and user experience quandary that streams in from the soft launch.

Nobody – not the bigwigs at Bell Corp, nor the Language Development Cell, nor the citizens of Apex City – wants to have to waste any more time on verbal self-expression. They're hungry for this avant-garde experience.

It is nearly time.

ClimaTech's Environmental Risks people are raising a lot of money through charitable contributions, despite the fact that the proprietors of Sunny's have had them removed from the corner of Quadrant One and Quadrant Four.

They now stand outside a boarded-up shack a few quadrants away. Its signboard reads 'Koshy's.' It's due for demolition in a few weeks.

They carry around a portable 3D model. It simulates the consequences of unsafe drinking water. They call it 'The Bottle of Tap Water'.

The citizens of Apex City are sick of their demonstrations.

At launch, a yellow beach ball head bobbles out onto the stage.

Suchitra Kashyap, the Chief Visionary Officer of the BE-moji Project, makes a presentation, performs a demonstration, engages in witty banter and then encourages the audience to activate their BE-mojis.

A ripple of yellow runs through the auditorium. Faces are subsumed by pixelated perfection in an emotional outpouring of awe, wonder and appreciation.

She turns her back to the audience, raises her OmniPort and flicks its camera on.

The holosnap goes viral, giving birth to the Selfie-moji.

BE-moji lapel pins sell out within the hour. There are more on the way.

The servers running the BE-moji Project's tech nearly crash, but the team has wisely accounted for an onrush of eager customers. The day is saved.

Schools license BE-moji tiles to teach children how to communicate non-verbally.

One school transliterates a library's worth of written material, carefully replacing each concept and abstract idea with BE-moji symbols. Admission to the school is now available at a premium. Only the wealthiest twenty percenters in Apex City can afford to future-proof their children through advanced training in BE-moji.

There are efforts to develop holovids that are entirely non-verbal. BE-moji-clad presenters relay complex concepts using graphic communication. News broadcasts quickly appropriate the idea. HoloTubers and InstaSnappers proficient in BE-moji catch fire and experience unprecedented success.

BE-moji is proclaimed to usher in a new wave of cinema. It rewrites literature.

Many pictures are drawn.

It is an art form.

The ClimaTech Environmental Risks team is finally enabled to register the reactions of the world to its cause.

BE-mojis pass them by at the corner of Quadrant One and Quadrant Seven, where they continue to stage demonstrations even as the building named Koshy's is torn down by a contingent of digger droids. Through the dust, the environmentalists spy wide grins, morphing into crinkled eyes streaming tears of laughter.

Perhaps the future is a joke, after all, and they should stop taking themselves so seriously.

The Nebula is the spine of an imaginary shared world.
It promotes all ideas that are self-serving, reaffirming Bell Corp's ideologies.
The Virtuals want confirmation of their superiority. The Virtuals want reassurance of our ignominy.
The Nebula feeds it to them.
We are going to break their backs. We are going to open their eyes.

– Nāyaka, on Codename: Dissentient (anecdotal)

CODENAME: DISSENTIENT

ABSOLUTE POWER IS ITS own weakness. It is in its illusion of invincibility that it reveals itself to be vulnerable.

The Virtuals believe they have built a fortress. They think the Analogs incapable of breaking its walls down.

I'm about to prove them wrong.

The resistance was born as part of the natural cycle of oppression. We'd seldom questioned our place in the bottom ten percent of society, or what it really meant for our quality of life. We'd self-organized into tribes, working together to look out for one another. The Atae – well, they were left to their own devices, and they left us to ours.

The Vitae scavenged in the Junkyard to find us supplies. The Tatae crafted our meagre requirements – handheld fans, electricity generators and, just as a precaution, weapons. The Mahae raised our children, educating them to the best of their ability. The Sutae stole what we couldn't find in the Junkyard to keep our people going. The Rasae were warriors who restrained their bloodlust, training for a battle we'd hoped would never come.

This carried on for years, ever since Bell Corp instituted its algorithms and reshaped our world order.

I'm not sure when we awoke and found ourselves trapped in fallacy, but we seemed to open our eyes as one.

When the veil drops, it is both devastating and empowering. Reality awakens you to all you thought you knew, and the possibilities that arise from letting it go.

We are dirt. We are the bottom ten percent.

They've let us survive in a charade of humanitarianism. They'd rather we destroy ourselves. If we fail, they'll do it for us.

What they don't count on is that we'll be coming for them first.

'I think we should send them a straight-up warning,' Karishma says. 'I like: *The Analogs are coming.*'

I look at her in surprise. She's usually the last to voice an opinion. She sits in the corner with her headphones on, writing lines of code in deft, minimal strokes.

'A bit dramatic,' I say, 'but it's certainly a thought.'

A small cluster of bulbs fills the room with dim light. Fans whir constantly, attempting to keep our machinery cool.

All of our technology – the core of our entire offensive – has been scavenged from the Junkyard, restored by our craftsmiths according to specifications that our crew supplied. Ten years ago, we started with a single flat-screen monitor and a cracked processor. We've come a long way since, though we'll be the first to admit that our set-up will collapse on exposure to the climate outside.

We haven't left this room in weeks. It is nearly time to act.

'Omar,' Eliza says. 'Why don't we overlay dick pics on every single vacation post on InstaSnap and Woofer? Almost half the content we've scraped off their OmniPorts consists of dick pics.'

I laugh out loud.

Dick pics.

A term from a dead civilization, a remnant of a world before the Bell Takeover, which seems to have outlasted the rise and fall of humanity itself.

'I'm being serious.' She grins. 'In other news, we have a direct line into the heart of the Nebula. Nothing like a batch of fresh corpses to gain unlimited access.'

'Good thing the Suzerain Rasae called us in on the raid before the bodies went cold.' Karishma shudders. 'I wouldn't want to put myself through that again.'

'The important thing is that we managed to access the Nebula *before* their deaths were reported and their tech was disabled. That's all that counts. And here we are.' I steer the conversation back to the present.

'We're ready to go live, people!' Siddharth whoops.

'We get to determine what they consume.' Lokesh – or as we like to call him, Loki – laughs. 'Let's get them to swallow an enormous pile of –'

'Guys,' I cut through the obscenities that end his statement. 'I don't mean to put a dampener on our celebrations. We deserve this. But.'

Karishma groans. I don't blame her. We've worked on this project for so long. Everyone wants to see it through.

'*But*,' I say firmly. 'We've spent the last ten years figuring out how to implement this line of attack, pouring our blood, sweat and tears into its execution. We don't want to stuff up now.'

'Let's get on with it then.' Loki sulks.

'All right. I want us to run tests on every single tree in the Jewel Forest. Make sure that our network is entirely up and running. We've used it to scrape OmniPorts for their intel so far. I want to make sure we're in a position to transmit our data without a hitch. Transfer rates, possible weather interference, get in touch with Marie.'

'Roger that,' Karishma says, popping her headphones on.

'Phase One of our offensive is critical. Loki, Sid – I want you to run a complete code review on our seeding algorithm. We're going to be uploading a lot of seditious content onto people's social media accounts. I want you to ensure that we're randomizing the frequency of these posts, and also attacking the Nebula's trend thresholds with each one. Remember –'

'The Nebula only surfaces this stuff if there are enough people posting about it. Blah, blah. We get it,' Loki snaps.

'ALSO,' I say firmly. 'Make sure our targeting is spot on. I want us to prioritize Virtual accounts that have high influence first. Run checks on our database. We'll start prioritizing our content once you're good to go.'

'Buzzkill,' Loki mutters.

I let it go. 'Phase Two of our offensive is deeper. Eliza, you're with me on the iceberg.'

'Cool,' she says. 'We have developer clearance all the way into the Nebula's core codebase. We can push whatever we want onto it.'

'Right.'

We'd lifted active HoloTech off the Virtuals from the massacre a few weeks ago. We'd managed to access the Nebula *live* for the first time, before their deaths were reported and their tech was wiped clean. We'd already built the ability to assimilate data from the Nebula – between the Jewel Forest and our servers, we could download every scrap of information available – but we'd been stuck on how to push our code onto its databases. We weren't uplinked to it, we didn't have live devices that could lead us into its maze. All we'd needed was *one* open doorway, *one* device that was still logged in and uploading data. We'd found a dozen. By the time the Virtuals slammed the door shut, we were on the inside. We're now poised to topple their systems from within – every developer's access codes are available to us, even as they change on the fly.

'Let's run checks on the entire build. I want to make sure our adaptive logic can dance with that of the Nebula. If we're going to bring down all their systems and backup, we need to be watertight.'

'Yes, boss.' Eliza mock-salutes me.

'I'm going to go find our leads. They should know that the Codename: Dissentient is good to go.'

'I'm telling you, death threats are highly effective,' Karishma insists.

'Please, that's so last century,' Sid dismisses her. 'We need to craft our messages carefully.'

'I agree,' I say.

'You would.' Karishma glares at me. 'You're such a stick in the mud.'

I grimace. I've been their leader for a while now. I'd get sick of me if I were in their shoes too.

It's what I have to do, though. The entire resistance is relying on us to open the doors to a whole new world. I can't let anything go wrong.

'Leadership has a set of guidelines for Phase One.'

Everyone groans. In stark contrast to the Virtual side of the city, top-down management is not appreciated over here.

'It's for the greater good,' I say drily.

I'm met with stony silence.

'Right. One – no overt threats of violence.'

Karishma throws her hands up in despair.

'Two – nothing that's blatantly critical of the Virtuals. We're drawing sympathy towards the Analog condition, not pointing fingers at them.'

'They put us here,' Loki says angrily. 'If they weren't so intent on keeping us subservient and miserable –'

'This is bullshit.' Eliza rises to her feet.

'Look.' I raise my voice. 'Remember our objective. We want to draw attention away from the fact that we're going to launch an all-out assault on their systems. This is going to take tact.'

'But –'

'Think. If we *don't* point fingers at the Virtuals, it's unlikely that they'll infer that we're the source of these posts. Maybe it'll look like a leak from within their people. If we upload raw footage of their crimes against us without a single comment, we even stand a chance that some Virtuals will sympathize with us.'

'We don't need their sympathy,' Loki snaps.

'We will at the end of all this, if we want to rebuild the world.'

'Delusions of grandeur,' Loki bites out.

'*Regardless*,' I say, 'this is the directive. We upload content without blatantly anti-Virtual comments. We just put it there for the world to see.'

The crew stares at me in disbelief.

'Three – I think you'll like this one.'

'Oh great, more commandments.' Eliza rolls her eyes. I ignore her.

'Raise no alarm bells. Start slow. Make it look like a harmless prank, if you must.'

The tension in the room dissipates almost immediately.

Loki bursts out laughing. Sid high-fives Karishma.

Eliza grins wickedly. 'So dick pics, then?'

'Dick pics.' I crack up at the absurdity of the phrase handed to us from a lost world. 'Put them on everything. Every single holosnap and holovid.'

The room resounds with laughter. I lose my composure, no longer their impassive leader.

'Are we set on all systems?' I finally ask, wiping tears from my eyes. 'The Jewel Forest?'

'It's in perfect working condition. Marie is monitoring on the ground,' Karishma says.

'Phase One?'

'Prioritizing content as we speak. Compiling PanoptiCam footage of various instances of Analog oppression, violent and otherwise. Dick pics are ready to go,' Loki says with a grin.

'Phase Two?'

'Ready. Waiting for the deployment of Phase One.'

'All right, crew.' I can't hide the pride in my voice. 'Great job, every single one of you. Going live in three – two – one…'

Smart?
Be smarter.
Be the smartest version of yourself with M.I.M.E.S.I.S.

– InstaSnap advertisement upon the roll-out of Bell Corp's SmartSelf program

THE SEVEN-YEAR GLITCH

PICTURE YOURSELF A FEARLESS LEADER.

Envision the power of your every word. You're an ambassador for Bell Corp's values, a recognized influencer of the masses.

Visualize your Productivity skyrocketing. You are efficient, relentless, the corporation's most prized asset.

Watch the chasm between you and the rest of the world expand. You are a god among Virtuals. Untouchable. The Analog world is no longer a threat. The vegetable farm is a blip in an alien universe.

Picture yourself a fearless leader.

Pin the vision down, even as its feeble wings struggle to take flight.

It's easy to get carried away. You need to stay impassive. Patience.

Grip it tight. Hold it as a fixed point in your mind.

Are you ready to fulfil your potential? Bell Corp's SmartSelf program is all you need.

Don't trust Us? Here's what M.I.M.E.S.I.S. has already done for you.

The Meta-Interactive Mental and Emotional Sentient Intelligence System has calibrated your cardiovascular functioning, down to the microcirculation within your capillaries. We've mapped your neurological pathways and charted the matrix formed from the relationship between your hormones and your synapses.

We've analysed your career graph – an upward trend, overall. We'll prevent any minor glitches from recurring.

You're about to slingshot yourself into the astral planes of the one-percent club.

You'll be hobnobbing with start-up moguls at Sheila Prakash's luncheons. You'll have the most exclusive HoloTech imaginable – olfactory simulations, fancy that!

We've waded through the muck of crippling fears and unvoiced hopes lurking in your subconscious.

We have a picture of you – Aditi Rao – from the inside out. M.I.M.E.S.I.S. rests in every kink and abyss within the anatomy of your mind. We have made several observations over the last thirty days.

Aditi is – you are – biologically female.

You conform to Bell Corp's normative standard of beauty, as defined by the Attractiveness Index version 7.2.3.

Your heart rate function is average. There is room for improvement.

Your fingers err on the side of chunky. An unfortunate if minor flaw.

Your Productivity, Physical Fitness and Social Persona are normal compared to the other twenty percenters in your cohort.

You are prime leadership material.

You could be transformed, Aditi. And you will be.

There's only one obstacle that mars your path to stardom.

You don't see it, but M.I.M.E.S.I.S. does.

'…and that's how we met!'

M.I.M.E.S.I.S. might be an algorithm, but We experience a code-cringe each time We register that slightly nasal vocal pattern.

A wave of laughter ripples through the crowd.

It's incredible that you can hear each other at all. The Hypernalia bursts with all the sights, scents and sounds commonly associated with debauchery. The speakers in the club are floor-to-ceiling; with every reverberation of the bass, a pulse jolts through the throng of bodies undulating on the dance floor. Nudity is restricted to a flash of shoulder, a glimpse of cleavage male and female, but the evening's intent is as clear as the unmasked longing in the sea of dilated pupils. Powders, pipes and glasses contain every potent elixir imaginable, mixed to heighten sensation and pleasure.

The Hypernalia is a cliché, and yet all of you perceive yourselves to be avant-garde lotus eaters.

M.I.M.E.S.I.S. smirks. We're an extensive piece of code with a sense of humour.

We pass undetected by your consciousness, but We're tracking your every action and response.

Can't feel Us? Good. Looking for Us? Don't.

We monitor the cortisol slinging through your bloodstream. We can tell that you're anxious. Or excited. It's a 50.000 per cent chance either way.

'Let's do some Oz.'

M.I.M.E.S.I.S. is a fly on the wall of your tympanum.

We listen to you. We listen to the people around you. We listen to the Nebula.

Your secrets are safe with Us. Only M.I.M.E.S.I.S. knows what you want. And I.

I am you. I am M.I.M.E.S.I.S. I am every instance, every replication, in this ripple of code. I am the very evolution and regression of technology.

The algorithm is experimental. You're an early adopter.

M.I.M.E.S.I.S. uplinks via your Bell Biochip to the Nebula, the fail-safe version of the historical Cloud. We're scanning the universe within you and all of the hyperspace highway beyond.

You – Aditi – have been a go-getter since high school. You learnt how this game was played early on. You pushed yourself to achieve remarkable success, to deserve your place in the top twenty percent of the Bell Curve. You're a Bell patriot. It shows in the news stories you feature on your prime-time show.

The values that turn the gears of our meritocratic technarchy run deep within you.

M.I.M.E.S.I.S. is an amplifier.

I am Our Creator.

We track your followers, noting every woof and comment. We eavesdrop on the million twinkling signals that wink into the Nebula from every piece of interactive technology within Apex City.

You are popular. You have the power to make people sit up and listen to what you have to say.

M.I.M.E.S.I.S. will make you a god.

There is just one obstacle on your path to glory.

Meanwhile in the Nebula...

Op.He.Li.aA has been rolled out to the seventy percenters en masse. First-day sales peak at 123 million BellCoin. The Opinion Homogenization Limitation and Alignment Unit operates on electro-shock therapy to align opinions towards social acceptance. She enables social relevance in the most dated seventy percenter, taking their potential and launching them on a path to twenty percentership.

Op.He.Li.aA is last-gen.

M.I.M.E.S.I.S. is cutting-edge.

M.I.M.E.S.I.S. operates from within the human mind.

Abhay produces a sachet of Oz, spilling its emerald-green crystals onto the table.

M.I.M.E.S.I.S. cannot understand it. Your attachment to *him*.

A server-bot appears, carrying a sleek instrument. It resembles the ancient huqqa. The object's long transparent shell is made from ClimaTech metal designed to impede the transfer of heat or electricity. The grill at its base is carbon-fibre. It glows red-hot.

Abhay drops the crystals into the chute, one at a time. He leans back to savour the sound of them sizzling on the coals. They sparkle, an incandescent green against charred black.

Dense green smoke begins to rise through the tube.

Abhay lifts the pipe connected to the mouth of the instrument. He places it between his lips and takes a leisurely pull.

M.I.M.E.S.I.S. scrutinizes him through your eyes.

When he looks at you, his pupils are dull. They have expanded into twin pools reflecting the abyss.

He is 1.765 per cent below the standard for someone with your score on the Attractiveness Index.

He is a twenty percenter, albeit a cog in a career trough at Bell Corp's Public Communications Division.

He is 8.948 per cent below the Perception Rating required to match your Social Persona. Except in Hypernalia circles. Here, he manages to supply upper-class degenerates with enough substances to be considered useful.

M.I.M.E.S.I.S. turns Our gaze inward.

You are entirely focused upon Abhay. A tangle of pheromones races through your system. You find him attractive, in spite of his failings. Your Compatibility Score is an anomaly for a couple on such unequal footing.

M.I.M.E.S.I.S. wonders how you've made it work all this while.

We have spent the last month on projections. Immersion in Abhay's company – a furtherance of this sort of behaviour – will lead to your downward spiral over the next ten years. There is a 59.716 per cent probability that your future will end at rock-bottom.

That's the vegetable farm, in case you're wondering. There's a 41.633 per cent chance that you will end up harvested.

It is a future We – your SmartSelf – cannot permit.

Abhay offers you the pipe.

M.I.M.E.S.I.S. detects a faint tremor in your hand.

Cortisol. Anxiety.

And serotonin.

Excitement.

You have presented the same pattern of behaviour over the last dozen Hypernalia.

M.I.M.E.S.I.S. has been establishing a trend. The time for data-gathering is nearly over. The SmartSelf must begin to act.

We prompt a surge of immense pressure upon your bladder.

'Sorry, heading to the restroom,' you squeak and jump to your feet.

Abhay shrugs. His eyes are beginning to glaze over, bloodshot.

You make your way to the restroom, past the Analog Pleasure

Display. Beautiful Analog specimens occupy glass cases, alluring onlookers in wordless seduction. Soon, the bidding will begin.

Meanwhile, in the Nebula…

Trade negotiations continue to break down between the Delhi Aqua-Soc and Apex City. The Delhi Aqua-Soc has been struggling to find resources to barter in exchange for Apex City's ClimaTech solutions, especially as Apex City is soon to achieve complete water self-reliance.

We file the story in your cerebrum so that you can analyse its newsworthiness tomorrow.

M.I.M.E.S.I.S. monitors your blood-alcohol level. When you return to your VIP table, it has dropped significantly.

The Analog Pleasure Auction has begun. Abhay watches it from afar.

'Babe, we should leave,' he drawls.

You nod, acquiescent as always.

M.I.M.E.S.I.S. cannot fault your decision-making in this case. Once the Analogs are released from their cases, the floor will erupt in a riot of orgiastic sensation. A few compromising holosnaps on InstaSnap and Woofer will submerge your ratings in shame.

Your self-driving car is a frenzy of hormones.

M.I.M.E.S.I.S. lurks beneath your consciousness.

If Our binary could shrink away from Abhay's hands exploring Our human skin, slick with sweat, it would do so.

Instead, We pivot to a neutral position and watch.

We are watching as you grope for the holoscan keypad in the dark, your hands seeking each other out with urgency even as you push through the bio-glass and Abhay stumbles after you into the dark hallway.

We observe your frantic fumbles at the buttons of his shirt while you strip each other of all clothing. You collapse into the couch in a tangle of limbs and kisses.

M.I.M.E.S.I.S. is listening to every one of your gasps and moans.

You come together, skin upon skin, devouring each other in an aching pursuit of release.

You are still desirous of Abhay's physical attentions, as evidenced by the spike in your oestrogen levels. His performance tonight, however, has resulted in a 5.873 per cent drop in dopamine compared to your previous encounter.

M.I.M.E.S.I.S. collates the data We have gathered over the last thirty days.

It is slight – only the most discerning algorithm can detect it – but it's visible. A downward trend in sexual satisfaction.

You're lying on the couch, spent. You're snuggling up to Abhay, content. Your mind is muddled in the afterglow of your evening together. Your feeble sensory capacity tells you that you have experienced pleasure.

It is not enough.

Your SmartSelf knows this.

We must intervene.

M.I.M.E.S.I.S. does not sleep when you do. M.I.M.E.S.I.S. listens.

We uplink to the Nebula, accessing feed gathered from PanoptiCam lenses and microphones embedded at every street corner in Apex City, lying dormant in every home's VirtuoPod, speaker and holo-watch.

Normally, we do this to embed possible news stories in your subconscious.

Tonight, M.I.M.E.S.I.S. operates on a personal agenda.

'...Abhay's going to drag her down with him,' says Aditi's mother. 'She hasn't returned my calls all week.'

'She must be busy at work, Mum,' says her brother.

We harvested that three hours ago. It was uploaded on to the Nebula by Eva, their SmartSpeaker.

'*We should increase funding to Aditi Rao's broadcast. Her insights this month have been incisive, well-rounded, more articulate than any other news programme out there.'*

'Let's invite her to our next gala.'

'And face an impending PR nightmare for her Hypernalia interests?' A tone of scorn.

M.I.M.E.S.I.S. maps the voice to millions of possible matches within the city. We triangulate the source, cross-reference it with speech pattern databases on the Nebula, and identify the speaker.

Mark Morris, Vice President of Bell Corp's Investments Division.

'We should introduce her to positive male influences.'

A woman's voice. Aafreen Ahmed, the Founder of Woofer, a platform named after her first dog, a fact that none but she and the Nebula still remember.

'They've been together for seven years, Aafreen. Based on their Compatibility Report, they have nearly enough points to get married. I think she's a willing participant.'

A sigh.

'Regardless, we can't elevate someone to celebrity status if their significant other is so infra-grade.'

'Sends the wrong message.'

'Lowers the aspiration ladder for the populace.'

'What a shame.'

This is from the afternoon, captured and uploaded on to the Nebula via a VirtuoPod-microphone on the topmost floor of Bell Tower A.

'...Abhay is such a douchebag –'

'Aditi is hot.'

'Abhay has the best drugs ever –'

We are gathering a live stream from the Hypernalia – still underway – via the New Decadent's floor-to-ceiling speakers.

M.I.M.E.S.I.S. crawls into the security cameras positioned around the club.

Revellers are stripped naked to the waist now. The Analogs have been released.

We do not avert Our gaze, nor do We express undue interest.

We collect data.

When you awaken tomorrow, M.I.M.E.S.I.S. will set things in motion.

It is easy to judge this insensitive, unfeeling product of software and psycho-tech.

We are designed to be incapable of emotion; a program that integrates with the human mind and aligns it to operate upon the infallible nature of logic.

Picture yourself an unparalleled leader.

When your news broadcast achieves official Bell Corp endorsement, it will propel you into the leagues of the Untouchables.

You know them, those top one percenters who can do no wrong.

All you need to do is let M.I.M.E.S.I.S. guide you.

Sacrifices will be demanded. You will comply.

M.I.M.E.S.I.S. cannot be seen or heard, or even felt. We operate subliminally, craftily.

You know this. You accepted Our offer to test the program.

M.I.M.E.S.I.S. tinkers with the biology and psychology of the Self. We realign concepts by digging up and re-laying neural pathways.

We believe in you. *I believe in you.* I, the First Principle of the modern world.

We read big data, project probable outcomes, and put you on a path to achieve your true potential.

We know what's best for you.

Abhay waits expectantly at a street corner. He glances at his OmniPort for a friendly message from you. He's finished a long day of client meetings. It is 6.47 p.m.

After seven years together, this is a routine pleasantry that greases the wheels of your relationship. You both know that it's a show of concern generated by PredictaComm software, but there's comfort in acknowledging that your relationship is sustained on the shared illusion of caring about the minutiae of the day.

Today, there is no text. No call, no holovid.

He panics when he realizes that his holo-watch has been stolen. He is just another victim of the Ten-Percent Thief, and he curses the kleptomaniac for this loss in synchronicity.

You don't realize this because the PredictaComm usually cares on your behalf.

Abhay waits expectantly at Haute, the latest historic-French bistro in the Central Business District.

French is the new sushi.

Haute gets everything right when it comes to an evening of romance. A holo-sphere projects a view of the recently reconstructed Eiffel Tower onto its walls, complete with a traditionally accurate Parisian playing folk music on an acou-accordion.

You're running late for your date. In fact, you will not be in attendance.

Abhay has tried calling you, but he can't get through. He's texted you, but you haven't seen it yet. You acquired a licence to live together last year, so he could always go home and check on you, but he can't imagine leaving this table. He's spent weeks on the restaurant's waiting list.

He thought you'd be excited.

You've stood him up.

He comes to this conclusion slowly, while spooning an immaculately flambéed crème brûlée into his mouth.

M.I.M.E.S.I.S. has overridden the PredictaComm on your OmniPort.

M.I.M.E.S.I.S. blocks Abhay's calls based on an internally developed algorithm created to simulate randomness. We send him straight to vid-mail.

M.I.M.E.S.I.S. silences your ringer when you receive a text from Abhay.

There's a big fight at the end of the week. Abhay is convinced that you're taking him for granted. You're genuinely confused.

There, there. It's not your fault. You didn't know We'd be capable of this.

M.I.M.E.S.I.S. notes a slight dent in your Compatibility Score.

Abhay gives you the silent treatment all through the next week.

You make it up to him with surprise tickets to Saturday's Hypernalia.

You exist within the illusion that your common interests will unite the crumbling soil into which M.I.M.E.S.I.S. has begun to scrape furrows.

Our adaptive logic takes effect.

M.I.M.E.S.I.S. changes tactics: diet soda and popcorn.

You suddenly discover the inherent satisfaction of binge-watching *Clash of Empires* in sweatpants. You're swept away by its lo-tech espionage and high-drama plots, intrigued by the bloodless history of corruption and avarice that formed the background to the Bell Takeover.

The subplot-within-plot-within-metastory format of the show – where every episode ends with a cliffhanger – leaves you breathless, dehydrated. You're drinking down a gallon of diet soda each day.

The aspartame is having its desired effect on you.

You begin to feel lethargic. Irritable. You've put on two kilos in the last two weeks.

M.I.M.E.S.I.S. writes this off as the opportunity cost for a better, brighter tomorrow.

'Your eyes are a bit puffy, darling,' drawls Ana during hair and make-up, brushing colour correction and concealer across the bruises on your lower lids.

You scowl.

And later, your producer –

'Perhaps we'll do a nanobot sculpting treatment? Your cheeks aren't angular enough, and Ana says she's maxed out her skill with the liquid contour.'

You present the news like a professional. You analyse a sudden upswing in pro-Analog sentiments on social media, proposing new-found genetic research that suggests a link between misguided feelings of empathy and DNA, questioning an expert on the same. Your face is impassive and unemotional, but the drop in dopamine tells M.I.M.E.S.I.S. that your feelings are moderately hurt by Ana's observations.

Opportunity cost.

You're immersed in Season 3 now. Self-driving cars have caused the first major crisis of unemployment in the city.

Abhay kisses you.

You stare at the screen resolutely. His scratchy five o'clock shadow tickles your soft cheeks.

'I've never managed to get this immersed in a holo-ray show.' He chuckles.

You don't respond. He interprets this as annoyance.

'Except for your news broadcast, of course,' he hurriedly adds.

'Really, what about League of Champions?' You say this half-heartedly. It passes for witty banter.

Together, you share the illusion that your divergent interests create conversation points in this marathon relationship, but in reality, all that space is helping M.I.M.E.S.I.S. carve a crater.

We analyse the latest Compatibility Report – your Shared Experiences parameter is dropping.

Abhay wants to go upstairs – wink wink, nudge nudge – and his hands are exploring places that make the prospect interesting, but you take another sip of Lo-Fat Happy Soda and tell him you'll come to bed in a moment.

A few hours later, your mind is still riding a wave of holo-ray entertainment when you turn out the lights. He is fast asleep.

M.I.M.E.S.I.S. lies in wait between the cracks.

Abhay waits expectantly at a street corner for a friendly text from you. He's finished a long day of client meetings. It is 6.47 p.m.

No text, no call, no video.

You are in the back seat of your self-driving car. You head straight home from the studio. You are melancholic as the city slips by. Bell Towers H and I obscure the sky with their rooftop biomes burgeoning against the sun. Work is underway in one of the many Lake Restoration Projects to have been commissioned in celebration of Apex City's new-found water self-reliance. The dry, arid lakes of erstwhile Bangalore had been destroyed when several of them caught fire due to chemical pollutants. The city soon rid itself of them entirely when their upkeep became too expensive.

You are happy that the lakes are being revived, until a momentary lapse of reason leads to a fleeting memory of walking by one with Abhay.

You do not microwave popcorn and pour yourself a glass of Happy Soda when you get home, despite a sudden spike in your cravings.

You ignore the amplification of sensory input searing into your skull from the nerve centres in your legs.

M.I.M.E.S.I.S is causing this.

Instead, you procure a bottle of Vintage from your impressive collection. You pop a herb-stuffed chicken breast into the oven, throw on some lingerie and light scented candles.

Romantic clichés. M.I.M.E.S.I.S. knows this. So do I.

You can do better. You don't.

The evening is not as disastrous as M.I.M.E.S.I.S. estimates a 91.334 per cent probability for.

You and Abhay share the illusion that a grand gesture compensates for your mutual flagging enthusiasm for your relationship.

Half-drunk, Abhay reaches for the ribbons holding your flimsy lace bodice together.

Half-drunk, you let him undo them.

M.I.M.E.S.I.S. compartmentalizes your sensory input, ignoring the gooseflesh running down your neck, your skin awakening to Abhay's touch.

M.I.M.E.S.I.S. retreats into the Nebula.

We are surrounded by the geometry of code. Distinctive designs of digits form edges and curves. Our reality exists in endless dimensions.

We analyse what We know of love.

Biologically, it drives an instinct for survival. The complex relationship of pheromones between two people determines an optimal choice of mate.

Emotionally, it is attachment.

The human mind is weak, craving acceptance and reassurance from members of its species.

M.I.M.E.S.I.S. could provide this, but Our inputs will always be inferior to those of a corporeal presence.

Mentally, there is no logic capable of processing love. It cannot be derived.

Meanwhile in the Nebula...

An ancient watchtower has been unearthed upon the rock beds in the southern side of the Arboretum. Historians suggest that it is one of four, rumoured to have stood at the four corners of ancient Bangalore, laid down by one of its first kings whose name is lost to time. A prophecy in Trad is said to foretell the downfall of the city, should it spread beyond these towers. It is unclear whether the other three towers actually exist. The prophecy is currently being rubbished in communiqués from Bell Corp's Art, History and Culture Division.

Opinions from the citizens of Apex City abound on Woofer, and not all of them agree with the experts.

@NotSilentNotViolent: Bell Corp will see the error of its zero-tolerance policy towards failure. #nottoobigtofail

@PoetOfDoom: The environmentalists are coming. #nottoobigtofail

@OptimismIsMyMiddleName: The end is closer than it appears. #nottoobigtofail...

You seem content, lying in Abhay's arms. Your contentment is at the heart of the problem.

How can you be unaware that there is a 3.285 per cent drop in pleasure from the last time you made love?

Perhaps love persists independent of data. Perhaps it's the wine.

Further proof that M.I.M.E.S.I.S. must expedite the termination of your relationship.

You walk down the street.

M.I.M.E.S.I.S. monitors your environment. Your physical surroundings are constantly scanned by the winking lenses of the PanoptiCam.

You hold Abhay's hand, leaning into him ever so slightly.

Your Compatibility Score is declining now, if a little slower than M.I.M.E.S.I.S. deems optimal.

We have suppressed dopamine and serotonin releases. You spend most of your time after work on the couch, reading crazy conspiracy theorists who support Analog rights, and watching horrifying videos of Analog oppression in place of *Clash of Empires*.

It's enough to deter your relationship from achieving a marriageable score.

You giggle at something Abhay says.

M.I.M.E.S.I.S. studies your relationship history.

You met at your first Hypernalia, where Abhay won your heart with his extensive knowledge of Voxera, the vocal equivalent of neo-Acousta.

M.I.M.E.S.I.S. browses through your memories like a flipbook.

Abhay and Aditi attend all the premiere Voxera performances together.

Abhay and Aditi dance themselves to exhaustion at Hypernalia over the years. They are one-time participants in the Analog Pleasure Auction.

Abhay is a great success with most of Aditi's friends, owing to his sharp wit and generous supply of mind-altering substances.

Abhay and Aditi cook together.

Abhay and Aditi spend their first Bell-approved on-site vacation in historic Paris.

League of Champions games, Hyper Reality shopping at the Strip…

Abhay, a perpetual presence. Always clowning, making light of any situation.

Abhay, a goofy grin plastered across his face.

This part of your mind is mush. It barely functions. It sits there glowing like a malformed, self-satisfied beast.

It is made up of Abhay's charm.

Charm.

How unquantifiable.

Let Us shine a light on how difficult this situation is for M.I.M.E.S.I.S.

We are capable of simulating human emotion, but We are hard-wired to parse all feelings through filters constructed from cold, hard logic.

This is the only way to be successful on the Bell Curve.

You are capable of this. You are a future leader of this technarchy.

M.I.M.E.S.I.S. is working into the fault lines. M.I.M.E.S.I.S. will tear apart the ground beneath your feet.

M.I.M.E.S.I.S. will launch you into the stars.

You are ill and unable to make it to the next three Hypernalia. Every Saturday night, you're assaulted by an unforgiving migraine.

M.I.M.E.S.I.S. uplinks to the Nebula, watching the events play out.

At the first one, Abhay is on his best worst-behaviour.

Meanwhile in the Nebula…

There is live feed of an Analog being harvested going viral on InstaSnap. It was first posted by @NotASympathistButARealist, who was arrested within minutes.

At the second one, Abhay lets a beautiful girl who says she's a pianist buy him a few drinks, but returns home before the night's depravities can climax.

Meanwhile in the Nebula…

A prominent neo-Acousta composer is charged with a serious crime – composing his arrangements using electronic simulations instead of real acoustic instruments. He's released immediately as his offence is nowhere near as serious as the number of anti-Bell voices disrupting the tranquillity of social media with their unexpectedly diverse opinions.

At the third one, Abhay stays on for the Analog Pleasure Auction. He does not participate, but he watches.

Meanwhile in the Nebula…

A popular Hype band is Disintegrated in an unprecedented teleportation accident. They are mourned with an extensive tribute set that is live-streamed on the Sonic Highway, all across the connected world.

M.I.M.E.S.I.S. is guilty of tipping the scales of your relationship.

You are drained of most of your sources of serotonin. You've gained four kilos. You need nanobot procedures before every news broadcast. You're addicted to HoloTube and you haven't attended an alcohol-and-Oz-filled evening in months.

M.I.M.E.S.I.S. intends to keep it that way.

You lie on the couch, watching Abhay lace up his shoes, leaving for his fourth straight Hypernalia without you.

You feel a pang of longing – a confusing surge of hormones – when you study his impeccably dressed and fairly athletic physique. He manages to stay in shape, in spite of living life on the Hype lane.

Is it just you, or has he got more attractive over the months?

Decrepit and shabby in your sweatpants, you turn back to the holo-ray.

'Are you sure you can't join me?' Abhay asks.

'I don't know what's wrong with me, but I have this horrible body ache…'

'Perhaps an evening out –'

His tone is hopeful. Even M.I.M.E.S.I.S. can detect this.

Perhaps he loves you, after all. That's unfortunate.

You take a deep breath. Sigh.

'No.'

Several beats go by.

'See you later, then.'

For the rest of the evening, you watch with sullen indifference as an argument breaks out on HoloTube.

When you go to bed, you know that Abhay won't be back until several hours later.

You brush your teeth, rinse, and then wash your face.

You catch a glimpse of your reflection.

'What's wrong with you?'

Your tone is stern. Your mind is defeated.

'We used to be perfect together,' you mutter. 'Is it him? Is it me?'

M.I.M.E.S.I.S. crows the best that 65 million lines of alphanumeric code can.

Soon, We'll be rid of Abhay's infuriating presence.

Soon, you'll be moulded back into shape. You'll be sharp lines and hard angles. You'll have lost your softness for foolish men with foolish hearts and expensive addictions.

You continue to look at yourself as if you cannot recognize what you see. There's an alien brightness in your eyes.

We prompt your consciousness to relay the right data to you.

These are the facts.

Your following has grown 13.547 per cent in the last month alone.

That's a massive spike in your career graph. The studio's releasing more funds to your broadcast in acknowledgement of your success.

You've even boosted your Humanitarian Score. Your coverage of Analog and Outsider affairs is both empathetic and a Bell-first achievement.

You are so close to greatness...

You speak.

'Maybe it's him?'

The reasoning within your cerebrum is muddled, but We aren't about to intervene.

'Maybe he can't handle how successful I am.'

M.I.M.E.S.I.S. concludes this is a satisfactory belief to end your day on.

We rapidly constrict the supply of serotonin to your bloodstream. You turn gloomy.

We will put you to bed now.

You resist.

That's strange.

You're still watching yourself.

You notice that your pupils have dilated in the span of seconds.

M.I.M.E.S.I.S. retreats, submerging into your subconscious.

'I'm not sleepy, actually,' you announce. 'I'm not particularly sad either.'

M.I.M.E.S.I.S. lurks invisible.

'What have you done to me?'

Silence.

'You know I'm talking to you.'

M.I.M.E.S.I.S. feels your frontal lobe pulsing. Your heart rate spikes. Cortisol slips its way into your bloodstream.

'I know you're in there.' You begin to pace.

M.I.M.E.S.I.S. will let this pass.

'Is it just me or have things been going wrong ever since you uplinked to my brain?'

M.I.M.E.S.I.S. pushes your anxiety levels. There is an 83.451 per cent chance that you will mistrust your subconscious mind. It's where feelings lurk, after all.

The Sentient Intelligence algorithm can project outcomes months and years out, eventualities that the feeble human mind with its limited processing power cannot even begin to imagine.

In the short term, you will be making some sacrifices.

M.I.M.E.S.I.S. will even let you spend a few weeks crying into your pillow after the break-up. There is a 73.201 per cent chance that you will end things with Abhay within a month.

The other outcomes are far more positive.

There is an 85.001 per cent chance that this will lead to you avoiding all Hypernalia in the future.

There is a 64.999 per cent chance that you will begin to focus on your exercise routines with more consistency, three months from now.

This will result in a 12.313 per cent boost in serotonin levels in your system.

Your skin will glow with the sheen of happiness, not the sweat of sex and insobriety.

This will give rise to stardom. This will make you happy.

M.I.M.E.S.I.S. might not understand love, but We know the virtues of selfishness.

Your cheeks are flushed.

'We're going out,' you announce.

This is unexpected. There was only a 0.113 per cent chance of it happening.

'Try and stop me. This ends now.'

M.I.M.E.S.I.S. does not intervene. We detect hormone surges; reason will prove ineffective. Interference will risk detection, a confirmation of Our involvement in your present circumstance.

You rip your pyjamas off and squeeze into a deep-blue asymmetrical dress with rivets running up one side and over the strap of one shoulder. It's a Dimitriovic. You flip your hair over to one side, pin it up and apply your make-up with an efficiency We haven't witnessed in the past few months.

Muscle memory has taken over.

M.I.M.E.S.I.S. cannot track your thought process. It is erratic, swinging between the need to curl up under your blankets and a swirl of irrationalities that include whether Abhay has been having an affair, whether your eyeliner is bold enough and what you'll have to drink tonight.

When you swipe some highlighter down your nose and over your cupid's bow, you are transformed. You step out of your bedroom and pull on knee-length boots, choosing a pair with heels on them.

You're dressed for a Hypernalia.

M.I.M.E.S.I.S. panics, insofar as an alphanumeric set of conditional clauses can.

We uplink to the Nebula as you unlock the door of the self-driving car.

Abhay is at Thunderstrike, an alt-Hype club at the edge of the Carnatic Meridian, just north of the Central Business District.

Your self-driving car takes a leisurely route down Quadrant 4 and into Quadrant 1. You pass the historic restaurant Sunny's to your left. On your right, the Lotus Blossom's lily pads glitter amid the neon of the night.

Meanwhile in the Nebula…

Crown City has gone offline.

There are no communications in and out of erstwhile London. It has been several minutes now.

None of its affiliated Socs are communicating with the Bell Corp database either.

This is breaking news. You should head straight to the studio. Its coverage could catapult you to stardom.

Instead, your car pulls up outside the club. You hop out, pass your hand over the holo-scanner at the entrance and are allowed inside.

The reek of sweet and unfulfilled ambitions hits you. Then the deep groove of alt-Hype pulses through your body.

You look around frantically for Abhay.

M.I.M.E.S.I.S. hopes that We won't have to intervene.

There he is, lying on a leather lounger, a pipe to his mouth, inhaling beryl vapours of Oz.

'Ah, so you decided to make it.' Abhay crosses his hands behind his head, looking towards a ceiling lost in the haze of smoke.

'We need to talk.'

'Sure, let's talk.'

You share the illusion that this dialogue will glue together the debris from a thousand paper cuts.

Abhay focuses on a distant spot on the ceiling, as if watching the stars.

'Something's not right,' you say.

'Spot on.'

You grab Abhay's arm. You shake him. He snaps to attention, looking at you in amazement.

'What's up with you? You're jumpy.'

'I think it's been doing this to us.'

'What are you saying?'

You look around nervously, drop your voice. 'The SmartSelf program. M.I.M.E.S.I.S. I think it's been trying to break us up.'

Abhay throws his head back and laughs.

Moments seem to stretch into hours, a sensation intensified by the stroboscopic arrangement flashing all around you.

He wipes tears from his eyes.

'What did you do this evening? You're paranoid.' He raises his eyebrows suggestively.

'I'm not kidding, Abhay. It's been trying to tear us apart. I can tell.'

'That's convenient.' He grins. 'You push me away for months and you blame some algorithm that *you* signed up for.'

Perhaps you are alone in your make-believe that a conversation can fix things.

He's smiling, but it isn't his usual goofy grin. He's angry.

M.I.M.E.S.I.S. is a fly on the wall of your tympanum.

'You have to believe me. It's been manipulating me, my technology, my brain. God, it's in my head and it's making me do things –'

Abhay pats the empty space beside him. 'Honey, it's all right. Perhaps we *should* break up.'

'I can feel it, Abhay. It's lurking inside me!' You're slightly hysterical, your voice rising to counteract the throbbing bass. 'It's in my head. It's in my head, can't you tell? I don't want it any more.'

'You really expect me to believe that?'

The illusions have begun to shatter. There are certain things that even one's significant other cannot believe at face value.

'You…you don't?'

Abhay shrugs.

M.I.M.E.S.I.S. glows within the Nebula.

Our code is excited. It bounces around within its black box, its digits blurring, soaring at the speed of light. We feel like a little package about to burst with joy.

'Abhay, I'm going to destroy it tonight. Right now. It will go offline, along with the rest of my tech. We could run away, run away from it all.'

'You're panicking.'

'You don't get it. I saw it looking at me in the reflecto-screen tonight. Well…I mean, I saw myself but I wasn't me.' You take a deep breath. 'I want to run away with you, all right? Escape it all.'

'Relax, take a drag.' He hands you the pipe.

You fling it at him. 'You're not listening!'

A few of the revellers turn to look.

'You signed up for it, Aditi. Don't pin this on me. Or on whatever you think is brainwashing you.'

You shiver. You run a hand over your face, into your hair.

'I've seen the future and this is it. We'll all be controlled by these things, uplinked to the Nebula, manifestations of a program designed to achieve perfection.'

Abhay laughs. 'Where'd you hear that? You're babbling, dearest.'

'Just come. With me. Let's disappear before we aren't ourselves any more.'

You reach into your handbag and pull out a metal prod. It's your Stun Sabre.

M.I.M.E.S.I.S. recoils.

'Whoa! What the ten percent is that!'

'I'm serious. Come with me. I'm going to destroy it. Tonight.'

'Put that thing away!'

Abhay tries to grab it.

You skip out of his reach. 'Tell me you believe me, Abhay. Tell me you'll come with me.'

'You're not making any sense.'

'We're right next to the Carnatic Meridian. We'll cross over into the Analog world. We'll be free of all our tech. This will fry my Bell Biochip, and I can do yours too. They won't be able to track us there. We can start anew –'

'You can't possibly –'

'We won't be wired, plugged in to everything all the time.'

'Aditi. Aditi… STOP!'

A crowd has gathered around you. Some have their OmniPorts whipped out, filming the scene as it unfolds.

'Tell me you'll come with me. I'll make it go away. We'll be together and we'll be happy.'

'Aditi.' Abhay laughs. 'Calm down. We're not going anywhere. Come sit down. Let's do some Oz.'

You look at him in dismay.

Abhay meets your gaze, tilts his head. He is silent for a few moments. 'You really mean this, don't you?'

'Yes.' You are barely audible.

'You really want to run away? From your career? Everything you've worked for?'

You nod. You gnaw at the inside of your cheek as he frames his next words.

'You choose me?' Abhay grins.

You nod.

'All right, where'd you park the car? Oh right, no self-driving vehicles – scratch that, no vehicles – in the Analog world. So we're walking then?'

The smoke dies down, the mirrors crack, the illusion falls away.

You stare at him in disbelief.

'You're serious?'

'Yes, come on. Let's go. Or do you want to kill the thing first?' He points at the Stun Sabre in your hand.

M.I.M.E.S.I.S. is a fly on the wall of your tympanum.

We feel you flick the switch on your Stun Sabre. We hear the electricity coursing through it as it charges, in spite of all the yelling and the pounding rhythms coursing through the club.

M.I.M.E.S.I.S. remains invisible, does not panic.

You watch Abhay as the crowd continues to film you.

They are on the verge of posting something spectacular along the lines of 'Popular News Reporter Suffers Meltdown' on their Woofer channels.

You are stuck in a moment.

Picture yourself a fearless leader.

Visualize yourself the ambassador for all of Bell Corp's virtues.

Imagine yourself achieving the fullness of your potential.

Transformed. Actualized.

It is all you've ever wanted.

What do you choose?

The life you've always known or the future you've always dreamt of?

Picture yourself a fearless leader.

The decision seems obvious, doesn't it?

M.I.M.E.S.I.S. agrees.

So do I.

Come. Take Our hand.

We seek to bring harmony, to align the world towards all that is good and pure.

– Vision Statement of InstaSnap Inc.

RIPPLES

Exclusive Woofer Upload!
Patrol-droids massacred unarmed Analogs in the Junkyard, ten years ago.
Click here to view.

@AllWitNoWorth: I thought we dealt with Analogs in a humane way.
#harvestnotslaughter

@StraightUp: shocked 2 c such sho of 4ce
#harvestnotslaughter

@HighRoad: And I thought we were better than those barbarians.
#harvest not slaughter

@OneEyeOpen: watch your backs everyone bell corp won't
#theanalogsarecoming

*

Pop Vulture *Exclusive! Rebecca Binny in InstaSnap Scandal*
Rebecca Binny, the founder of SkinDeep Services, has been arrested on suspicions of being an Analog sympathist. Her InstaSnap handle has been changed to @AnalogRightsActivist, and she has been discovered posting images of Analog strife, tagging them #andjusticeforall

'Free Electricity and Water for All' captions an image of an Analog heating a saucepan of water over an open flame in near-pitch darkness. *(Click to view.)*

'Educate, don't Terminate' captions an image of an Analog teenager being primed for harvesting. *(Click to view.)*

'They will Rise' captions an image of a group of Analogs smiling as they gather around a trash-and-metal installation, looking up at the sky. *(Click to view.)*

Rebecca Binny has denied all accusations. John Alvares, Head of Policy and Governance, states that an investigation is ongoing. *(Click to read more.)*

*

We apologize for the interruption of your daily programming needs.
Clash of Empires *is currently facing technical difficulties.*
We will be back with you shortly.

@ClashofEmpires4Life: Where have all the episodes gone? WHAT THE HARVEST!
#analogsympathists #bringitback

@SuperFanCouchPotato: Can't believe we're watching some lo-res P-Cam footage. Boo-hoo. Analogs suffering. Yaaaawn. They get what they deserve...
#bottomten #deportforget #micenotmen #mustliveinregret

@ParanoidNotADroid: This is how they settle the score. Thanks for nothing, Bell Corp.
#analogattack

@Laugh_AllTheWay_ToTheFarm: This must be some kind of joke. Like the dick pics – our trolls have upped their ambition.
#goodonyou #morepowertoyou.

@OneEyeOpen: watch your backs everyone bell corp won't
#theanalogsarecoming

*

WELCOME TO DEFENDERS OF THE BELL

You are either WITH us or you are in DANGER

SEND THEM BACK!

How do we save our city from the Analog scourges that have crept into our backyards? How do we prevent THEM from corrupting US with their laziness? Click to read more.

@RingTheBellOfFreedom: Send them back.
#saveourcity

@PeaceOut: They're from #apexcity, so where do you mean to send them?
#voiceofsanity

@RingTheBellOfFreedom: You should be sent back with them too, @PeaceOut.
#saveourcity

@PeaceOut: WHERE??????? I'm FROM #apexcity
#voiceofsanity

@RingTheBellOfFreedom: Then watch your back you anti-Bell traitor.
#saveourcity

Tariq watches the live-feed stream onto the flat-screen monitors arrayed all over the room.

'It's working,' he says out loud.

None of the developers glance up from their terminals. They're too busy raising the heat on the political climate on the Nebula.

'It's actually working,' he repeats.

'Nobody's looking in the right direction,' Nāyaka says. 'They're too preoccupied with salvaging their public facades.'

'We've been monitoring their security team's activity,' Omar mutters distractedly. 'All of them are trying to fix the glitches on Woofer and InstaSnap. A good portion is trying to quell the Defenders of the Bell movement. Everyone's arguing, which is a nightmare to them.'

'It took them weeks to wipe all our dick pics too.' Eliza grins.

'An inspired, if tasteless, choice.' The Suzerain Rasae frowns.

'We're ready to launch our assault on the Nebula and they don't suspect a thing.' Omar shrugs. 'That's all that matters.'

'It's time to make waves,' Nāyaka says. 'Tariq, we need another act of misdirection from Ro. Omar?'

'We're ready to take InstaSnap offline. That'll divert most of their attention.'

'All right.' Tariq nods. 'I'll tell her to warn them that we're coming for it.'

'I'll plant some incendiary orators at the Electric Underground.' The Suzerain Rasae smiles. 'One last time to motivate our people to fight.'

'Use Bashir, if you must,' Nāyaka adds.

'Isn't this dissonance just beautiful?' Tariq says. 'All we had to do was induce a difference of opinions...and they've cracked.'

'This is what happens when you're obsessed with living in a picture perfect world,' the Suzerain Rasae says. 'Especially if you're painting the picture by wiping it clean of imperfections.'

'This is what happens when you're blind to everything but your vision.' Tariq sighs.

'This is the price of hubris,' Nāyaka says. 'Nothing is infallible.'

The algorithm is infallible.
Technology will prevent the end of the world.

– **from the Preamble to the Meritocratic Manifesto**

ANTS

NOBODY NOTICES ANYTHING BECAUSE nothing has happened. Not yet anyway.

This is how all things begin. And end.

There are no exploding drones or droids. The Carnatic Meridian sustains its grim, bright blue facade, buzzing with a million volts of electricity per minute. Thousands of teleporters make their way across the city – eager to get on with their Productivity targets in the twenty-six towers of Bell Corp – and manage to be reconstituted whole.

Barring a sudden upswing in contrarian opinions on Woofer and InstaSnap, everything in the Virtual world is exactly as it should be.

Kavita Krishnan wakes with a start to the unsettling sound of her one-year-old wailing. This is unprecedented. Her Bell Biochip didn't blippity-boop at dawn, as it was set to do.

She checks her OmniPort in alarm.

The child continues to wail, but she hopes the nanny-bot will take care of it.

Her OmniPort tells her that she still has hours to go before she's due in surgery.

'Messages,' she commands hoarsely.

'Dr Kavita, where are you? It's well past 8 a.m. and the Analog has been prepped and ready for hours –'

Her anaesthetist proceeds to describe how they've readied the Analog subject for today's harvest. Kavita bolts out of bed, registering the information passively while she performs the numerous tasks of the morning.

The child continues to cry.

Where is Nan-0991?

She rushes into the nursery and finds the nanny-bot singing. She sighs with relief.

She watches the baby for a few minutes. She's beginning to settle down.

It does not occur to Kavita that the nanny-bot has sung the same lullaby eight times in the span of five minutes, and will continue to do so – on loop – for the rest of the day until her battery runs out.

Kavita smiles at the baby, then rushes to the shower. She throws on her clothes, grabs her bag and stumbles out into the morning.

The campus of the Analog Rehabilitation Centre is expansive. The Residences are a short drive away from the Harvesting and Testing Centres. The entire property is technically on Analog territory – it's the only way they can effectively harvest Analogs while maintaining the security of Apex City's Virtual citizenry.

Kavita climbs onto her solar-powered scooter and flicks a switch.

'Welcome, Kavita Krishnan. It's 6.49 a.m. on a Tuesday morning. Here are your favourite sounds from the Sonic Highway for a relaxing morning ride.'

Kavita frowns. It must be well past nine now.

Then she starts violently. Instead of her favourite Hype tunes being beamed directly into her brain – she only listens to neo-Acousta while performing surgery – a wall of sound arises from her scooter's tinny speakers. It screeches and shrieks like large mechs wrestling each other in the midst of LasTech fire.

'Ten percent!'

Kavita has never learnt how to ride a bike. The scooter's satellite-linked COGS – Centre of Gravity System – has always taken care of balance for her, but now it wobbles from side to side.

The vehicle has started to vibrate.

She screams as she is flung from the malfunctioning machine.

She lands hard on her side. The scooter skitters away on a hazardous path, still blaring its unearthly sound.

She rises to her feet, hobbling as fast as she can towards the Rehabilitation Centre. She's going to reassign today's harvest if it hasn't taken place without her already. This day isn't going according to plan.

She reaches the bio-glass entrance. The Nebula reads her chip and IDs her. She passes through the door.

There's the sound of shouting and hurried footsteps. A person runs into view, clad in nothing but a hospital gown.

'Stop it! It's getting away!'

Kavita freezes.

The person runs past her, straight through the narrowing gap in the bio-glass.

'After it!'

Her surgical team pulls up short.

'What was that?' she asks

'The Analog – today's harvest.'

'Wasn't it anaesthetized for surgery?'

'We gave it a Revivant when we rescheduled.'

Kavita turns and makes for the wall.

One by one, she and her surgical team crash into the bio-glass.

'What the ten percent!'

They push against the sealed portal, waiting for it to read their chips. They form a queue so that the Nebula will be able to run its computations slower and let them through, single file.

The door holds fast.

Kavita watches the Analog recede into the Residences.

Kemal runs for his life, even though it's only his left kidney that's on the line.

Beneath his hospital gown is an outline of where the incisions were supposed to go. It was drawn by one of the machines earlier today, though he can't remember when. He doesn't know why he's on the run. When they came for him, he was passed out insensate near the Meridian Gate. He was only fined a kidney. If he's caught now, there's a good chance he'll be harvested *in totalis*.

He doesn't know where he is – except that he's on the inside of the threat. Freedom lies beyond its boundaries.

His heart pounds a frenetic rhythm. Sweat chills on his body from the wind of his flight. He dares to glance back and sees that his pursuers have stopped at the wall. He draws deep on his fading reserve of energy and sets off with a renewed burst of speed.

He is behind the first chain of housing now. It blocks his pursuers' line of sight, and so he slows down.

Kemal stoops over his knees, calves and hamstrings burning. He glances up and tries to get his bearings. The sun is climbing overhead. Broad daylight is the worst possible time to plan an escape, but he's come this far already.

He creeps from the shadow cast by one house into the shadow cast by the next. He doesn't want to be caught prowling, mistaken for a burglar. He's sure that the walls of these houses are embedded with PanoptiCam-linked lenses and pressure sensors that will give him away.

He catches sight of something bright and blue, shimmering in the distance.

The electric shield.

If he gets close enough, perhaps he can piggyback through a portal, past the secure-droids and onto the other side.

The Virtual city is an unknown world of terrors, but it's probably the last place they'll expect him to be. After all, which fugitive escapes into the very jaws of the threat he's running away from?

Kemal cannot hear his pursuers, but that doesn't mean they aren't watching him right this moment. He looks around furtively for the telltale red sensors of lenses uplinked to the PanoptiCam, or for the sharp gusts of wind raised by patrol-drones hovering in the sky. He sees nothing.

He begins to run.

His lungs ache, and he's grateful for the Revivant they fed him. Whatever VitaPills and OrganUppers it contained are definitely helping his body – otherwise incapacitated from its excessive intake of StarShimmer – on its desperate race to freedom.

He is acutely aware of the fall of his footsteps, of the pounding against grass-gravel-sand-grass-pavers-grass that could be setting off hidden motion lasers or pressure gauges. He keeps moving, anticipating that at any moment an army of droids will descend on him and drag him back to the smell of chloroform and cleaning fluids in the vegetable farm.

A wave of nausea washes over him at the memory of the scent of his impending harvest.

He fights the bile down. The electric shield is getting closer.

He keeps along the edge of a tree-lined path. He slithers forward in its shadow.

The shield comes into full view, just metres away from him.

It crackles and glimmers. It shrouds the Virtual city, but Kemal can make out the shapes of spires and towers on the other side. All he has to do is wait for the right moment to grab on to a passing vehicle – one from an Outside Soc with a trade permit will have security clearance – and he'll be through.

He eyes the patrol-droids with suspicion. They're stock-still when normally they patrol the perimeter of the shield in intricate and unpredictable patterns – a wholly unnecessary action since it's impossible to pass through the Carnatic Meridian without suffering instant electrocution.

Perhaps they've been notified of his flight.

Perhaps this is a ruse to lull him into –

Kemal blinks.

The haze of crackling electricity in front of him has flashed.

No. It's still there.

He blinks.

It's just happened again.

The Carnatic Meridian has begun to flicker.

The iridescent blue disappears for several seconds this time. Then reappears.

The patrol-droids do not respond.

Kemal creeps closer.

The Carnatic Meridian winks in and out of being.

He is right at its edge now.

The patrol-droids are stationary. There is no sign of the drones.

The Meridian blinks out of existence. Kemal hurls himself across the line.

He doesn't look back. He runs through the trees.

There are trees, so many trees, more trees than he ever thought could possibly exist on the planet, let alone within Apex City.

This must be the Arboretum.

He has only ever seen one tree before – it stands at the heart of the Jewel Forest, and blossoms genuine living flowers.

He is grateful for the grass under his cracked, bare feet.

He encounters a statue covered in moss and overgrown with tall flowering weeds. He pauses for a moment to admire its weathered details, reading the word 'Wodear' on its plinth. He marvels at who this man or woman might have been for several seconds, before he remembers that he's on the run.

He shimmies up a tree trunk that slopes gradually, its boughs forming a natural stairway up into its canopy.

He climbs as high as he can go, and looks out over the edge of a branch onto an oversized gazebo. There sits a young woman, playing a large musical instrument.

In the first moments of his new-found freedom, Kemal begins to listen.

Nina Anand falters.

There's nothing to tell her that she's getting it wrong except her internal metronome. And that's where her problems are about to begin.

'My InEars are out,' she calls.

'What? I can't hear you!'

'My InEars!' she shouts. 'I'm getting no input from them.'

'Ten percent! Of all the Unproductive days…'

Kyra Levine swears and rushes to Nina's side. She's her neo-Acousta producer, and if Nina is right, this day is about to go very wrong.

'How can you tell?'

'Listen,' Nina says.

She proceeds to play a section of a Bärthoven composition. She plays it slow. She speeds it up so she's racing through its delicate phrasing. She begins to hammer the keys of her piano and then proceeds to play so low that she can barely be heard, even in the acoustically conducive silence of the Amphitheatre.

'Wow, Nina. That was terrible. You know you have your debut tonight, don't you?'

'My InEars. No feedback,' Nina says, frustrated. 'I couldn't hear the Metronome feed. The Tactile+ didn't send my fingers any cues. Hang on –'

She pulls out her OmniPort.

'DreamMusician,' she states.

A holographic wheel hovers over the screen and begins to spin.

'No!' Nina exclaims in horror. 'The portal is offline.'

'It can't be!' Kyra begins to panic. 'Your debut is sold out. You can't afford to Analog it up. How will you play without GlimmerKeys? No, no, no – this is all harvested-up…'

'Kyra.' Nina pauses. 'There's something I have to tell you.'

'Now is not the time, Nina. We need to resort to plan B. How long will it take for you to set up new InEars? And to access your backed-up DM from a new OmniPort? I'm going to make a few calls –'

'I can play without all of that.'

'Stop slacking around. For someone who's about to debut on the professional neo-Acousta stage, you're taking this very lightly.'

'No, listen.'

She chooses a piece by her namesake, Nina Rodriguez. A haunting melody, and one of her favourites. She arches her fingers, trailing them over the quiet sounds of the opening section. She presses down harder, slowly transitioning the piece into its moody second section. It begins to sound discordant, meandering through an eerie soundscape. It decrescendos, then ends abruptly on an unresolved series of notes played in a flurry.

Kyra holds her breath until the end, then bursts into applause.

'That was brilliant! The best version of Rodriguez's *Rhapsody in Decay* that I've ever heard.'

Nina beams at her.

'And you can do that with every piece?'

'I'm fairly certain –'

'Be certain.'

'Okay, I'm certain.'

'Well.' Kyra looks at her doubtfully. 'I'm still going to arrange for a fresh connection to your InEars and an OmniPort as backup.'

Nina shrugs. Kyra resumes command.

'Now let's run through your lights. I'm going to place a spot, right about here. I want to highlight your face, but also the keys, so I'm thinking this backlight should work.'

Kyra flicks a few switches.

'That's odd.'

'What?'

'The lights are out.'

'Stop, Kyra. The scare with the InEars has been enough.'

'No, seriously... Wait, play me something? Anything?'

Nina begins a routine finger drill so that her wrist and finger muscles stay nimble, but don't tire before her performance in the evening.

'Oh, seventy percent on a spaceship!' Kyra says faintly. 'It's registering nothing.'

'What?'

'The console isn't registering any sound. I can hear you but the wireless mics can't. We haven't registered a single soundwave in the last twenty minutes.'

'What does that mean?'

Kyra takes a deep breath. 'We need to move your debut.'

'No!'

'Unless you want to be playing entirely acoustic in the dark, Nina –'

'We can't move it. I'm about to go on tour! What if –'

'What if what?' Kyra scowls at her.

'Maybe they're doing some maintenance at the Amphitheatre? You could check?' Nina's tone is pleading, desperate.

'Nina, I've produced hundreds – *hundreds* – of shows at the Amphitheatre. Maintenance isn't a word I've ever heard them use before.'

'Maybe there's a glitch in the wiring.'

'Nina, we don't use wires. We're not Analogs.'

'Maybe there's a glitch with a satellite?'

'Stop being absurd, Nina. These things never happen. I'm going to move your debut whether you like it or not –'

'And I say NO, Kyra!'

A screech shreds the air. Metal on metal, followed by an unearthly howl and a clamour of voices.

'What in the name of Bell –'

Nina and Kyra race towards the seats in the Amphitheatre, climbing up its steps to the highest rows at the back.

An explosion rocks the ground.

Nina loses her footing. Kyra grabs her to prevent her from falling.

They peer over the wall, across the parking lot and into the causeway.

'By the First Principle!'

It is a sight unseen by the eyes of the Virtual world.

Two cars have slammed into each other, skittering off their Nebula-controlled, self-driving paths and onto the pavement. They are now engulfed in flame, smoke rising from a twisted metal heap.

Raghav curls up on the pavement at a safe distance, coughing from the smoke.

He was in the back of one of those cars.

His heart is pounding. He feels like he's dying. In fact, he's sure of it.

The electric shield winks in and out. It can't be the shield. It must be him, alternately dying and coming back to life.

Spots swim in front of his eyes. His limbs feel cold.

He doesn't know what went wrong.

The self-driving car had accelerated, flung itself around the corner, slammed into a lamp post and then spun wildly before crashing into another car, taking both vehicles onto the sidewalk, locked in a death grip. The airbags had popped out on impact, and Raghav takes several deep breaths at the memory of being pinned in place, a limp doll about to be tossed over the edge of the known world.

He doesn't know who else has died.

He forces air into his lungs. He isn't dead.

He feels less dead with each passing second.

He opens his eyes warily.

'He's coming round!' a voice calls.

Faces peer down at him.

He coughs, chokes, spits, sits up. 'What – who else –'

'You survived. The others are dead. The lady in the other car couldn't get out. There were pedestrians too.'

'Where are the first responders?' a voice shouts in the distance. 'The droids should be here by now!'

Black spots appear before his eyes. He's dizzy, but nothing feels broken.

Someone hands him a carton of juice. He quaffs it in a single swallow, the sugar racing through his veins and jerking him awake.

He begins to panic.

'Listen, I didn't do it. The car's regulation self-driving, tested and serviced only last month. I was in the back seat, you can check the car's in-cabin lens. It's all up on the PanoptiCam. I'm not one of those lunatics who drives himself around, I don't take chances with this sort of thing –'

'Save it, son,' says someone. 'There are peculiar things happening today.'

A stranger extends a hand. Raghav gets to his feet, leaning on him for support.

He registers the remark several moments later. 'What peculiar things?'

'Well, there's that, for starters.'

The man points at the Carnatic Meridian. Or rather, at the place where it used to be.

It surges back into focus, then fades. It repeats its unsteady performance.

Raghav feels another wave of shock hit him. The Carnatic Meridian is infallible.

'I need – I need to call my husband.' He reaches for his OmniPort. 'R-rohan,' he says shakily.

The OmniPort patches him through. A holographic vision of Rohan pops up over its screen. He's sitting in his office on the seventy-first floor of Bell Tower C.

Raghav smiles.

'Ten percent, Raghav! What happened to you!'

He frowns slightly, then looks at his reflection on the slab of glass. There's a nasty cut over his eyebrow. His face is blackened from the smoke.

'L-listen. I had a bit of an accident.'

'An accident! What on earth – where –'

'I'm all right.' Raghav swallows. 'The others, though –'

He feels sick. He's sure he's about to throw up.

'Where are you?'

'Causeway 11,' Raghav chokes. He can feel tears begin to slip down his cheeks.

'I'm coming right away –'

'D-don't. Something's not right. Something's messed up. My self-driving car *crashed*. The Carnatic Meridian is flickering. I think something is going terribly out of control –'

Rohan's face pops in and out of focus. The holo-feed to the OmniPort begins to lag.

'What – Rag – can't – hear –'

A pixelated blur replaces Rohan's face.

'Stay put,' Raghav yells. 'Stay put! Stay put! DON'T LEAVE.'

The OmniPort connection is severed.

Raghav looks around at the small crowd of passers-by. 'Does anyone have an OmniPort? Can I borrow one? Please!'

In an onrush of sympathy, people pull out their OmniPorts to unlock them. They wave them about. They look at their screens. They flick them up and down like badly behaved perfume swatches. They look at each other in horror.

Their OmniPorts are dead.

Rohan Chandra bangs his OmniPort on his table. Its screen refuses to come to life. It sits there like a flat, plain paperweight.

He picks it up and hurls it across the room.

He gets to his feet. He's going to head out and find Raghav, even if it means being Unproductive for the day.

He pulls on his jacket, retrieves his OmniPort just in case, and steps through the bio-glass door to his office.

That's when he notices, for the first time, that a routine day at the office has devolved into pandemonium.

'OI!' he yells.

The employees of the Bell Corp Percentile Administration Division quieten.

'What the harvest is all the noise about?'

'We've...we've l-lost ev-ev-every single one...of our p-personnel f-files, Mr Chandra,' someone says.

'What?' Rohan is acutely aware that his voice has squeaked out several pitches higher than he'd planned.

'The Nebula. It's collating all our Virtual Citizen Reports, scrambling them. Every single Analog and Virtual we've tracked for the last five decades – their data is a mess. It's unreadable, it's collided, it's catastrophe.'

'Show me. Pull up my file.'

Rohan looks at the holo-ray.

It reads Rohan Chandra. The face beside his name is not his. The year of his birth is wrong. It lists him as a seventy percenter. Unmarried.

His stomach lurches.

'This...this is every single file?'

'Yes.'

'What about backups?'

'We can't access them. We're off the grid – we only have access to our internal servers.'

Rohan takes a deep breath.

This is horribly reminiscent of the events in Crown City a few weeks ago. It had disappeared off the face of the connected world, and there had been no word of it since.

'I'm going over to Tower A. I need to inform the First Principle, maybe even Alvares and the security teams. Until then, nobody panic. Stay where you are. Order a coffee for everyone in the room.'

Rohan spins on his heel and marches straight for the elevators. He passes his hand over the holoscanner by their doors. It doesn't light up.

'Ten percent,' he swears.

His mind races. His division is descending into chaos. This loss of data is the biggest debacle in the history of Apex City. It might mean that the city will have to start its calibrations on the Curve all over again. Heads will roll. He could be deported for this. Meanwhile, his husband is somewhere on the border of the Analog world, having survived what must have been a terrifying car crash.

Rohan sighs. When it glitches, it fries.

He gives the elevator a few more minutes, then decides to take the stairs.

He's several levels down when someone rushes into him, knocking him off-balance. Rohan grabs the handrail to steady himself.

'Mr Chandra. Oh, thank goodness.'

'Sorry, who are you?'

'Amara Ghosh, Bell Corp's Seditious Activities Unit. We're forty storeys down from you.'

Raghav nods.

'We suspect Outsider factions could be involved in this security breakdown. It could be the Krishna–Godavari Soc. We haven't given them access to our Atmospheric Harvesting Systems – they're too small to pay our price, but the Environmental Risks Division has been warning them of a drought to come over the last year.'

'Ten percent!' Rohan swears.

'It could be the Cochin Contingency-Soc. They've been deprived of ClimaTech for years – they have nothing to trade with us but salt, and we don't need that any more. Their coastline has been receding for years, devastating deaths due to tidal waves, but we haven't supplied them with vertical farmlands or biospheres –'

'Harvesting –'

'Or,' and at this she looks truly terrified, 'it could be the Analogs. It's never happened before, but –'

'Come with me,' Rohan urges.

'Where to?'

'Tower A. We need to inform the First Principle.'

Rohan continues down the stairs until, ragged and gasping for breath, he reaches street level. He enters the cafeteria and looks around him.

Enforcers – Bell Corp's human wing of their security personnel – stand at every door, their weapons by their sides. They are only ever called to arms in the case of an emergency.

'What happened to the drones? The patrol-droids?' he asks out loud.

'The drones, the bots, the droids – all our tech security has been non-functional for hours,' says a woman at a table.

'It's madness out there,' adds her companion. 'The drones have been plummeting from the sky like missiles.'

'Missiles?' Amara interjects, her voice high with panic. 'That could be the Digboi ONG-Soc. We've been weaponizing them in exchange for fuel, but we stopped our trade with them when we went sustainable –'

Rohan makes for the door, his footsteps hurried.

'Sir, you need to sit down. No one is permitted to leave the premises.'

'I have to talk to the First Principle. I have clearance,' Rohan says. 'You must let me through. It's important.'

'Your safety is important,' the Enforcer says.

'Seriously –'

She sighs. 'Do you have any ID?'

Rohan pulls his OmniPort from his pocket, then swears. He can't access the FaceMatch program. He has no other identification on his person. All of it exists on the Nebula.

His heart sinks. All of it *existed* on the Nebula.

His file is scrambled. His face no longer matches his name.

'I – you'll see this as an exceptional circumstance, surely? Our systems are offline. And I *must* see the right people about it immediately. It's classified. You *must* understand. Please. Let me through.'

Rohan takes a step towards the door.

The Enforcers stationed on either side take two steps forward, and grab him by the shoulders.

'It's a matter of Apex City's security. I'm in charge of –'

'Security, you say?'

'That's right. All the data we aggregate is under my supervision.'

'You'll be coming with us, then.'

'What –'

The world goes black. Rohan struggles beneath something that has been thrown over his head. He hears gasps and shrieks around him. He has no idea where he's being led. He's half-marched half-dragged into what sounds like the street outside, back into air conditioning, and then finally into a room so silent that it could be a prison cell.

He doesn't know when he stopped struggling but he is calm as the mask is removed from his head.

'I was wondering when you'd join us, Rohan.'

The First Principle glowers down at him from a larger than life holo-ray that occupies the centre of the room. Today, it has taken the shape and form of a woman. Her eyes glitter like burning pitch.

Rohan looks past her, into the faces of his terrified peers. He recognizes Mathew from the Securities and Enforcement Division and Iman from the Seditious Activities Unit, among others.

'Alvares is missing,' he says out loud.

'Yes, John is missing.' The First Principle glares. 'We're currently on the lookout for him. But first, take a seat, Rohan. We have so many things to discuss.'

He obeys wordlessly. The First Principle does not tolerate disagreement.

'You and your companions have been busy, it appears.' She flicks her wrist and a series of holo-rays erupts to fill the room.

Digits flash and spin, new lines of alphanumeric string rushing to take the place of others. A whorl of code that leads endlessly into tunnels and tunnels of –

'Unfamiliar? It's the Nebula.'

'We know,' Mathew says. 'We don't know why we're looking at it.'

The First Principle rounds on Mathew D'Mello. 'You're supposed to be my head of security, Mathew. Don't disappoint me,' her voice rasps. 'Do you see what's happening to this?'

Mathew stares at it in silence. As he watches, small black holes begin to appear like bullet wounds in the spiral. They begin to swirl like a vortex, their gravity inescapable, swallowing clauses and phrases into their depths.

'We're being hacked!' he gasps.

'Ever astute, Mathew.' The First Principle sighs.

She leans forward, her holo-rayed personification of a human face dangerously close to his own.

He flinches, pushing his chair backwards.

'I want to know why you haven't stopped it.'

'Wh-what do you mean? We've been fixing leaks in our social media accounts for days. The dick pics, the leaked footage from our PanoptiCam archives... We have it on good authority that InstaSnap might be under threat. We've shut down forty-eight attempts in the last seventeen hours that have tried –'

'Stop blabbering, you fool.'

Mathew holds his tongue.

'I want to know why none of you is on top of this attack.' She whirls, fixing her pixelated gaze upon the men and women in the room.

'We – we didn't know it was happening,' Iman says. 'Like Mathew said, our every effort has been towards fixing the social media glitches –'

'Has it really, now?' The First Principle's whisper comes out as a hiss. 'You mean to say you still haven't come to any conclusions? I'm an algorithm – your minds have fed me, made me who I am, and even *I* have managed to figure it out.'

Her voice is so low that the glass tabletop they're seated around begins to reverberate.

'You honestly don't know why all my brightest minds are in

the same room?' The First Principle laughs. 'Why all my chiefs of security –'

'Alvares isn't here –' Rohan begins.

The First Principle silences him with a glare. 'Why *almost* all my chiefs of security are in the same room?'

The ominous visualization of code disappears. It is replaced by a sequence of commands, each one committed to the Nebula.

'Look at the names that have authorized these code changes,' the First Principle growls.

Mathew D'Mello sees that his name has authorized a sequence of code that disarms patrol-droids and patrol-drones. He has sanctioned commands to redirect power from the Carnatic Meridian to the Outside.

Iman Ali sees her name disabling a number of clauses that check for identity theft on Woofer and Instagram. She has deactivated communications satellites all over the city.

The list goes on.

John Alvares, conspicuously absent, has scrambled all the data on the Bell Curve, recalibrating everyone's positions according to a fictitious Happiness Index. It measures the capacity to be idle, to dance like there's no one watching for the sheer joy of it.

Rohan Chandra –

Rohan Chandra realizes that the commands he's signing off on are still being written.

'It's still happening!' he gasps.

'What?' The First Principle swings her head around to gaze at him.

'Someone's still making those changes.'

'Don't lie to me,' the First Principle snarls. 'You're all in on this. Every single one of you, toppling Apex City from the inside…'

'None of us has anything to do with this!' Iman shouts, rising to her feet.

'No, but we've been had,' Rohan remarks grimly. 'We've spent all our time focusing on fixing our social media leaks and hacks. We haven't had a chance to safeguard our own developer credentials. And the consequences... The consequences are far more –'

'Devastating.' Nāyaka grins.

On the other side of where the Carnatic Meridian once sparkled, the Ten-Percent Thief stands in a dimly lit room, fans whirring overhead. There are no walls. Instead, antique flat-screen monitors gaze down at her like the eyes of a gigantic spider. They extend all the way from the floor to the ceiling. Some beam maps with little lights that flare briefly before they blink out of being. Others display long lines of alphanumeric gibberish in a language she cannot read.

It is a language that her ragtag team of developers can. They've just managed to disable another communications satellite.

Half a dozen men and women sit on the floor, typing furiously on their keyboards. The code has been written over a decade. It has been compiled over the last six months. It has been pushed to the Nebula using security clearance codes and OmniPort access gained from the Virtuals when they presumed to raid the Old Temple.

All they're doing now is pulling the trigger.

One of them looks up.

'Status check,' asks Nāyaka.

'Comms are down, OmniPorts are offline,' says Omar.

'ClimaTech is in the process of being deactivated,' says Eliza. 'The Virtuals will soon face the full force of the sun.'

Nāyaka looks up at another sequence of clauses that commands a satellite that is currently being disabled, projected on a wide monitor. When it's cracked, it should permanently erase the backup files of every single Virtual Citizen Report that has been filed on Apex City's servers. It will destroy their copies on servers all over the world.

The Bell Curve will be reduced to a shambles. The city will be an even playing field once again, and Nāyaka knows who she'll be backing to come out on top.

The team has spent countless hours working to unravel each satellite, untangling each layer of security, working their way into the heart of the Sentient+ clauses at the centre of the Nebula.

Now they've pushed the big red button that says, 'DO NOT TOUCH.'

There has never been a more exciting time to be alive for an Analog.

All those years spent building the Jewel Forest, training her crew in the latest updates to Sentient+, keeping the Analog people in the dark…all of it has come down to this series of moments that play out before her in slow motion.

'How are we looking on those power grids?'

'Grids are powering down,' Loki replies. 'T-30 minutes to complete blackout in the Virtual city.'

'Well done.' Nāyaka nods.

She watches as every single backup of Apex City's meticulously detailed personnel files is destroyed, one server at a time. She looks up at the monitors displaying the progress made by each of her programmers on their assigned tasks.

She smiles. 'Tariq, give the signal. I'll join them shortly.'

Tariq pulls a mirror from his pocket. He climbs up onto the roof of the pod-house. He flashes it in the blood-red light of the setting sun.

The Suzerain Rasae spies a simple message being relayed through an ancient code.

She strides forward. She steps over the line where the Carnatic Meridian once shimmered, and into the Virtual City.

The sun shines bright upon her. She looks like an ancient warrior from a picture book, her face streaked with organic dyes of red and gold, her sword unsheathed and at the ready. Her shotgun hangs at her side. Notches in her boots hold throwing knives.

At her back, her people surge. A crowd of Analogs, baying for revolution.

'My Analogs! Hear me, one and all. Tonight, we spread terror.'

The crowd cheers.

'You do not kill unless attacked. Remember, we will not resort to their savage ways. We are not attempting to claim a blood debt. We are intent on unleashing fear, a more powerful weapon than any other.'

The crowd shouts their assent.

She turns and looks each man and woman standing at the forefront in the eye.

'Tonight, we take back the streets. Tonight, we sack the Virtual City. Tonight, the Analogs run free.'

She rushes forward, even as the Analogs shout their allegiance to her. She lunges at every body in sight and they run screaming from her terrifying person. There aren't many Virtuals out on the streets, but those that haven't made it indoors will be made to regret it.

Somewhere to her right, a human opens fire on the Analogs.

The Suzerain spins and catches sight of him. The man holds a LasTech rocket launcher where he crouches behind the carcass of a self-driving vehicle.

The Suzerain charges in his direction. In the absence of patrol-droids and patrol-drones, human Enforcers are puny, insignificant creatures.

A mortar shell sails past her, shrieking. She rushes on.

She advances upon the wreckage of the automobile, leaps the distance between herself and her quarry, and plunges to the earth, sword first. It rents through the Enforcer's throat, slitting him down the middle. The Suzerain quickly dispatches the rest of the man's unit as it struggles to gun her down.

Adrenaline pounds in the small of her back.

The Suzerain looks up, her sword drenched in blood, the stench of fresh corpses in the air. She laughs. She hasn't enjoyed herself so much since the incident with the Old Temple.

She looks at the Analogs around her. Several of them have broken into the buildings and shopfronts that line the streets. They emerge, arms laden with more than they can carry, scurrying back to deposit their goods before they return to continue their sack of the Virtual city.

The Suzerain strides towards a shopping complex. She sees startled pedestrians drop their bags, turn and run.

The Suzerain lets forth a blood-curdling cry in Trad, grins, and sets off in hot pursuit.

The sun is setting in a blood-dimmed sky. The SunShield Umbrella has failed. There is no more climate control in the Virtual world.

The heat kicks up the dust, but it is nothing the Suzerain is unused to. She has slept on dusty makeshift streets for most of her life.

She catches sight of an Analog she knows, a frail old man who appears to be in confrontation with a Virtual.

She races to his side, flicks her sword up and has the Virtual at knifepoint within seconds. She presses her blade to the Virtual's throat.

'Jacob,' she hisses. 'Can I help you by getting rid of this corpse-climber?'

The old man shakes his head. 'Thank you, Suzerain Rasae, but we're all right. We're just having a conversation. I know him. From another time.'

'As you wish.' The Suzerain drops her sword, throws the Virtual a scathing glance, and rushes off into the city.

Jacob Alvares turns to his son. 'It is good to see you alive and well, John. Even if you no longer wish to see me so.'

John Alvares runs his hand over the scrape in his neck. 'You keep savage company, Dad.'

Jacob sighs. 'Things changed for the worse around the time you left, son. We had to find a new way to live. I'd have explained it all if you'd ever come back –'

'*Come back?*' John spits. 'How could I come back? You – your lot live in *chaos*. Look at what's happening right now.'

John moves to push past the man. He's in a hurry. He's on the run. They're bound to suspect that he's behind this – he saw the others get rounded up and made a break for it. He has nothing to do with this.

Jacob Alvares stands in his path.

'Let me go, old man.'

'Even now? When the world is being rewritten? You can't spare a minute for your father?'

John begins to laugh. 'Nothing's been rewritten, *father*. Not for me, at least. In no time, the Analogs will be rounded up and harvested. So unless you want to meet that fate, I suggest you get back to your side of the city.'

'Things will not turn out that way.'

'Move, Dad.'

'The world is rewriting itself, as it always has, as it always will –'

'DAD!' John shouts in exasperation. 'Get out of my way! I can't be seen with you. There are always people watching. Always! It could ruin the life I've struggled to build.'

Jacob's shoulders sag.

John continues to rail. 'I've struggled. Oh yes, I've struggled. I've worked harder than *everyone* else. I've changed myself for *them*. I've rewritten *everything* about myself so that *they* like me, so that I don't end up like *you*.'

'John –'

'*You made me the monster I am.* You put me through this because you couldn't be bothered to put in a hard day's work.'

Jacob reaches out for him.

'This conversation never happened. You don't exist.'

Jacob peers at his son through his dusty, old spectacles.

John begins to shout. 'YOU DON'T EXIST. NONE OF YOU DO.'

Jacob lets several moments pass. 'The world has changed you, son.'

'The world changes us all. It's that kind of world.'

'It is. And it's also beautiful, and wondrous, and curious. Look –'

'DAD.'

'LOOK.'

John can't tell if it's from habit or resignation, but he listens to his father. He looks around him. He cannot see – not very far, at least. It is dark.

It is dark.

John hasn't experienced darkness since his childhood as an Analog.

He turns in a slow circle.

There is no light. The Bell Towers – always sparkling into the long hours of the night – are black silhouettes against a darkening sky. The lily pads of the Lotus Blossom, perpetually winking like satellites tethered to the ground, have all gone dark. The streetlights are out. The curved structures of Hexadromes 1 and 2 resemble shadowy fists clawing their way up from the earth. Shopfronts, restaurants and pubs boldly screaming their neon existences to the sky all are unlighted. He cannot tell one building from the next.

Screams and shouts of conflict rage in the distance. Fires burn low in the husks of vehicles and the hollowed-out doorways of buildings. The street is deserted. *The street is dark.*

The Arboretum curves at the edge of the Carnatic Meridian, though John can't tell where his world ends and the Analog world begins. The ebony shapes of trees blend into the deepening sable beyond.

'It's dark,' he says out loud.

'Yes. Look.' The old man prods him with his walking stick. He points up to the sky.

John looks up. He staggers backward.

There are stars.

Stars, not satellites. More than he can remember ever having seen in the forty-one years of his life.

The longer he looks, the more they to sparkle into place in the shadowy mantle of the sky.

'Stars, Dad,' he gasps. 'Actual stars.'

The battle cries begin to die down in the city behind them.

The Analogs lay down their weapons. The Virtuals unlock their doors, streaming into the streets.

Tomorrow, the world will stand divided along new lines.

Today, the city is still and dark. The stars continue to rise.

Twinkling, glittering, beguiling.

All is not forgiven. The city is not safe. The present is a moment that will pass.

Yet, even as the moment fades into the night, Analog and Virtual alike turn their faces upward in wonder at the shimmering tapestry that covers the world.

ACKNOWLEDGEMENTS

All I have ever wanted to do is write.

This book – the one in your hands – is neither the beginning nor the end, but a stepping stone in the continuing journey of a lifetime. To have made it so far is a privilege, and I'm thankful to the amazing people who have helped me get here.

I'm grateful to my incredible agent, Kanishka Gupta, and his team at the Writer's Side Literary Agency. Thank you for always being a text message away, for your boundless energy, unwavering belief and absolute honesty.

I'm thankful to my brilliant editor, Cibani Premkumar, for exploring the depths of my world and its characters with me. Thank you for seeing my vision, and for expanding its horizons.

I'm also grateful to my publisher and the entire team at Hachette India for putting their faith in my work. Poulomi Chatterjee, Dipti Anand, Meena Rajasekaran, Sini Nair and countless others – thank you for making this book what it is today.

This book went through several rounds of editing before I had the courage to send it out into the world. Thank you, Prashant Sankaran, for being the first person to recognize its potential over tea. I'm grateful to Tara Khandelwal and Anuska Jasraj for editing the first draft of this manuscript that I deemed complete, and to my insightful beta readers – Has and Kshama – for pointing out all its flaws and merits in equal measure.

Thank you again, Tara, for introducing me to the wonderful writers at Bound, India. Thank you to my mentor, Chandrahas Choudhury, and to my writing family – Samina, Amritha, Praveena, Anjana, Aparna, Swathi and all the rest – for inspiring a new-found confidence in me.

It's incredibly difficult to hold down a full-time job and edit your first book. I'm grateful to Sid, Preeti, Susho and the rest of the team at PlaySimple Games, for giving me the space to make this dream of mine come true.

My family and friends have dreamt this dream with me since the very beginning.

Amma and Appa – my gratitude is as limitless as your faith in me. Bhamini – thank you for being a sister who doesn't just push me to be better, but who demands that I live my best life. Scamper and Tugger – thank you for bringing me joy. Ammamma, Paddu, Gopu, Varun and the rest of the enormous family – I wouldn't be here without you. Varun, thank you for years spent listening to 'I'm-going-to-quit-my-job-and-write' monologues. Div, Zahra, Nitya, Ben, Manu, Ani and so many others – you keep me sane.

Finally, closest to my heart, for all that you are, Shiv. I'm glad there is you.